New Leash on Life

The Dogfather · Book Two

roxanne st. claire

New Leash On Life
THE DOGFATHER BOOK TWO

Copyright 2017 South Street Publishing

978-0-9981093-3-6 – ebook
978-0-9981093-4-3 – print

COVER ART: Keri Knutson (designer)
and Dawn C. Whitty (photographer)
INTERIOR FORMATTING: Author E.M.S.

Critical Reviews of
Roxanne St. Claire Novels

Dear Reader:

Welcome back to the foothills of North Carolina where The Dogfather, Daniel Kilcannon, is once again pulling some strings to help one of his six grown children find forever love. Once again, I am delighted to inform you that a portion of the first month's sales of all the books in this series is being donated to Alaqua Animal Refuge (www.alaqua.org) in my home state of Florida. That's where these covers were shot by photographer Dawn Whitty (www.dawncwhitty.com) using *real* men (not models, but they are gorgeous!) and *rescue* dogs (now in forever homes!).

Publishing is a team effort and mine is superb. Special shout out to editor Kristi Yanta, who makes me dig deep for that emotional gold; copyeditor Joyce Lamb, who keeps every scene on track; proofreader Marlene Engel, who finds and fixes my many mistakes; and cover designer Keri Knutson, who understood exactly what I wanted to wrap around these stories. Huge hugs to my friend and neighbor, real estate maven Barbara Wall, who provided invaluable brainstorming help, love during our dog walks, and wine.

Sign up for my newsletter on my website at www.roxannestclaire.com to find out when the next book is released!

xoxo
Rocki

Dedication

For Ginger, the precious ball of furry fun who writes
every book with me. Her soul is sweet, her bark is
loud, and her love is unconditional.

Chapter One

Chloe Somerset needed an idea. A big, wild, brilliant, jaw-dropper of an idea. But for a woman whose bread was buttered with creative concepts that transformed lackluster locations into tourist magnets, she was feeling kind of uninspired after one interminable Tourism Advisory Committee meeting.

The town of Bitter Bark, North Carolina, was in dire straits, and not one of the local business owners had given her anything to work with so she could help them. Usually in Chloe's first meeting with a new tourism client, someone would say something that sparked a firestorm of promotional possibilities.

Nothing had sparked, except maybe a little chemistry between the egotistical undertaker and the spa owner with bright red hair.

Now that they'd all left, Chloe sat at the town hall conference room table, reaching absently for some hand sanitizer in her bag. While she rubbed it on her hands, she stared at the rows of business cards she'd lined up like little soldiers, trying to think of ways to remember all the names.

Ned, the newspaper editor. Nellie, the librarian. Jane, who owned the B&B, and Dave Ashland? Which one was he? Oh, the real estate broker who spent the whole meeting looking at his phone. And that man who owned the dog place—

"Whew, they're gone." Aunt Blanche swept back into the room and closed the door behind her, her sweet blue eyes glistening. "And you were magnificent, young lady."

Chloe held up both hands to stop any compliments she didn't deserve, and to let her hand sani dry. "All I did was listen," she said. "And make promises I hope I can keep."

"I hope so, too," Blanche said, sliding into a chair next to Chloe. "You can see we're in big trouble and, as mayor, I'm taking the brunt of it. I'm sure they all left here to go gossip about how much they want me to step down."

Chloe searched her aunt's face, marveling, certainly not for the first time, how sisters could be so different. Blanche Wilkins was warm, kind, caring, and accomplished. Doreen Somerset, Blanche's sister and Chloe's deceased mother, had been none of those things.

"I'll come up with something," Chloe assured her, realigning the cards again. "I need a few days to think and get familiar with the town."

"I'd think after that info dump, you'd be familiar enough."

Chloe smiled. "There was a lot, but the major takeaway I got was you want to be 'the next Asheville.'"

"Did you hear that expression often enough?" Blanche asked on a snort.

2

"Let's just say if it had been a drinking game, you'd have to call the ambulance."

She didn't laugh. In fact, Blanche's expression grew serious. "We have to share ambulance service and trash pickup with the next town, Chloe. That's how bad it is." She dropped her head into her hands. "I feel like I let Frank down," she whispered. "He was the best mayor this town ever had. And the best husband. I shouldn't have run for mayor and taken the job after he died, but I knew that was what he wanted."

Chloe offered a comforting touch. Blanche had always been Chloe's lifesaver when things got really bad when she was a kid—which was often—and Chloe had longed to return that kindness. She couldn't let this dear woman down.

"We'll make Uncle Frank proud, I promise. I do this for a living, Aunt Blanche."

"But we're not even paying you."

She waved it off. "You can pay me after the tourists pour into this town. I'm a tourism consultant and run my own business, which means I can dictate my schedule and pick my clients. I have a few weeks until I hear from some island in the Caribbean that I'm sure will hire me, and this is a perfect way for me to use my free time."

"Your clients are islands in the Caribbean, and yet you're taking on some two-bit town in North Carolina as a favor to me." Her eyes welled up. "How can I thank you?"

"I'm thanking *you*, Aunt Blanche," Chloe said softly. "You're my godmother, and we both know that on more than one occasion, you were a savior to me."

Blanche averted her eyes, keeping their unspoken agreement of never really talking about the literal mess that had been Chloe's childhood. Her mother's inability to throw anything away or organize her life into some semblance of sanity wasn't exactly an elephant in the room. It was more of a black hole of shame that they both tiptoed around so they didn't fall in.

But it bonded them. Blanche was the one person on earth who understood Chloe, and Chloe clung to Blanche's "normalcy" as a way to remind her that those lovely genes were in her DNA, too.

"Just let me immerse myself in Bitter Bark for a few days," Chloe added. "And I'll dream up something that will knock their socks off and get tourists crawling all over this town."

But Blanche still looked doubtful. "Frank put his heart and soul into the gentrification project. He got all those businesses to take a chance on his idea to turn the whole Bushrod Square area into something special."

"And from what I saw when you drove me through town today, he did a great job. It's quaint and inviting, all that red brick and scalloped awnings. There's a nice theme with almost every business being called Bitter Bark Something, and that grassy common area with the fountains and walkways is small-town Central Park. Uncle Frank's vision was brilliant."

"But vision isn't enough," Blanche said on a sigh. "He knew how to pull strings, to get people to make deals and take chances. But it's been two years without his leadership—"

"It's not a leadership issue," Chloe said. "You simply haven't hit on a way to really position and promote the town. Once we do that, you'll easily compete with places like Asheville and Blowing Rock and Boone."

"Once *you* do that," Blanche corrected. "We don't have any ideas, and *you* are the tourism expert."

"Then I better get to work." She started lifting the cards one by one, glancing at the names of business owners. "Will they all really have to move out and go belly up if we don't bring in more business?"

Blanche shrugged. "Some of them will. Maybe not Mitch Easterbrook. People will always die and need an undertaker. But the spa? The bed-and-breakfast? Yes. And we need the local newspaper on board, so I had to have Ned Chandler here. And I invited Nellie to the committee because she knows the history. Andi Rivers was one of the architects who worked on the design of Bushrod Square, and Daniel Kilcannon's family has been here for more than fifty years."

Chloe picked up the card of the handsome older gentleman. "Waterford Farm?"

"It's a dog training facility on the outskirts of town."

"What about Dave Ashland? The real estate guy? He seemed pretty disinterested."

"He shouldn't be, since his client is an old coot who lived here years ago and retired to Florida, but still owns that whole block of Bushrod Avenue along the square, and Dave manages the properties. Rent won't get paid if those businesses go under."

"But if real estate values go up, Dave could help

him negotiate higher rents or even sell the land. He definitely has a lot to gain from tourism."

Blanche gave in to a deep sigh. "It's make-it-or-break-it time for Bitter Bark, and I don't want to let Frank down."

"And I don't want to let you down, Aunt Blanche."

She squeezed Chloe's hand. "You're a good girl for helping me. When I called, I only wanted an idea or two. I never expected you to leave your fancy apartment in Miami and your exciting life."

But Chloe had heard the desperation in her aunt's voice and known this was one thing she could do to help a woman who'd helped her so many times. "It's not so exciting. My life is mostly one hotel room after another."

"And here you're staying in an old, empty house. I hope it's clean enough for you. I know how you like things just so, not that I can blame you, what with the way…" Her voice trailed off.

The way you were raised.

Chloe could well imagine how that sentence should end. "It's fine," she promised her aunt. "I'm happy not to stay in a hotel for once, and it's nice of your friend to let me live there while she's traveling."

"Taking care of an aging mother, not exactly a European tour. And she's thrilled to have someone in the house," Blanche said, glancing at her watch. "Oh God. I have the dreaded Finance Committee coming in here to make my life miserable, even though it's already five o'clock."

"Then let me leave and go wander the streets of Bitter Bark in search of an idea."

Blanche gave a shaky smile. "Where do you find things like that, Chloe?"

"I have no clue," she said with a wry laugh. "But if I find one, you'll be the first to know."

A few minutes later, Chloe walked down the wide stone stairs of town hall and took a good long look at Bushrod Square, which, she'd learned from Nellie, the librarian, had been named after the town's founder, Captain Thaddeus Ambrose Bushrod.

Bushrod. Oh, the places she could go with that. None of them G-rated or tourist friendly.

Spreading out over the equivalent of several city blocks and anchored on four sides with stately brick columns, the square included a playground, benches, a fountain, gazebo, and a large statue next to a massive tree in the center. That would be Captain Thad, she guessed, and the famed bitter bark tree that gave the town its name.

Except that looked an awful lot like a hickory to her, not that she was a botanist. But she'd never heard of a bitter bark tree. Was there something there?

Come see the world's only bitter bark tree? Strolling through the square, she snapped some pictures and stared at the tree and paused to read the plaque that described how Captain Bushrod founded the town after the Civil War, seeking a place of peace for his family.

The most peaceful town on earth?

Which would be the most boring tourism campaign ever.

She continued on to one of the four streets that ran the perimeter of the square. Along the avenue, there was an abundance of cutesy mom-and-pop stores, with green and white awnings over precious window displays. She wended around a few tables outside the Bitter Bark Bistro, meandered past window boxes full of pansies at Bitter Bark Books, and stopped to take a deep inhale of the buttery deliciousness of Bitter Bark Bakery mixed with an overpowering scent of honeysuckle from Bitter Bark Buds 'n' Blooms.

Maybe old Uncle Frank took this name thing a little too far. Or was there a certain kitschy quality that tourists might like? Bittersweet Days the Bitter Bark Way? Bitter is Better than Butter? Take a Bite of Bitter Bark and Die of Happiness?

Oh boy. She was tanking here.

She stopped in front of a pub-type place called, no surprise to anyone, the Bitter Bark Bar. A glass of wine to kick her creativity back to life, perhaps? She'd earned it after today.

Praying the place met her impossibly high cleanliness standards, she pulled open the door and blinked into darkness. Clean enough, with booths and tables and an expansive hardwood floor that looked scuffed from dancing.

She opted to sit at the mostly empty bar, and as she picked a stool, a man came out of the back room wiping his hands on a towel. "You're all set back there, Billy," he called to the bartender, who was at the register, counting bills. "I found the problem and fixed it."

Chloe eyed the back-bar fixer in well-worn jeans and a filthy white T-shirt, inching back at the impact. Because...*whoa*. A shirt that dirty in the back of a restaurant ought to be...illegal. And one that fit like that? All tight around too many muscles? Also illegal, but for entirely different reasons. By the time she made it up and down over all six, no *eight*, of those abs outlined by the sweaty shirt, she reached his face and discovered his gaze locked right on her.

"You got a customer, Billy," he said, staring right back at her. "I'll take care of her for you."

He took three slow steps closer, a hint of a smile pulling at his lips. Beautiful lips. Soft, sexy lips. Lips that were moving and she didn't even hear what he said until she realized his broad, strong shoulders were shaking. In laughter. At her.

"Woman clearly needs something strong, Billy." His voice was low, but still a little playful. "Let me buy it for her."

"No, that's…" Good God, her voice came out like a strangled goat's. "You don't have to."

"I want to." He wiped his hands on his shirt, which just made them—or the shirt—dirtier. "Newcomer's special. We give one to all the tourists, right, Billy?"

Billy grunted while he counted, and Chloe nodded. "All right, then. A pinot grigio, preferably dry and crisp, please. And from a fresh bottle."

He lifted both brows like she had to be kidding.

"Okay, anything white," she relented. "Do you really give a free drink to all the tourists?" Because that was a decent hook.

He snagged a glass and pulled the cork out of some cheap Chardonnay that had probably been in the bar fridge for days. "Only the beautiful ones, right, Billy?"

Oh. He was flirting. Well, she *had* stared at him like he was wrapped in gold with a red ribbon and Godiva stamped on his abs.

"He doesn't even work here," Billy said, as if his friend needed an explanation.

"I just clean up the messes in the back," the man shot back at the bartender. "And, whoa, that was a wreck."

"I know, sorry." Billy stuffed his bills in the cash register and slammed it shut. "Thanks, Shane."

Shane. Dirty, unshaved, cocky Shane with short chestnut hair and a riveting gaze the color of oxidized copper. Not gold. Not green. Not bad.

"S'okay." He looked right at Chloe and not the glass that he filled to the top. "I love a challenge."

He put the drink in front of her, forgetting a napkin but not a smile. One that was sexy and sly enough that she failed to notice where his finger had touched the rim and now she'd have to put her mouth on him, er, it.

"So what brings you to Bitter Bark, gorgeous?"

The bartender, a husky older man, made his way over and gave his grimy pseudo-employee a poke. "Do your pickup work on the right side of the bar, Shane."

He flipped the service bar up and stepped out. "Then gimme a Bud Light, Billy, and I'll keep an eye on the tourists."

"I'm not a..." Oh, let him think that. Maybe thinking like a tourist would help her figure out a plan to attract them.

He slipped onto the next barstool. She braced herself for a whiff of blue-collar sweat, but a surprisingly musky, masculine scent hit her, and she shivered involuntarily as his arm brushed hers when he settled in.

Because it was covered in dirt, of course.

"So, what's your name, buttercup?"

She closed her eyes. "Chloe," she said. "My name is Chloe. Not Gorgeous. Not Buttercup."

Billy snorted as he put down a beer in front of Shane. "And not interested."

Undaunted, Shane turned his barstool to face her. "Chloe." He said it slow, drawing out the syllables like he wanted his mouth around each one. Then he gulped some beer, eyeing her over the bottle. "That's perfect," he said after he swallowed.

"The beer or the name?"

"Both." He eyed her again, openly. "It's the perfect name for you."

Okay, now he was just yanking her chain. "What's that supposed to mean?" she countered.

"It means what it says. It's a perfect name for a perfect woman."

She angled her head and met that mesmerizing gaze. "I'm sorry. I'm not from around here and may not speak your language. Was that sarcasm?"

He laughed. A sound that came from his chest and managed to roll right through Chloe from head to curling toes. "Do you have a hair out of place?" he asked.

She didn't have to touch her long dark hair, still pulled back into a neat ponytail the way she wore it for meetings, to know the answer. "Of course not."

He reached for her hand and took it in his, shocking her with the unexpected contact and the roughness of calluses. Examining a flawless French manicure she'd gotten the day before, he nodded. "Not a chip in sight."

"I have standards."

He lifted a brow. "I bet you do."

She tugged her hand free and stared down at the manhandled wineglass. That drink looked awfully damn good right now and maybe the only way to manage the onslaught of Dirty Shame.

Oh hell. Alcohol kills germs, right? She gulped, a little shocked at the cold, light wine and how delicious it tasted.

"So, New York or DC or Boston?" he asked, studying her intently enough to cause a slow warm burn to slide up her chest.

"Miami," she replied.

"Miami?" He sounded stunned. "Who leaves Miami to come to Bitter Bark?"

"Exactly what I'd like to know," she replied. "So tell me five amazing things one would find in this town."

"Other than me?"

She had to laugh. "Then just the other four."

"Okay." He took another sip and thought about that. "This new section around Bushrod Square is pretty. Weather is perfect, and you can see the Blue Ridge Mountains from anywhere you stand."

The "mountains" that had been called the "Appalachian Highlands" when she grew up on the other side of them in Kentucky. Proving that a simple and marvelous name change could transform a place from dull to desirable.

"We have water sports and hiking in the summer and skiing in the winter," he continued. "And a whole bunch of cute little stores. Was that four?"

"It was *standard*." She let out a sigh and shook her

head. "None of that makes this place different or even remotely competitive with Asheville."

He rolled his eyes. "What is everyone's obsession with Asheville?"

"It's on the map," Billy chimed in. "*That's* the obsession. The bars are packed, the stores are crowded, and streets are lined with gold."

"That's ridiculous," Shane replied. "You can't move in this bar on a Saturday night, crowded stores means long lines, and our streets are lined with…"

"Dog poop," Billy said, cracking himself up. "Yours are, anyway."

Shane glared at him. "What my esteemed colleague is trying to say is that we also have a world-class dog training and rescue business that brings in people from around the country."

"Oh yeah." She nodded, remembering they'd talked about it in the meeting. "The dog place that old guy owned. Daniel something."

"Kilcannon," he supplied, lifting his glass to his mouth, but not hiding a smile. "That *old* guy?"

Billy gave a soft hoot and walked away to serve a new customer. But Chloe frowned, looking down at her wine as an invisible thread tugged at her brain. A tendril of possibility. A direction. The very first cloudy fog of an idea. What was it?

"Yeah," she said absently, digging deeper into her subconscious like a dog rooting for a bone that he'd once left. Yes, exactly like a…*dog*. "They talked about some farm with lots and lots of dogs," she said.

"Waterford Farm," he supplied. "It's not really a farm as much as an elite canine facility."

But she forgot the man next to her for a moment as

something completely different, and wonderfully familiar, rose a few thousand chills on her skin. It was the blissful, delicious sensation of a brilliant idea about to hatch.

"If you like dogs," he said, "I'll take you there."

She curled a lip, not really thinking about her response, because all of her brain power was hard at work on something much more important: exploding with a solution to her problem.

"Was that face because you don't like dogs?"

She just shook her head as the idea took shape in her brain. Still...*she* didn't have to like them. "But..."

"Because if you don't like dogs, we don't have a chance, darlin'. I mean, Chloe."

"Dogs." She barely heard the comment and ignored the pet name, because a concept was crystallizing, taking shape, and growing. And that made her whole head buzz. "Something like..." She snapped her fingers, closing her eyes, words popping into her head. "The Town That Went to the Dogs? Who Let the Tourists Out? Get a Better Bark in..."

And there it was. Wham, a flashing light snapped on in her brain, shining nothing but brightness on an absolutely glorious idea.

Better Bark.

"Oh my God, that's it. That's it! That is an absolutely on-the-money freaking fantastic idea!" She pushed back from the bar, standing from the sheer power of the concept. He was right next to her in a second and, without thinking, she clamped both hands on his broad shoulders. "Oh, I could kiss you!"

He smiled. "Now *that* is a good idea."

"Yes, yes, it is!" Still holding on to him, she

squeezed, realizing the very genius of the idea had made her a little lightheaded. Or maybe it was the wine.

Or maybe it was this man.

Stupidly, she tightened her grip, looking up at him. "Really, I can't thank you enough."

He let that gorgeous green-gold gaze drop down her face and settle on her mouth. "Sure you can," he whispered. "That kiss you just mentioned, for example."

She opened her mouth to suck in a shocked breath, but he lowered his head like he was about to make good on the suggestion.

"Just one," he whispered, "really quick, but unforgettable, kiss." A little closer. "It's our newcomer's special."

Chloe Somerset didn't kiss strangers. She didn't kiss filthy strangers with hard muscles and soft whispers. She didn't tilt her head, close her eyes, and...

And then she did all that and more.

His arms slipped around her, pulling her into his powerful, masculine chest. And his lips landed on hers, taking ownership of her openmouthed gasp with his soft, skilled lips. Everything spun, so of course she reached up to steady herself by holding on to...those *shoulders*.

She forgot where she was. Forgot *who* she was. Forgot the idea, the bar, the world around her. Everything disappeared except the searing warmth of this stranger's lips that made her stomach flip around like a helpless fish hanging on a hook. Her chest grew warm. Her legs grew weak. And, God help her, she opened her mouth and let their tongues touch so that she could taste beer and mint and something dangerous and thrilling.

When it ended, she stayed right where she was, eyes closed, reeling.

He let her go very slowly, as if he knew she was unsteady. As if he didn't want to let go.

What the hell was wrong with her? "We're square now," she said breathlessly. "And I have to go home and work."

"Where's home? I'll take you."

Not a chance. She'd never come out alive. "I can walk there." She hoped. She managed to let go of him, peeling away, praying for steadiness but ready to blame the wine if she stumbled. "Thanks. And, bye...Dirty Shame."

He grinned at the name. "See ya around, Perfect Chloe."

But he wouldn't. She didn't know his last name. Or where he lived. Or what his deal was, except that he was a back-bar fixer and a damn good kisser. And she'd sucked up his inspiration and tongue like a woman who'd lost every shred of self-control.

The one thing Chloe Somerset never gave up.

She took off like a scared cat, still tasting him on her lips.

Chapter Two

Three days after one hot kiss and Shane still couldn't shake that beautiful brunette out of his head.

What the hell?

It was eight a.m. during a training class, and he was surrounded by five new dogs and their five fairly clueless owners seeking guidance and help from him. But he was standing in the July morning sun wondering how to find Perfect Chloe. She'd never gone back into Billy's bar—God knew he'd asked Billy enough times. A few unnecessary strolls past the Bitter Bark Bed & Breakfast offered no glimpse of her, but it felt way too stalkerish to ask Jane Gruen if someone named Chloe had checked in recently.

And that left him cold. Or hot, as the case may be. He knew nothing else about this woman from Miami who seemed interested only in what made Bitter Bark special. Then walked away when he tried to show her.

Maybe he'd lost his touch.

He snapped his fingers as if to make sure they still worked, and a schnauzer named Garfield instantly dropped the chew toy he'd been playing with, trotted to Shane, and looked up as if he was a private in the army waiting for his drill sergeant's next instruction.

"How did you do that?" Garfield's owner, an older woman with zero training skills, cried out in exasperation. "Are you wearing that special spray that makes dogs listen to you?"

Sure hadn't been wearing special spray the other night, or he wouldn't have woken up alone and wondering about a stranger every morning since.

"No pheromone juice, Mrs. Freeman. It's all natural talent at Waterford."

"Well, you sure are good with dogs."

He didn't argue. Dog whispering was his gift, one that had only been a handy hobby until three years ago, when his father convinced almost all of his kids to return to Bitter Bark and build a first-class canine training and rescue facility. Shane had walked away from practicing law and now worked as the head of civilian dog training at Waterford Farm, side by side with his father, two of his brothers, and two sisters.

Would Perfect Chloe have given him a chance if she had smelled money and a law degree instead of dogs and sweat? No doubt. With her expensive clothes and shiny hair and perfectly made-up big brown eyes, she was a judgmental woman who cared only about appearances and made assumptions about people that were wrong.

So if he'd been sitting on the other side of the bar in a two-thousand-dollar suit and a legal brief in front of him, would he have been able to get her out of those clothes and mess up that hair and see those big brown eyes spark with arousal?

Probably. And that pissed him off even more. In

fact, everything pissed him off, including the fact that he'd never get another chance with her.

Mrs. Freeman got down to pet Garfield, but Shane's attention was drawn to Rin Tin Tin, the battered yellow Jeep that they used to transport dogs to new homes or here from shelters. His younger brother Garrett was at the wheel, pulling onto the road that ran behind the kennels.

Next to Garrett, his fiancée of one month, Jessie Curtis, sat with her tan and white Aussie shepherd, Lola, on her lap. But Shane's gaze was drawn to the back, where an unfamiliar new arrival sat on haunches, looking around.

He handed Mrs. Freeman some more treats. "Try again, but this time hold his eyes while you give Garfield the reward," he said. "I'll be right back. Looks like we have a new rescue I want to meet."

Even from a distance, he could see the distinct brown and white coloring and the familiar head shape of a Staffy. He didn't have any memory of Garrett saying he was picking up a new dog, but then Garrett had been pretty damn distracted with Jessie these past few weeks. She'd moved to Bitter Bark, got an apartment in town, and Garrett was never around the house he and Shane shared near town.

He ambled across the training area just as Garrett and Jessie climbed out. When Shane reached the Jeep, they opened the back door to let the dog out, but the new arrival didn't move until Garrett gave permission.

"Well trained," Shane noted, seeing now that the dog was female with stunning two-toned coloring that divided her face into an almost perfect split of chocolate and vanilla. Of course, she'd have to go through life being called a pit bull by judgmental people who made assumptions based on appearances. Like Perfect Chloe.

He shook the woman out of his brain and focused on the dog, who still hadn't so much as barked. In a brand-new place with at least ten other dogs in sight? This one was an angel.

"What's her name?" Shane asked, immediately coming to his knees to greet the dog.

"Daisy."

Shane smiled and eased his hand around her head, knowing exactly how to reach without any aggression, but a steady, kind hand. "Crazy, lazy Daisy," he said softly, holding her dark gaze to establish a bond. "Rescue?"

"Long-term boarder," Garrett said. "Jessie and I went over to Greensboro last night to have dinner with Marie Boswell and celebrate our engagement, and we came home with Daisy."

"Sounds like dinner with Marie." Shane laughed, thinking of their family friend who volunteered in shelters and frequently sent dogs to Waterford for the rescue program that Garrett ran. "How long term?"

"Could be a month," Garrett said. "Marie broke her foot, a fact she forgot to mention to me until we arrived. The woman has four dogs and can't handle any of them until she's out of a cast. She was able to find temporary homes for all the others, but she wanted to keep Daisy. Impossible, since this dog is incredibly active."

"Most Staffies are," Shane said, curling a finger around the terrier's ear. The misunderstood Staffordshire terrier, like its cousin the American bull terrier, had been Shane's weakness ever since...Zeus. He swallowed hard at the memory of the dog, as he always did.

No, it wasn't fair that these dogs got saddled with a name and a bad rep. No one knew like Shane that it wasn't the dogs that were monsters. The real animals were the people who didn't know jack shit about them.

"She's never been in a kennel in her life," Garrett said. "But I couldn't let Marie struggle with her, and Daisy wasn't happy with no playtime."

Shane made a face, knowing Daisy would have to be inside plenty at Waterford.

"I can keep her at night," Shane offered, already planning to take her for long walks and Frisbee tosses. But during the day, she'd have to stay in the kennels while other dogs were training. She'd hate that, and he knew it. Being penned up during the day would make her restless and anxious, and then, if she made one mistake...someone might say it was because of her breed and not her situation. Not anyone who worked at Waterford, but a guest.

When he used both hands to rub the dog's head, she instantly leaned forward to show her gratitude with a juicy lick on Shane's cheek. A kisser, like all happy Staffordshire terriers.

"Good girl, Daisy." He reached into the treat bag hanging off his pants and slipped out a tiny biscuit. She gobbled it out of his hand and rewarded him with a direct, grateful gaze and a little pant of love.

"I'm going to check her in and show her shot record to Molly," Garrett said, referring to their sister, the Waterford vet. "Where are you going to be, Jess?"

"Lola needs some exercise," she said. "I'll take her down to the creek and wait for you."

"Okay." Garrett leaned forward to kiss Jessie on the lips. "See you in a bit."

"Oh, the smooching," Shane whispered to Daisy as Jessie took off. "Don't tell me they did that all the way from Greensboro."

"Shut up," Garrett said, snapping a leash on Daisy's collar. "You're jealous."

"Not at all." Shane stood to look his brother in the eyes. "As a matter of fact, I was kissing someone myself recently."

One kiss. But Garrett didn't need to know that. Or the fact that "recently" was three days ago and he was still thinking about her.

"Someone with two legs, not four?"

"Screw you," Shane joked. "The king of celibacy falls hard, and the rest of the world is on the receiving end of his teasing."

"Not teasing, Shane. You should try something more than meaningless sex sometime." Garrett's gaze shifted to the figure of Jessie, disappearing around the tree-lined path that led to Crescent Creek. "It's life-changing."

"Only if you want your life to change, which I don't." Wouldn't mind having his empty bed change, though.

"Hey, you two!" They turned to see their father walking across the expansive lawn behind the house where Daniel and Annie Kilcannon had raised six kids and more dogs than anyone could remember. "Have either of you seen Liam?"

"It's explosives training today," Shane told him,

which meant the oldest Kilcannon would be far from the facility all day, doing canine bomb-sniffing training with some officers and trainee dogs.

Dad frowned, shaking his head as he came closer. "New rescue?" he asked, looking at Daisy.

"She's Marie's dog," Garrett said, giving the dog's leash a tug. "We're boarding her for a month or so, and I have to get her checked in and over to Molly. Come on, Daisy." He started walking, and Daisy followed at a nice, even trot.

"That's a good girl," Shane said, watching them go and appreciating how well trained Daisy was. If only people could see that dog when they thought of a pit bull, they'd change their stupid preconceptions in a hurry.

"That's a happy boy," Dad replied, his gaze on Garrett. "I really couldn't be more pleased with Garrett's engagement."

Shane eyed his dad, suspecting, as they all did, that the possibility of a romance was the real reason Dad had encouraged his middle son to consent to the in-depth profile that Jessie, a journalist, had wanted to do on him. The whole thing had damn near exploded as badly as one of Liam's sniff-training devices, though.

"So, Liam's out all day?" Dad asked, sounding a little disappointed.

"They'll come back for lunch, or you can text him. What's up?"

Dad shook his head. "That won't work. I need him this morning."

"For what?" They all had various specialties at the facility, but most of the jobs were interchangeable. And if Dad, who was the de facto boss of all of them, needed something, Shane was always willing to help. "I'm almost done with this training round, and I can give you a hand."

His father leaned against the split-rail fence that no longer enclosed much of anything, but it was the original fencing they'd had around the old yard when they were kids, and Dad kept it for sentimental value. He gazed at Shane, considering the offer, a frown making the creases around his eyes deeper. He didn't look fifty-nine, nor did he act it. He sure wasn't "an old guy," as a judgmental stranger had called him the other night.

"I really wanted Liam," Dad said.

"I can do anything Liam can do," Shane said, adding a grin. "Usually better and with way more personality."

"But you're not the one I want."

Shane's competitive streak shot up his spine. "But I'm the one you got. What do you need?"

"I really believe Liam would be the right choice for this…situation."

"For *what* situation?" Even in the early morning, summer heat made him sweat. Or maybe that was his frustration with Dad, who was obviously meddling, pulling strings, and being the man they called the Dogfather. He got the nickname for his love of dogs and his desire to get people to do what he wanted, like The Godfather of the Mafia. Only, Irish without the bloodshed and way more fur.

"It's that Tourism Advisory Committee I'm on," Dad said. "I have a conflict and need to back out of today's meeting and, honestly, I thought it would be a good idea for Liam to take my place."

"Liam? Don't you have to talk in those meetings?"

Dad shot him a look. "He's the best for this...task."

"If the task is training German shepherds how to kill on command so we can sell them for ten grand a pop, yeah. If you need someone to represent..." Something clicked in his mind. "The *tourism* committee, you say? What's this meeting about?"

Dad waved a hand as if the actual reason for the meeting wasn't that important. "Mayor Wilkins brought her niece up from Miami, and she's some kind of tourism expert who's going to help Bitter Bark get more visitors."

Oh, hello, manna from womanly heaven. I thought you'd never fall into my lap.

"Her niece from Miami?" Shane actually had to stop himself from fist-pumping in victory.

"Yeah, and she's supposed to give some presentation at eleven today. Seems she has some ideas to help build tourism."

"I'll go." Nothing would stop him, in fact.

"I really want Liam to go."

Like hell Liam was getting near her. "Dad, you are looking at the best possible representative for Waterford Farm. I'll be there at eleven, no worries."

Dad lifted a brow as if he was trying to say something but didn't want to. "Andi Rivers is on that committee."

The architect? "Yeah? So?"

"*Andi Rivers,*" he repeated, as if Shane didn't hear him the first time. "Liam's Andi Rivers."

Oh, so that was Dad's game. Shane laughed softly. "Subtle, man. Unbelievably subtle."

"I know they used to date, and I thought..."

"I know what you thought. And you need to let it go. Andi had her shot at that big dumb ox and missed it. But I, on the other hand—"

"*You* want to go out with Andi Rivers?"

"No. But I want..." One more shot at Perfect Chloe. If only to let her see what she missed. "I want to help Bitter Bark," he said.

"You do?"

His father wasn't the only one in this family who could manipulate. "This town's in trouble, Dad. We need tourists. We need to get on the map like Asheville."

"You sound like you were a fly on the wall at our last meeting."

"I know what Bitter Bark needs." He could still see her eyes light up as she grabbed his shoulders when he'd handed her...an *absolutely on-the-money freaking fantastic idea.* "I'm an idea guy, and you know it." And *she* knew it. "I'll be able to really judge whatever she's presenting."

Just like she judged him and found him...only good enough for one kiss.

"You're right, Shane. And we'll need more if her idea fails."

His idea, actually. Whatever it was. "I'll go. I have to see what she's presenting."

His father's brows, still much darker than his salt-and-pepper hair, drew together. "I would never have thought you'd be so interested in Bitter Bark's tourism program."

He wasn't. But he sure was interested in the tourism expert. "Count on me. I got your back."

"All right, but..." He looked past Shane to the

distant hills where the explosives-sniffing was going on. "But I like that Andi Rivers, and she got a raw deal."

When the guy she picked over Liam was killed? "She chose poorly," he said simply. "I'd say I'd put a good word in for him, but Dad, when are you going to quit trying to fix us all up?"

His father frowned at him. "Your mother wanted you all to be as happy as we were, and if I can help that along, then I will."

Shane puffed out a breath, as if he had to make space in his chest as he always did at the mention of his mother, gone three years now. "Look, what you and Mom had was one in a million. A billion. Nobody else will ever get that."

"Not with that attitude," Dad chided with a sigh. "Okay, you are officially on the Tourism Advisory Committee, Shane. Thank you."

He gave his father an easy pat on the shoulder. "No, thank *you*."

He turned to finish the training class, unable to wipe the smile from his face. He had at least one more chance to mess up Perfect Chloe.

Chapter Three

Chloe checked her PowerPoint presentation one more time, straightened her notes, and took a deep, slow breath. She'd arrived early for the meeting, and Aunt Blanche's assistant had ushered her into the same conference room they'd been in a few days earlier.

But what a difference a few days made. Chloe had nailed this one, working nonstop to put together a presentation that would wow them all. Like nothing they'd expect and, if they had a vision, everything they needed.

Excited to present, she'd dressed to impress with a crisp white suit over a silky black tank top and sky-high heels.

Now, she just had to do what she did best and deliver a brilliant proposal.

As she walked around the table, murmuring some of the key messages she wanted to get across, Aunt Blanche came in, her pale skin flushed and her eyes sparkling as she closed the door behind her.

"I can't stand the anticipation." Blanche rubbed her hands together. "Please give me a sneak peek."

"Not a chance," Chloe said. "I want to read your reaction along with everyone else's."

"Oh darn." She brushed back some hair that had more silver than blond strands these days. "Can you give me a hint?"

"Not a word," Chloe teased, counting her business cards and making sure each one was perfectly lined up with the edge of the table. "Eight committee members and you, right?"

"Yes, but we had a change on the committee this morning."

Chloe gave her a sharp look of concern. She'd geared this presentation to really appeal to the businesses that were present. "Who is it?"

"Daniel Kilcannon, the man who owns Waterford Farm, won't be here."

Disappointment thudded. Daniel Kilcannon was the *dog* guy. "Oh no. I was counting on his support."

"I know, he's one of our exemplary local citizens, having raised six kids right here in Bitter Bark."

"Six?"

"Oh, such a wonderful family, the Kilcannons. Annie, Daniel's wife, died so tragically about three years ago. Heart attack at fifty-five."

"How sad," she said, barely registering the news as she kicked herself for not going out to Waterford Farm while she was preparing her presentation. She hadn't wanted to give her hand away.

"It was, but then the most amazing thing happened. Five of those six kids—one is in the military overseas—rallied round him and moved back to Bitter Bark. That's when they turned their homestead, which has always been called Waterford Farm, into that dog training facility. You know, people have called Daniel the Dogfather since he's a veterinarian and had foster dogs forever out there at Waterford."

With each bit of local color, Chloe's heart sank. She *had* to have this man they called the Dogfather on the committee.

"I'm so disappointed," she admitted. "I think he would have loved my idea."

"Not to worry, dear," Blanche assured her. "He's sending one of his sons in his place. His name is—"

The door to the conference room popped open, cutting Blanche off, and they both turned to see a man entering the conference room.

No, not a man.

The man. That man. The very man who...holy sweet merciful heaven, he cleaned up nice.

"Shane!" Blanche clasped her hands together. "I was just telling our new tourism expert that you'll be stepping in for your father."

Chloe gripped the back of the chair in front of her, holding on for dear life as the impact hit her. *His father?*

"And how'd she take that news?" he asked with a half smile as he inched to the right to see all the way around Blanche and pin Chloe with that mystical, magical, way too dizzying green-gold gaze.

She opened her mouth, but not a damn word slipped out.

"I was filling her in on your wonderful family," Blanche said. "So let me introduce you. Shane Kilcannon, this is Chloe Somerset. Shane is the top trainer at Waterford Farm, but before that, he was a corporate lawyer. He went to Georgetown Law school. Pretty impressive, huh?"

She literally had to work to speak. "Very…impressive."

She tried not to stare at the crisp, expensive white shirt, open at the collar but fitted over shoulders she still remembered holding on to for support when he kissed the daylights out of her. He'd shaved today, which gave him a whole different look. Handsome. Professional. Clean.

And Clean Shane was as hot as Dirty Shame.

"I hope your father filled you in on our committee meeting yesterday," Blanche said, stepping to the door.

"He told me all about the tourism expert you brought in, Blanche." He held Chloe's gaze with enough humor in his that she almost felt herself smiling. Almost. "So of course I jumped on the chance to join the committee."

His eyes narrowed in a secret message she heard loud and clear: *I'm here because of you.*

And that did some wild and unexpected things to her insides.

Taking a steadying breath at the thought, she finally held out her hand when he got close. "I believe we've met already, Mr. Kilcannon."

"You have?" Blanche asked. "Well, that's wonderful."

"Briefly." Chloe slipped her hand into his, feeling the calluses and strength again and having the same reaction she did the other night. Worse. Because now she knew how he kissed.

"And please call me Shane. Or, some might say,

Shame." He gave a sly wink that only she could see, and it sent a whole cascade of chills down her entire body. Not fair. So not fair.

"And you can call me Chloe. Or, some might say, *buttercup*." She whispered the last word, and he grinned.

"Oh, here's the rest of the committee," Blanche announced, thankfully not paying attention to their exchange but making Chloe realize she had to let go of that masculine hand before someone noticed. And her knees got wobbly.

Rooting down to her toes for composure and focus, she forced herself to forget how Shane Kilcannon kissed. Right now, she had a concept to sell, and he was…the very person who gave her the idea.

Would he try to kill it? Love it? Take credit? Or distract her every time her gaze landed on him?

Definitely that one.

She turned her attention away as the room filled with the Tourism Advisory Committee members. She now knew every name and job…except for the new arrival.

The *lawyer* named Shane. Not a back-bar fixer, and he sure looked like he was getting a kick out of her surprise.

"Nice to see you again, Chloe, and so soon after we last met." Ned Chandler, the editor of the *Bitter Bark Banner*, came up to her first to shake her hand. "I respect a person who rises to a challenge."

She shook the man's hand, sizing up how he'd react to her idea. This guy was early forties, and not a local, having moved here from Upstate New York to take over when the last editor of the local paper retired. He seemed to really like the town and relish his role, and she was definitely counting on his support.

Right behind him was a young woman Chloe had immediately connected with in the last meeting. Andrea Rivers was in her mid-thirties, a smart, quick-witted, and easy-to-talk-to architect who'd been involved with the gentrification of the Bushrod Square area. They gave each other a warm hello, and then Chloe turned to the one she thought of as the undertaker.

Mitchell Easterbrook, owner of Easterbrook Funeral Home, the fifth generation of Easterbrooks to bury the dead, was conservative and staid, which probably served him well in the funeral business, but might not win him over to her plans. He'd take a little wooing.

And speaking of wooing...Chloe felt the burning heat of someone watching her as she worked her way through her greetings. She didn't need to turn and look to know that Shane had her right on his radar.

Would anyone else pick that up? Had anyone seen her with him that night? The thought was sobering, and she squelched it, fast. She couldn't get distracted.

She said hello to Jane Gruen, who, along with her husband, owned Bitter Bark Bed & Breakfast, and Jeannie Slattery, with her violent red hair. For the owner of Bitter Bark Body and Mind Spa, Jeannie seemed wound pretty tight. And Jeannie once again had a hard time resisting eye contact with big Mitch the Undertaker. Definitely something going on there.

She greeted Nellie, the librarian, who was as quiet as her workplace and a little mousy, probably a red flag that she was anything but. Finally, Dave Ashland, the large, slightly overweight Realtor who already had his phone out.

And that was nine total, including Aunt Blanche and...Shane. She stole a glance at him, and they locked eyes, his sparking with humor and interest as he took a seat right next to where her laptop was. Of course.

Blanche started things off with some small talk and chitchat. During that, Chloe opened up her computer and checked behind her to see that the connection was still working and her first slide was on the screen.

"You nervous?" Shane whispered under his breath so that only she could hear.

"Should I be?" she replied in the same *sotto voce*.

"Could be a tough crowd."

"At least I know *who they are*." She slid him an accusatory side-eye.

"You never asked who I was." He tipped his head. "You merely assumed I was in the back..."

"Fixing beer taps," she finished for him. "And I *kissed* you."

"Imagine what you would have done if you'd known the truth."

She eyed him. "Is *that* why you're here?"

Blanche cleared her throat, bringing their whisper volley to a halt. "And without further ado," Blanche said, "I'm turning this meeting over to our expert, who assures me she has come up with a strategy and idea that will change our image so that we can compete with the very best tourist towns in North Carolina. Chloe?"

She took a deep breath and pushed her chair back,

vaguely aware that her leg brushed Shane's expensive trousers. She smoothed her skirt and tapped the remote she held in a hand that was surprisingly damp.

"I know you all would very much like to be 'the next Asheville,'" she started, clicking to her screen that displayed those very words. "But I have a *better* idea." Another click showed a big red X over the word *Asheville*, making someone—she thought it might be the librarian—gasp softly at the heresy of it all.

Baby, just wait.

"There already is an Asheville," Chloe reminded them. "And it's arguably one of the most beautiful places in this state." She let her gaze move from person to person, comfortable in this role that she'd learned at her first marketing agency job right out of college and had perfected during the years she'd been on her own. "But what we need in Bitter Bark is something to differentiate us from all the other sweet little tourist towns tucked into these lovely foothills. All the precious towns in the state. On the entire East Coast. In fact, something that will set us apart from every other tourist destination in the whole country."

Taking a breath, she got some nods, some exchanged looks, a little skepticism, a lot of interest.

Then she risked a look at Shane and saw something else. Some...heat. It made her stomach do a flip, so she looked away to avoid the response she couldn't afford when she clicked to the next slide.

"I propose to make Bitter Bark the town known primarily for one thing and one thing only...the unabashed love for and welcome of that one member of the family that inevitably gets left out of every vacation."

She clicked to a slide of a little puppy with big eyes and a sweet face. It did nothing for her, but the chorus of "awwws" in the room boosted her confidence. She sneaked a look at Shane and noticed his expression had softened somewhat, and included a knowing smile.

Well, he had given her the idea when he mentioned the dog training facility. He just failed to mention his family owned it.

"We're going to the dogs?" Jeannie joked, getting a nervous laugh from the rest.

"It's a doggone good town?" This from the undertaker, making everyone moan.

She let them settle down before taking ownership of the room again. "You're close," she said, so as not to alienate the mockers. "I propose we position Bitter Bark as the most-dog-friendly vacation spot in the state of North Carolina and, in fact, the entire US."

"How?" someone asked.

"By making dogs welcome in restaurants, in shops, at all businesses, all around the campus of our local college, at the river rafting, on the hiking trails, and in every single shop. Not simply welcome, but a focus. If families know they can bring their furry companions and come as a whole family, then they are so much more willing to book a vacation. We have a dog training facility..." She nodded to Shane. "Which I understand is world-class."

"It is," he agreed.

"And we have one more thing that no other town has."

They all stared at her, some definitely mesmerized, some processing this idea. Or stunned speechless. She still didn't know, but had a feeling she was about to find out.

"We have the name. Or at least we will." She clicked to the next slide showing a large map of the state of North Carolina with *Bitter Bark* in big, bright letters. "Let's seal our place on the tourism map as the number-one family destination for people who love dogs when we change the name from Bitter Bark...." She clicked again, this time with the new name. "To *Better* Bark."

The room instantly exploded.

Chapter Four

She was serious. She was dead-ass serious, and Shane didn't know whether to throw his head back with a hoot of laughter or kiss her on the mouth, because the idea was hilarious and she was…sexy. Confident. Smart. And sexy.

Considering how badly he wanted to undress her with his eyes while she spoke, he couldn't get down to imaginary underwear, because the idea was so damn good he actually had to pay attention.

And now, all around him, the outburst around a table full of opinionated people who were arguably some of the town's biggest movers and shakers filled the room. The divide was easy to see and evident by the questions and comments.

"You can't change the name of a town that's about to celebrate its 150th Founder's Day!" sourpuss Nellie Shaker predictably squeaked out. She'd never *shaken* anything in her life, Shane thought, and wouldn't start now.

"That is the most inventive thing I've ever heard!" Andi may have smashed his brother's heart a while back, but she was cut from the same intelligent, professional cloth that Chloe was wrapped in.

"Inventive? Try ridiculous!" the news guy, Chandler, balked. "We'd change the name to the *Better Bark Banner*? Next you'll suggest editorials written from a dog's perspective."

Chloe brightened, unfazed by the criticism. "I love that idea, Ned."

"Well, I'm not going to be Better Bark Body and Mind," Jeannie Slattery snorted. "Unless I add dog grooming to my services."

"You might consider that and double your business," Chloe replied with a dazzling smile. She let the reaction die down, then placed her fingertips on the conference table and leaned a little closer to pin them with her sparkly ebony gaze.

Shane let his attention slip down to see how nicely her top clung to her figure under that white jacket, appreciating her long, thick ponytail the color of a freshly washed chocolate Labrador spilling over a shoulder. Everything about her was clean, crisp, orderly, and hot.

Oh, he would have so much fun undoing that hair and getting her out of her flawless white clothes and making her all messy and sweaty and—

"Ladies and gentlemen, will you please hear me out?" she asked, pulling him out of his fantasies.

"What kind of town changes its name?" Easterbrook demanded.

"A smart one," Chloe replied. "There's plenty of precedence of small towns who changed their name for a day or a month or a year, including Joe, Montana, to capitalize on a celebrity. Some have changed their name permanently, like North Tarrytown, New York, when they embraced a famous local legend and become Sleepy Hollow back in the 1990s. Check the record, because the economic lift to that community was tangible."

A few responses, some harrumphing, and the mayor tapped her hand as if it were a gavel. "We asked for a great idea," Blanche Wilkins said loudly. "So let's give her a chance to explain what she's thinking."

After a moment, the room grew silent again, all eyes on a woman who...had a pair. And Shane didn't mean the lovely breasts he was sneaking peeks at. Sure, she had big brown eyes and an angel's face and pouty lips that tasted like cotton candy. But that was only packaging. Chloe Somerset was no pushover and, whoa, he liked that in a woman.

It would make sex all that much sweeter.

She crossed her arms and started walking around the room as she talked, a technique that forced their gazes to follow her and one he'd learned years ago when he cleaned up in law school mock trials.

"When I heard there was a world-class dog training facility here," she said with a slight nod to Shane, "I admit that's where I got the idea."

Credit to him, he noted.

"And from there, the ideas rolled. There is no town in America like this, nowhere that could attract families for fun and activities that also includes this very key member of so many families in our country. Hear me out."

Back at her computer, she clicked to the next slide, one that he was quite familiar with: dog ownership in the United States.

"Over seventy million dogs in this country. Thirty-seven percent of homes have at least one, many have two dogs or more. Services for dogs are growing at an astronomical rate. And look at this." She clicked again and literally buried them in statistics he already knew.

Before they could breathe, she moved to the next set of statistics: family vacations. She obviously knew her stuff, snapping slide after slide and making her argument with such skill, he could practically feel the room shift in her favor. How many families would take a vacation to a new place if they were comfortable bringing the dog?

And, she added, celebrating the dog. "Because Better Bark won't just be dog-friendly," she added. "We'll be dog-*focused*."

She flashed picture after doctored-up picture of local businesses in the new section of town, all of the signs changed from Bitter Bark to Better Bark. She'd used photo-altering software to show where there could be "dog resting" stations, changes to the local parks, and even special "leave your leash" poles.

"Just think of the possibilities," she said with infectious enthusiasm. "Nothing brings in families like festivals and events. The towns you all want to emulate, like Asheville and Boone and Blowing Rock, all have jazz concerts, art festivals, 10Ks, and wine tastings. I'm proposing a year-round calendar of special events that all—every single one—have an emphasis on the universal love of dogs."

"Like a pooping contest in Bushrod Square?" Jeannie pushed back a lock of fake red hair, and most of the table, including Shane, shot her a look of disgust.

But cool-as-a-cucumber Chloe barely flinched.

Instead, she clicked to a slide of a giant twelve-month calendar, a different event highlighted in each month.

"The Better Bark Dog Show that's a sort of mini-Westminster," she said, gesturing to the slide. "Then we'll have a Bark in the Park art festival that features paintings, sculptures, and artwork of dogs. There will be Woofstock, our outdoor doggie concert. We've got the Doggie Olympics, a Bow Wow Beauty Contest, a 10K Run for the Rescues, and..." She pointed to December. "Santa Paws, a special adoption day just in time to have a new face in the family photo on Christmas morning."

Shane felt his jaw drop a little. This was friggin' *brilliant*. Every single person at Waterford Farm would love this...along with every single dog.

"Who's going to pay for all this?" Ned, the news guy, demanded.

"Sponsors like pet-supply makers and pet superstores and tourists." Chloe tilted her head as if that were obvious. "Lots and lots and lots of tourists."

"It's too much," the always-fun undertaker, Mitch, groaned. "A little dog thing, okay, one annual event. Anything else is going to alienate the people who don't like dogs."

"Then let them go to Asheville or Boone," Chloe replied. "If we only get the families who have dogs to bring on vacation, we'll have more tourism business than we can handle."

So deft, using the corporate *we*, Shane thought. And she was right.

"I believe in this idea." Chloe leaned her fingertips

on the table and stared Mitch in the eye. "I have created and run many successful tourism campaigns, and I know what builds visitors. This will work. I absolutely *guarantee* it."

Before they could respond to that declaration, she clicked to the next slide, this one detailing a national publicity campaign that included every imaginable form of media and how they would cover the story of a town so devoted to dogs that it changed its name.

She finished with a banner over the face of a ridiculously cute pug that said, "Hot diggity dog! Let's go to Better Bark!"

And every single person in the room sat in dead, stunned silence, flattened by the bulldozer that was Chloe Somerset and her ideas.

Including Shane. He'd listened, holding her little white business card in his hand, running his fingers over the raised letters the way he wanted to run them over her body. Slowly, carefully, and with great admiration.

She finished, closed her laptop, and sat quietly, looking from one to the other. "Any questions, ladies and gentlemen?"

"Yes," Jane Gruen said. "How quickly can we do this so I can get my B&B certified for dogs and advertise it?"

"You'd let dogs in the Bitter Bark Bed & Breakfast?" Ned shot back. "They'd chew up the furniture and piss on the rugs."

"Hang on." Blanche raised a hand as if she had to be the voice of reason. "A change of town name would require first an advisory committee vote, then if it passed, it would have to be taken to the town council for a hearing that allowed for debate from business owners and locals and, finally, a full citizens' vote. I'd have to look at the bylaws, but a name change is not something that can be done in this room, obviously. But we can take an initial committee vote."

"We don't have to vote." Mitch leaned forward. "This is a waste of time and will never pass."

"What?" Andi's jaw dropped. "This is the single most exciting idea I've ever heard."

"Forget the dogs." The librarian, Nellie, cleared her throat, fighting for their attention, color rising when she got it. "This town was founded in 1867 by Thaddeus Ambrose Bushrod. He named it after the tree that sits at the heart of the entire community. You can't change history."

Every eye in the room shifted to Chloe, waiting for her to volley back.

"Then you better change the tree." She crossed her arms and leaned forward. "Because that one is a hickory tree."

That caused another little uproar, but not from Nervous Nellie. She nodded repeatedly. "That's true. It may be that Captain Bushrod was mistaken about the tree. But he *thought* it was a bitter bark, and he named the town after that tree."

"Bitter bark is actually a shrub with wonderful medicinal uses," Chloe said. "If it would make you feel better, we could plant some all over the square and call it Better Bark."

That caused another round of arguments that Chloe silenced by holding her hands up. "Please, think of the publicity if we *rename* this town a hundred and fifty years after its founding...with a hundred and fifty dogs in the square," she added, her voice rising as if she just had a new idea. "The Barkiversary!"

Shane gave a soft hoot and clapped. "Damn, you're good."

"Well, of course you're all for this," Jeannie Slattery hissed at him. "Waterford Farm would only benefit financially. I suspect you're behind this whole thing, frankly. Tourists all coming in and going to see your place. It would build your business."

"It would build everyone's business," Andi Rivers chimed in. "That's the whole idea, Jeannie. It differentiates us in a way that no one ever dreamed of." She beamed at Chloe. "My head is spinning with ideas that we could incorporate into the next phase of development."

"That phase is on hold," Dave Ashland chimed in. "I've been texting James Fisker, who owns a little over twenty-five percent of Bushrod Square, and he's not ready to develop anything with property values as low as they are."

"But values can only go up if we're wall-to-wall with tourists," Blanche retorted. "We can't do anything if we don't do anything."

The pithy phrase got everyone mumbling and made Chloe beam at the mayor. "Exactly," she agreed.

"Wait, wait, wait." Easterbrook stood to take over the conversation. "I speak as the representative of the family that's been burying Bitter Barkers for five generations." He leveled a gaze at Chloe. "An Easterbrook put Thaddeus Bushrod in the ground under that tree."

"That *hickory* tree," she said softly.

He looked like he wanted to bury her. "We need to

vote," he said, adjusting the sleek tie that added to his tall and commanding presence. "By secret ballot, so there are no hurt feelings and no lobbying one way or another. Before we spend one more moment of our short and precious lives on something that will either turn everything upside down or become a distant memory. Every single one of us in this room, except you, Miss Somerset, needs to cast a yes or no vote. From there, we'll either take it to the town council or ask our esteemed specialist to return to her drawing board for more ideas."

Shane saw her shoulders sink a little at that possibility.

"Are we voting on the concept or the name change?" the librarian asked. "Because we could be dog-friendly without a ridiculous new name."

No doubt where Nellie stood.

"Yes, the concept would work without the name change," Chloe said. "But then you have no hook. No promise to the guest. No way to generate national news coverage, and I do mean a few minutes on CNN and at least an hour-long special on Animal Planet."

A few people leaned forward, like hooked fish.

"Animal Planet?"

"National news?"

"A promise to the guests," Jane Gruen cooed. "I love that concept."

Chloe nodded. "A promise is critical, Jane. It's at the heart of every tourism campaign, and I believe the name of Better Bark does that."

"We should keep the name," Chandler insisted. "The dog thing's a cute idea, and we still have 'bark' in the name."

"Bitter," Chloe replied. "Bitter is not better. It is a word that, by its very definition, is not friendly. It's hurting the town, in my professional opinion."

The statement, which had to have some basis in truth, silenced them all.

"That's what makes the whole idea a winner," Chloe continued when no one argued. "Anyone can say they are dog-friendly and have a few hotels or restaurants that welcome dogs, but I'm proposing you restructure this entire city around the universal love of dogs, and that starts with a name change."

"Then we'll vote by secret ballot," Blanche said, standing up. "I'll get my assistant to bring in ballots and a box. Chloe, will you step outside for a few moments?"

"Of course." She stood and shot one more warm smile at everyone in the room. "I want to remind you that I have created winning tourism campaigns for dozens of cities and a few countries. I know this will work. I am one hundred percent confident that within one year of implementing this change, tourism will increase by a thousand percent. Asheville will be scratching their head about how to compete."

On that, she left, and every person in the room—including Shane—watched her in wonder.

He was so attracted to her, it hurt.

Which made him certain he knew exactly how to vote.

When Chloe walked back into the conference room not ten minutes later, the adrenaline that had dumped through her veins after that presentation had finally settled to a low-grade tension that hummed through her.

She *knew* this would work. She had complete confidence in the idea and absolutely would bet everything she had that this idea would increase visitors to the town and help the local economy. And Aunt Blanche's job would be safe, and Uncle Frank's legacy intact.

But would they go for it?

Sure, a few of them would be old school and stick to the name of the town because they were distantly related to the founder or didn't care that the place was named after the wrong tree. But if they were truly the business professionals who cared about the growth and success of their companies, then they should recognize that this was a great idea.

Especially Shane, who'd been unexpectedly quiet during the presentation and discussions.

Stealing a glance at him as she sat down, she still wasn't able to read his expression. There was a warm glimmer of a tease in eyes that looked more green in this light and the slightest secret smile.

"The votes have been cast," Aunt Blanche announced, pointing to a covered box in the middle of the table. "Chloe, since you didn't vote, will you read them for the record?"

"Of course."

They slid the box toward her end of the table, and she stood, letting out a little exhale of nerves and excitement. "Is there anything formal that has to be done or said?" she asked.

"Just show us each vote," Ned said, as if she would stand there and lie to them.

She didn't dignify that with a response.

"Nothing special for an advisory committee," Blanche assured her. "This is merely step one to see if we will proceed. If this group votes for the idea, then we'll create a plan to take the concept to the town council. If the vote is against it, we'll table the discussion and ask that you come up with something different."

"Okay." Except something different wouldn't work as well. Taking the lid off the box, she leaned over to folded slips of paper, all the same.

She took out the first one and opened it. "Yes." She resisted the urge to add a slightly snarky smile as she turned the paper and showed it to Ned. Then she opened another. "Yes."

This time she bit her lip to keep from smiling.

The next one was a "no" and then another "yes."

"We are three to one for the yeses," Blanche said, a bubble of excitement in her voice. "When we reach five for one or the other, there's no need to continue to count."

Chloe gave her aunt a grateful look, touched by the support. "Okay," she said, opening the next slip of paper. "It's a no."

Three to two.

And the next one. "Another no."

Tied at three all. Chloe exhaled softly, but it sounded loud in the quiet room. She'd really expected more support from this group of professionals.

Certain they could all hear her heart pound, she reached into the box.

"Another no," she said, and it was impossible to hide the disappointment.

"That's four no's," the undertaker said firmly.

"One more, and we can be done with this," Ned added. "I have a deadline to meet for the *Banner*." He cleared his throat. "The Bitter *Bark Banner*."

There were two slips of paper left. She opened one, and her heart kicked as she read it. "Yes."

Not a single person in the room moved or breathed, the tension palpable in the thick silence of the dead tie of four to four.

"Okay," Chloe whispered. "Last one," she said, closing her fingers around it.

"Read it," Nellie insisted, leaning all the way forward.

She opened it and blinked, stunned. "Abstain."

"Abstain?" The echo came from at least five people in the room, two immediately on their feet.

She turned the paper to show them all. "Abstain."

"Who abstained?" Ned Chandler insisted.

"It's a secret ballot," Blanche reminded him.

"What do we do?" Andi asked, her frustration as evident as everyone else's.

"Let's break for lunch," Blanche suggested, the idea like a bucket of cold water on them. "We all need a little time to think about this, talk to each other, and come back and revote."

What they needed was to know who abstained and why so Chloe could work to change that person's mind.

"I think a break is a great idea," Chloe agreed, hoping it would give her a chance for private conversations. "And I'm available to answer any questions or offer additional information if you need it."

"We don't need it," Ned grumbled.

"We need lunch," Undertaker Mitch said, putting his hand on Ned's shoulder. "Let's go get a bite and talk about this. Jeannie, join us, hon."

Oh, that wasn't good.

"Of course." She smoothed her hair and looked at Nellie. "Make it a foursome and come with us."

No one else was invited to that party as the four of them walked out, leaving Chloe to assume they were the four nays. And unless she tagged along, she wasn't going to be changing their minds.

"Blanche, take me to an empty office so I can get some work done," Dave, the real estate broker, said. "I have more important things to do than chat about this." As he stood, he looked at Chloe. "If you ever give up marketing, I'll give you a job."

She nodded thanks as he and Blanche walked out, followed by Andi and Jane, who were deep in discussion.

"And that leaves us," Shane, who hadn't moved from his chair, said softly.

On a sigh, she sat back down and started to drop her chin into her hands, but stopped herself. Instead, she reached into her bag and grabbed the hand sani to squirt it on the palms that shook so many hands today.

"Well, I never saw that coming," she mused aloud as she rubbed.

"I gotta know something, Perfect Chloe."

She sliced him with a look. "Don't push your luck, *Counselor*."

"Aww. The other night it was Dirty Shame."

"The other night you were…a guy who fixed broken stuff in the back of the bar."

"Do you like me more or less now?"

"I don't recall ever saying I liked you at all."

He laughed. "But you have to answer my question."

She waited, studying him, hating the so completely female response that zinged through her as every hormone in her body perked up the very moment they were alone.

"What breed?"

She frowned, not following the question at all.

"Or is it just a sweet little mutt?"

"What are you talking about?"

"Your dog."

"I don't own a..." Oh, she'd walked right into that one.

He leaned right in, reminding her very much of a lawyer who'd made his point to the judge and jury. "So you don't like dogs."

"I didn't say that."

"You didn't have to."

"You didn't say anything about your father being Daniel Kilcannon."

"I didn't have to."

She launched a brow. "Technicality, Counselor."

"Have you ever even owned a dog?" he asked.

"No."

He exhaled slowly and geared up for the next cross-examination, but she cut him off. "I don't like shrimp, either, but I promoted Louisiana."

"Not even shrimp scampi?"

"I'm not a huge fan of the beach, but that didn't stop me from increasing tourism in the Bahamas by 38.4 percent in one year."

He choked softly. "Who isn't a fan of the beach?"

"Too much sand," she said. "It gets everywhere, and you can't get it off you."

"Plus all those waves that won't do your bidding," he joked.

"And not once in my entire life have I gotten on a pair of skis, but I singlehandedly turned Mount Ward into the ultimate winter-break destination for college students, adding millions to that town's coffers. I know this will work, Shane."

"But dogs are personal."

And dogs were not her *personal* thing and never would be. "I travel too much to have a pet. That doesn't affect my ability to come up with great ideas—"

"That I supplied."

She gave a dry laugh. "Yes, oh, great and powerful Shane Kilcannon. You inspired me."

He got even closer. "I kissed you."

"You certainly did." She inched toward him, just to let him know he didn't intimidate her. Much. "And I'd rather that didn't get all over town too fast."

He studied her for a minute, amusement in his eyes. "So letting me take you to lunch would be a conflict of interest."

"You're the lawyer, you tell me."

"I'm conflicted and I'm definitely interested, so yes. But I still want to take you to lunch."

She held his gaze, feeling the pulse in her neck thrum a steady beat and the palms of her hands dampen and that low burn in her belly that had nothing to do with hunger. At least not for lunch.

"Depends," she finally said. "How'd you vote?"

"I didn't vote yes."

Her jaw unhinged.

"And I didn't vote no."

Leaning back, she let that sink in. He was the abstaining vote. Why? "Then, by all means, let's have lunch."

He inched closer and ran a light finger over her knuckles. "Is that the only reason?"

God, no. "I'll abstain from answering that."

He smiled at her. "I like you, Perfect Chloe. Never liked a woman who didn't like dogs, though."

"I guess there's a first for everything."

Chapter Five

Before they reached the street, Shane's next great idea had taken hold.

Turned out, he really *was* an idea guy. Just how "perfect" was Perfect Chloe? Since he didn't believe in perfection, he already knew the answer, but messing with her was definitely fun.

"In here?" Chloe asked as they approached a sandwich shop not far from town hall.

"Let's do takeout. We can go across the street." He gestured toward Bushrod Square. "Sit under the shade of the *hickory* tree."

"Did you know that the whole town was named after the wrong tree?" she asked.

"I've heard the rumor," he said. "It's town folklore."

"It's town *fact*."

"Well, there already was a Hickory, North Carolina, so we ended up as Thaddeus Bushrod's mistake. Be thankful you're not trying to put Bushrod, North Carolina, on the tourism maps."

She laughed, the first time he could remember hearing that pretty sound today. "I might have an easier job getting the name changed. Anyway, I'm not going to sit in the park and eat, so we'll find a table in here."

"Why not? It's a beautiful day."

"I'm in a white suit."

"There are clean tables and benches." At her look, he gave a conciliatory shrug. "Clean enough."

"Nothing is," she muttered as they stepped inside to order.

"I noticed you're a bit of a clean and neat freak."

"A bit," she agreed, the understatement obvious in her voice.

He ordered a sandwich, and she got a salad, but as she turned, the last table was taken by an elderly couple.

"Come on." Shane nudged her to the door. "Outside. I'll clean your bench before you sit on it."

But she was already looking around the little restaurant, probably doing a dirt scan for the most spotless table.

"There isn't going to be an empty table for a while," he said.

"I'm just noticing how dog-friendly this place could be." Her dark gaze landed on him, those long lashes reaching up to arched brows, a hint of challenge in the look. "My plan would work, you know. You should change your vote."

"I might if you eat outside."

She huffed out a breath. "Fine."

"Question for you," he said when they stepped out into the sunshine. "Would *you* eat in a restaurant if a dog was at the next table?"

"It's not about me. It's about the town and the idea and building tourism."

True, but something about a non-dog person using

the love of dogs to her advantage rubbed him the wrong way.

Maybe Shane simply never met a challenge he didn't want to conquer, but why the hell didn't this woman like dogs? He'd suspected it from the first curled lip and he knew that's why he'd abstained.

They crossed the street at the light, and he put his hand on her back, the gesture natural and protective, but he noticed she stiffened as though it were unexpected, too. "You have to practice what you preach."

"Why?"

Was she that clueless? "I'm going to go out on a limb and guess that you have never lived in a small town before."

"Then that limb would break," she said. "I grew up in a town not much different than this one, though not as picturesque and our town coffers were probably in even worse shape. Little Fork, Kentucky, on the other side of those mountains."

"Kentucky?" His brows drew. "I don't hear that in your voice."

"Because I've traveled. After I graduated from UK, I moved to Miami when I got a job with a marketing firm down there. My first client was a hotel chain, then I landed my first tourism account, for the city of Miami Beach."

"A challenge to promote," he said dryly.

"I learned so much and discovered I was good at it. I helped get a lot of business for the firm, then I went out on my own when I was twenty-five, which was seven years ago. I spend about three hundred days a year on the road."

"Ugh." The idea was so unappealing he couldn't put it into words. "Don't you get homesick?"

She shrugged. "Not for where I grew up certainly. And 'home' is a lovely apartment on Brickell Avenue with a view of the water, but not…" Her voice faded, then she finished with, "It's more like home base and a place to sleep when I'm not on the road."

What kind of life was that for a thirty-two-year-old woman? "Well, have your world travels taught you about local politics?"

"Enough. Except for one abstained vote, which I fully intend to change"—she elbowed him lightly—"I didn't do too badly today."

That was today. She could win today, but the whole town? Doubtful.

A few minutes later, they found a bench and picnic table, and he spread one of his extra napkins for her to sit on. She thanked him, brought out her ever-present hand sanitizer again, then carefully took her plastic fork out of a wrapper and opened her salad.

All the while, he sat across from her, watching. "So are you this particular about everything?" He imagined her folding each piece of clothing as she undressed. Imagined it a lot, to be fair.

"Pretty much."

"Like, do you roll your underwear into perfect cylinders and stack them color-coded in your drawers?"

She looked up at him. "Didn't take you long to get to my underwear."

"But I'm right."

She smiled, which was all he needed to know.

Just then, an older woman came around the path with a beauty of a golden retriever on a leash.

Shane looked over Chloe's shoulder, tracking the dog. "That one's been well trained," he noted.

She turned and glanced at the dog. "How can you tell?"

"Experience." He clicked his tongue and snapped his fingers, and the dog slowed its step and turned to Shane. So did his owner, so Shane pushed up.

"He's a stunner," he said to the lady, who beamed with pride, as most dog owners did, especially if they'd taken the time and love to train their doggo. "May I?" Shane asked, already on the way over.

"Of course." As expected, the woman and dog came right toward him, and Shane got down and made eye contact.

"What's his name?" he asked.

"Jackson," she said warmly.

"Hey, Jackson." He knew where retrievers liked to be scratched and adjusted his tone to one a dog would recognize as friendly. "Want to meet my friend, Chloe?"

He turned to catch a flash of disbelief on her face, but she wiped it away quickly, along with her hands on a napkin. "Oh, that's okay. He's walking."

"Oh, no," the owner assured them. "Jackson loves to make new friends." She took a few steps and dropped the leash, which told the dog he was free to approach yet another stranger, and he loped toward the table.

"Don't give him any food, though," the woman added.

"I won't." Chloe twisted on the bench, discomfort already all over her body language.

Shane had seen it so many times in new dog

owners, usually people who'd been talked into a dog by their kids or a well-meaning spouse, and they were either scared, clueless, or simply intimidated by any dog.

Jackson went right up to Chloe and sniffed, pressing his snout on her leg and making her jerk away, both hands in the air.

"He won't hurt you," the lady said.

"I know…it's just…" She gave a helpless look to Shane, who immediately took control by getting back down with the dog.

"Here, Jackson. C'mere, boy." The dog instantly came to him and got some love. "Can you sit?"

He did, making the owner laugh with more doggie pride. "He knows a lot of commands," she bragged.

"Roll over," Shane ordered, and Jackson immediately lay down, turned over, and offered his belly for a rub. Of course, Shane obliged, talking quietly to the dog. "Give kisses?" he asked, knowing exactly what he'd get.

The dog got up and leaned in for a big lick of Shane's face, making the owner coo and Shane laugh and Chloe gape in horror.

After a minute, he got up and made small talk with the owner, whose name was Betsy, then said goodbye to Jackson before coming back around to his side of the picnic table.

Without a word, Chloe reached into her bag and pulled out her little bottle of trusty hand sanitizer, handing it to him.

"Only for you." He squirted some on his hand. "Nice dog, huh?"

"Oh yeah." Zero interest.

As he suspected, miles from "perfect," at least in his opinion.

"So," he said after a moment. "I'm changing my vote to a no."

Her plastic fork froze midbite. "What? Why?"

"Because you don't believe in your own idea."

She set the fork down and gave a frustrated exhale. "Because I didn't crawl all over the ground, touch an animal while I'm eating, and let it lick my face with a tongue that might very well have been covered with dog food or…worse?" She shook her head. "For that I lose?"

"Unless someone else changes their vote."

"Why did you abstain?" she asked. "Conflict of interest?"

"I told you already, I'm interested. You're the one who's conflicted."

"With your business, I mean. I think someone mentioned that my idea would help your business." She thought about that for a moment. "Would it?"

"Maybe. And our business could help your idea. That's not why I abstained."

"Then why?"

She probably wouldn't like the truth, but he wasn't a person to dance around it unless he was in a courtroom. "I knew how everyone in that room would vote, and I knew it would be a four-to-four tie."

"How did you know for sure?"

"Because I live here and I know the players. Would you like to know how they all voted?"

She picked for a dainty bite of lettuce, flicking red onions out of the way of her fork. "I can guess, but I'm sure you'll set me straight."

"The four who left together were your no's."

She thought about that, nodding as she swallowed. "Librarian is a stick in the mud. Spa owner Red Head is a pain in the butt. The funeral director is a stiff."

"Pardon the pun."

She laughed softly. "But you'd think the newspaper guy would be a little more progressive in his thinking."

"Damn media." He grinned at her. "On the other hand, you definitely have your aunt—"

"Whoa." She held up a hand. "How did you know she's my aunt?"

"My dad told me. You know, the old guy?"

Her eyes shuttered. "I meant that in the nicest possible way."

"Don't worry, I didn't tell him, and that's not why I'm taking his place."

She didn't respond right away, studying him for a moment. "Why *are* you taking his place?"

"Because of you."

A little color drained from her cheeks at his honesty. "Really?"

"Don't underestimate your power, Chloe Somerset. You're smart as a whip, extremely pretty, and you kiss like...like you need to do more of it but don't like to lose control. I'm here to help on both counts."

She shook her head and gave up completely on the salad. Instead, she took a drink from a water bottle, and he enjoyed watching the slender column of her throat move as she swallowed. She set the bottle down and, of course, screwed the top back on.

"So you're a shrink and a dog trainer and a lawyer."

"Guilty of all charges, only the shrink part comes from the other two. You can't train dogs or practice law without becoming a little bit of an expert on figuring out what makes all of God's creatures tick."

"And you think I'm a control freak because I don't want my hands covered in dog slobber when I'm eating?"

"Pretty much. Also, because you wanted to win that vote so bad today."

"I didn't want to win for *control*. I'm not trying to control this town."

"Your aunt is."

"Because she's the mayor," she replied. "She's a very dear person, the only real family I have, and I want to help her out of the financial jam Bitter Bark is in. And…." She pointed at him. "This idea is brilliant, and you know it will work. You *know* it."

He smiled. "You're welcome."

"It was up here all along." She tapped her temple. "You just helped me dig it out. And I did thank you, if you'll recall."

"Not enough."

She choked. "If you're implying what I *think* you're implying…"

"You think I want sex for that idea?" He managed to sound shocked.

"Yes."

"Well, you'd be wrong." He leaned back and crossed his arms, as smug as he could be. "You'd be dead wrong, like you were wrong about me being some guy who fixes Billy's beer taps."

"But you *were* fixing his beer taps or…something."

"I was fixing his contract with the liquor distribution company because he was getting screwed out of two percent of profits. I was dirty because I'd been rolling around in a training pen with six dogs before Billy called me." He shot forward again. "You made a wrong assumption. Admit it."

"Yes, I did, but I'm not wrong about you wanting to have sex with me."

Of course she wasn't. But that wasn't all he wanted. He needed help, and so did she. But he'd have to make her see it that way. "That is not how I want to be thanked and, frankly, I'm not looking for thanks."

She folded her napkin in a perfect square, her long, feminine fingers smoothing the edges. "Why did you abstain from voting?" she asked in a low, calm voice. "You still haven't answered that question, except you wanted to force a tie. Why?"

He considered all the ways to go. Then, of course, picked the truth. "I'm not sure I trust you," he said.

Her jaw loosened. "You don't trust me? You're the one who—"

"Didn't tell you who I was. I know. I had no idea I'd ever see you again, or that I'd want to so much."

Her eyes flickered at his admission. "Then why do you say you don't trust me?"

"With dogs. Dogs matter to me. A lot. I need to know you're not just using them for this tourism thing."

She didn't respond, but met his gaze.

"If you get this vote today, then you'll have to win over the town council. That's a whole bunch of people you'll have to meet and woo. And then, if you succeed there, you'll have to win over the whole town for a vote. Will you stay to make that happen?"

"I have a few weeks, maybe a month before my next client needs me, and I promised Aunt Blanche I can stay until I get that call. I'll put together a strategic plan and a calendar of events and maybe train an employee, if she can afford one, to run the program."

Which was ideal. "Where are you staying, with Blanche?"

"No, in a house not far from here. Rose Dixon, the owner, is Blanche's friend and is letting me live here while she's out of town."

He knew Rose, who'd brought her little Maltese to Darcy for grooming, and the house, which was perfect. "But before you can do all that, you have to convince the people of this town that your idea is a great one."

"It *is* a great one."

"Fifty percent of that conference room didn't agree," he reminded her.

She took a slow breath. "What are you proposing?"

"That you have a partner."

"A…partner." She laughed softly, shaking her head. "You really think I don't see right through you, Shane? A partner where? In bed?"

"I doubt very much you'll sleep with this partner, but then, I don't want to make assumptions. You could surprise me."

Her dark brows furrowed. "Who is this partner and how could they help me?"

"Her name's Daisy."

"Daisy. What does she do?"

A slow smile pulled. "She walks. She obeys. She barks. She might lick you, but only if she likes you."

"Shane." She angled her head and let out a sigh. "Fine. You win. I'm not a dog person. Guilty as charged, Counselor."

"*Exactly.*"

"What does that mean? You want to change me? Because not everyone is cut out to be a dog person, as I'm sure you know."

"I do know that." He leaned forward and took one of her hands in his. "But dog people can smell other dog people."

She curled her lip.

"Not that dogs smell," he added. "But, if you won't even say hello to a sweet ol' retriever in the square, you don't stand a shot at winning this. And you sure as hell don't get my support."

She opened her mouth to talk—to argue, he'd bet—then shut it, smart enough to see the wisdom in his thinking.

"And I'll be honest, there's something in it for me, and it's not changing you into a dog person."

"What is it?" she asked.

"I need a home for this dog, for about a month or so, until her owner is healthy enough to take her back."

She looked confused. "Don't you run a dog shelter?"

"Daisy's never been in a kennel in her life. She's a house dog and lives with a woman I know."

She lifted a brow. "Someone special?"

He almost laughed at the idea of Marie Boswell, a seventy-year-old widow with a passion for saving dogs, being what Chloe thought she was. "Very special," he assured her.

She didn't say anything for a long time, but she was considering the idea, he could tell. Points for not saying no outright. "I have issues with dogs," she said bluntly.

Clearly. But he understood that, all too well. "Have you had trouble with one? Been bitten?"

"No." She shook her head, then looked down at her perfectly folded napkin square before meeting his eyes again. "I don't think they're clean."

"Oh, is that all? A good dog'll cure you of a little germophobia."

"Look, I'm not germophobic. If I were really that crazy, I couldn't do this." She put her hand on his this time, adding pressure. "I couldn't shake hands with strangers, and I sure as hell couldn't have kissed you on the mouth *with tongue* the other night." She took her hand away and started stroking that napkin again, quiet for a bit.

"I know what crazy looks like," she said softly. "I'm not crazy. I do, however, like things…sanitary. Clean. Safe. I was sick a lot as a kid, had a ton of allergies, and I…protect myself."

He glanced down and watched those lean fingers shred one side of the napkin, and something slipped inside his heart. Oh, that need for control might run deeper than he even imagined. And dogs could test that, for sure. Help it, too, but she hadn't asked for his help, and maybe he was the one making wrong assumptions here, and just because he believed the world should love dogs like he did didn't make it so.

"You won't have to protect yourself from Daisy," he said quickly. "But I'm not going to force you if you don't like the idea."

"I don't *hate* the idea." She let out a soft sigh. "Would it get you to change your vote?"

"If it did, I'd be guilty of graft and corruption. And you'd be guilty of bribery."

She smiled. "Then I'd need a good lawyer."

He reached for her hand to stop the napkin shredding. "Why don't you just meet Daisy and see what you think?" He ran a finger along her knuckles and watched some chill bumps rise on her arm.

"I don't think I'll ever…" She glanced to where he had been with Jackson. "Rub them or let them lick me."

"You don't have to. Simply have her live with you, and walk her around every day while you make friends with people who live here. I'll help you get used to her and learn commands. I am a dog whisperer, you know."

She swallowed. "I think you're just a whisperer."

"Maybe a little."

"Daisy," she sighed. "She sounds sweet. I'll meet her, but no promises."

"She's amazing. And you're going to love her." He picked up her hand and brought it to his lips. "I bet you'll even let her kiss you."

"Not likely."

"How about me?"

She let out a sigh. "Pretty likely."

He grinned at the answer and the fact that he felt her pulse kick up at the admission. "Then let's go rock the vote."

"I thought that was bribery, graft, and corruption."

He scooped up her trash and dropped it in the nearest can. "See? One lunch and I taught you all about small-town politics."

Chapter Six

When Chloe wasn't sure of her next move, she did the one thing that allowed her to clear her head. She cleaned. Hard.

And there was plenty to do in Rose Dixon's two-bedroom bungalow on the edge of Bushrod Square. The house was what people liked to call vintage, or charming, or quaint.

Chloe could see that, but she thought it was a little more in the "grimy" camp.

Morning sun poured into the kitchen the day after her advisory committee victory, highlighting the cracks in the linoleum, streaks on the windows, and some bits of dirt gathered in the corners.

No one would call this house dirty, unless they were...*crazy*.

Which she was not. Merely safe and clean and organized.

With her hair pulled back in a ponytail, Formula 409 in one hand and a roll of paper towels in the other, she started in the kitchen, soothing herself by scrubbing, rubbing, spraying, and scouring. The whole time, the events of the day before played through her mind.

Shane had been true to his word, and the next vote had gone her way, with no abstaining. There'd been some grumbling from the no's—and he was right about who they were—but the meeting had broken up after scheduling a follow-up in a week to review what she had ready to take to the town council.

During that time, she'd work on a new version of her presentation, honing her ideas to the very best ones. She'd gotten some input from Blanche and a few other committee members, including architect Andi Rivers, who had some terrific ideas. In fact, she and Andi made plans to have dinner tonight to talk about them.

But not everyone had shown the love for Better Bark.

"You have your work cut out for you, young lady," the undertaker had said with a subtly ominous tone in his voice.

"Once this is public, you can expect the editorial board of the *Banner* to oppose the idea," Ned the Editor, as she'd come to think of him, had warned.

The librarian, Nellie, and Jeannie, the fiery spa owner, stuck close together and left in silence.

Since then, Chloe had visited the grocery store to stock up on cleaning supplies and food. And had reorganized Rose's pantry, which she hoped didn't upset the woman. But it had been a hot mess. So had her utensil drawer.

She'd found enough cans of dog food in the pantry to know the homeowner must have had a dog, so if she did end up taking the dog Shane had talked about, it probably wouldn't be frowned upon by the woman who lived here.

And that thought, like so many others, brought her thoughts back to Shane. He said he'd be in touch, and that was the last she'd heard from him or...a dog named Daisy.

She let out a sigh at the possibility. She agreed that having a dog would show she practiced what she preached. But that's not why she was seriously considering the idea.

A dog was in the category of "never, ever" in Chloe's life. And every time she ran smack into one of those walls, she had to suck it up and kick it down.

Otherwise, she'd never be...normal.

Speaking of which, she needed to stop cleaning *now*.

She opened the cabinet under the sink to put the 409 away, and something scurried in the dark. Chloe gasped, threw the doors closed, and practically fell on her backside scrambling away.

"Oh my God." She stood up, horrified. "Oh my God, what was that? What was *that*?"

It was a mouse, and she knew it. Instantly, her whole being itched. She spun around in a full circle, clueless what to do. She had a mouse? Mice? Her hand still pressed to her lips, she backed out of the kitchen, into the living room, toward the front door, and yanked it open to get air and—

"Shane!"

He was climbing out of a pickup truck, a blue baseball cap and sunglasses covering much of his face, but she recognized the body. There was every inch of muscle and man she'd been thinking about...before the mouse.

"Are you okay?" He slammed the driver's door and

took a few steps closer, tipping the brim of the hat a little.

"Mouse," she managed, shaking off the initial shock of the living creature in her kitchen as she handled the impact of this living creature in her driveway. He wore a dark bluish-purple T-shirt, shorts, and sneakers. Some whiskers created a shadow on hollow cheeks. He was all Saturday sexy and casual and...*think, Chloe.* "I have a mouse."

"Did you name it?"

"Please don't joke. It's under the sink. It needs to die." When his eyes flashed, she added, "Or live somewhere else."

He reached for the hand that held the 409. "Interesting weapon."

"I was cleaning."

"Shocker." He gave the slightest whisper of a smile and nodded to the house. "Let me look."

"Okay, but if there's one, are there more?"

"Maybe. We'll set traps."

She sucked in a breath. "In my kitchen?"

"Come on." He put a hand on her shoulder, but she steadfastly refused to move.

"I can't go back in there. I can never go in there again. I'll have to move. Maybe out of state."

He laughed and nudged her some more. "Another reason for you to have Daisy here. She's a terrier, and they were born to do one thing and one thing only: catch rodents. Of course, she might bring it to you and expect a reward."

This wasn't happening. Chloe pressed both hands to her mouth and literally held back a roiling stomach. "She *eats* them?"

"Nah, just kills and buries."

"I…can't. I absolutely can't."

"Can't what? Handle? Deal? Take Daisy? Express how happy you are to see me?" He slid his sunglasses off and let the glory of his hazel eyes hit her. "It's the last one, isn't it?"

"I am glad to see you," she admitted. "If you know how to catch and kill mice."

"I don't usually kill anything, but let me check it out." With that irrepressible smile, he went ahead. "Stay here and I'll see what's what."

She sighed, relieved, and gestured for him to go in, leaning against the column that held up the porch overhang.

A few minutes later, he came back to the door. "Safe to come in now."

She pushed off the brick and looked at him as the screen door opened and he came out. "He's gone," he said.

"How do you know?"

"I escorted him outside by the tail. Didn't give me much of a fight."

Her jaw dropped. "With your bare hands?"

He reached them to her and pressed her face, making her jerk back with a scream, even though she could feel they were wet and smelled of her antibacterial soap.

"With my big, bad, bare hands," he confirmed. "And I found a hole that is probably how he got in, which I can easily seal for you. Then we'll set a humane trap."

"So I'll have a live, trapped mouse in my kitchen? Then what?"

"Then I will rescue you again," he promised, making her stomach do another one of those flips that it did all too often around him.

"I don't need rescuing."

He lifted a brow. "Then don't freak out about a mouse."

Touché. "Why are you here?"

"To take you to meet Daisy."

She stared at him, spinning through every possible excuse for why she couldn't have a dog. But there really wasn't one except she didn't *do* dogs. Even cute little puppies named Daisy. A terrier, he'd said yesterday. Wasn't Toto a terrier?

"Only to meet her?" she asked.

"And see how you feel about her. But in case you want to bring her back today, I thought I'd check out the house to make sure the house is dog-friendly."

"I think the owner has a dog she must have taken on her trip."

"Ziggy, a Maltese," he said. "But Daisy's a different breed and we require a house check, even for a temporary situation or a rescue from Waterford. I promise you she's well behaved. Still, I'll look around and handle the due diligence since we're technically boarding her for our sick friend."

Dog rescuer. Sick-people helper. Mouse remover. He really was the whole package, wasn't he? Not to mention stone-cold gorgeous. And the way he *kissed*.

"Why are you looking at me like that?" he asked.

Um, out-of-control hormones? "Just wondering… what might she chew?"

"Shoes."

She blinked in shock. "Expensive ones?"

"If they smell nice and foot-y."

Oh, *God*. "The fun never stops with you, does it?"

"Never and you'll do well to remember that." He gave a cocky but somehow still-endearing grin. "Keep your shoes behind a closed door. Oh, and you have to be careful with any medication. I'll check for choking hazards, like window-treatment cords. No wires she could gnaw on, or dangerous substances around like chocolate."

"Chocolate is dangerous?" She'd bought a giant bar of Godiva that was right out on the kitchen table. *Unless the mouse ate it.*

"Deadly. Do not ever let a dog eat chocolate. No table food at all," he said as they walked back in. "It's best to never let her eat off your plate."

She coughed softly, making him laugh.

"I guess I don't have to worry about that with you."

"But there is chocolate," she admitted as they got to the kitchen and she pointed at the offending bar, which suddenly looked really out in the open and deadly. And huge.

"You'll eat that whole thing?" he asked, incredulous.

She shrugged. "I like my chocolate, okay?"

"Okay. But keep it behind a closed door with your expensive shoes. Can I look around?"

"Yes," she said, finally putting down her 409 and pulling her hair out of the ponytail on a sigh when he disappeared down the hall. "Maybe I'm not the best person for this dog," she called. "What if I leave chocolate out? Or there's a stray window cord? Or she brings me a mouse in the middle of the night?" She had to actually stop herself from wailing.

"She's really a good dog," he called back. "And you're only going to dog sit for a month or so, Chloe. Not adopt her." At her long silence, he added, "Just meet her, okay?"

She let out a sigh. She really did want to see this famous Waterford Farm. And a few hours with Shane wouldn't exactly be painful.

"You're good," he said, coming back to the kitchen. "And I was so right about that underwear drawer."

She gasped. "You looked?"

He laughed. "You might want to keep the bedroom doors shut since there's carpet in those rooms. The rest is wood or linoleum, so you're fine."

"Don't tell me. If she chews carpet, she'll get sick?"

"No, but you will if she pees on your carpet. At least on the wood or linoleum, you can easily wipe it up."

Her jaw dropped. "The dog is going to pee in my house?"

"Not if you take her outside." He picked up the 409. "You'll need something better than this if she does pee. You'll want to kill the smell."

"No, I'll want to kill myself."

Still laughing, he led her to the door. "Come on, I want you to meet my family."

She slowed her step. "Like this?" she asked, gesturing toward her shorts, sneakers, and cleaning top. Without a speck of makeup and her hair a wreck?

"It's a dog farm, Perfect Chloe. We don't dress up.

Although you might want to put jeans on, because Daisy will lick those legs like you're a human ice cream cone." He leaned in closer and pressed his strong shoulder against her. "Not that I could blame her."

She closed her eyes and prayed for whatever she'd need to handle what was ahead. "I'll change and meet you at your truck."

If Chloe was scared of a mouse, how was she going to feel about Daisy?

Shane knew he should at least tell her ahead of time, but something stopped him. Maybe he wanted to see her natural reaction when she saw Daisy and realized she was in the pit bull family. But maybe she had no idea what that meant and she'd immediately see what a great dog she was.

Or maybe Daisy would lick her and Chloe would turn tail and run away in horror.

He needed to know that before he invested one more minute in this woman. Changing the world's perception of pit bulls was his mission in life, and he did his best to convert every person he met.

Why should she be any different?

"So, how exactly did you go from lawyer to dog trainer?" Chloe asked as Shane drove his truck out of Bitter Bark and headed toward Waterford Farm.

"Easily," he answered. "I hung up my three-piece suits and law journals and put on boots and treat bags."

"Do you miss it?"

He'd been asked the question a million times, and the answer never changed. "Not for a minute. I still practice law by handling all the contracts and legalities for Waterford, but I wasn't cut out to be a litigator."

"Then why did you go to law school?"

Good damn question. "I've always had a thing about injustice. It makes me wild. Things should be fair. Life should be fair. And yet, it so rarely is."

She looked at him, a question in her eyes. "Has your life been unfair?" she asked.

Just once. Brutally, viciously unfair. But he shoved the thought of his mother's death away and threw her a playful look, far more comfortable with flirting than letting that hole open up.

"Unfairly good," he replied. "Do you think that's why I'm an arrogant bastard?"

"You're not a bastard."

He had to laugh at that. "I'm a little cocky, it's true. But you're a little obsessed with appearances, so—"

"I am not."

"Did you or did you not put makeup on when you changed into jeans?"

A slow smile pulled. "I bet you were a good litigator."

"I was fantastic," he said. "It wasn't about being good. It was about being miserable. My last job was as a corporate attorney with FriendGroup in Seattle and, whoa, can we talk about boring? Now I work with my family, and I spend my days around dogs, and I don't have to suck up to clients or judges or juries." He waited a beat. "Just tourism experts."

"You are not sucking up to me," she countered. "You're guilting me into taking a dog."

"No guilt at all, I swear. I'm helping your cause, and you're helping mine." He reached his hand over to pat her arm. "I really think you're going to love Daisy, and if you don't? I'll understand."

Wouldn't like it. Might not be so hot for her anymore, but he'd understand.

"I am excited to see Waterford Farm. My aunt told me it was your dad's idea to turn your family home into a dog facility."

"Everything is my dad's idea," he said with a laugh. "That's why we call him the Dogfather." He leaned closer and did his best Marlon Brando. "He likes to make you an offer you can't refuse."

She chuckled. "That's hilarious."

"It would be if it weren't true. Do you want to know why he backed out of the tourism committee in the first place?"

"Why?" she asked.

"Because he was trying to orchestrate a little get-together with my older brother Liam and the lovely Andi Rivers."

Her jaw dropped. "Really? Do they know each other?"

"They dated for a little while, but it didn't work out. Except, my dad hasn't quite accepted that. He's on his own mission in life."

"Which is?"

"Impossible," he replied. "But ever since we all moved back to Bitter Bark, my father has been on a quest to get all his kids leashed and collared."

"What does that mean?" She looked confused. "You mean...married?"

"He thinks the world will stop turning if his kids

don't somehow replicate his perfect marriage to my mom."

"I think that's sweet."

"So's a no-hitter and a hole-in-one. You can't catch lightning in a bottle 'cause you want to."

"Oh, cynical, are you?"

"Realistic. But we all humor Dad and let him try."

"Okay, who's 'all'? You said Liam is older than you. Is he the oldest?"

"Yeah, he's in charge of our K-9 training unit and our protection dogs, which he trains and sells for astronomical sums to rich people who want vicious German shepherds patrolling their estates. He's the strong, silent, and courageous type. So are his dogs."

"Duly noted. Will I meet him today?"

"Not sure who'll be around, but probably you'll meet Garrett, who's about a year younger than me, making us genuine Irish twins. He runs all of our rescue operations, handles placement and adoptions. We share a house not far from here or, hell, we used to. I never see him anymore."

"Why not?"

"He got engaged about a month ago, so he's always with Jessie, his fiancée. Which is great for him, but sucks for me."

"Oh? So someone caught that lightning in a bottle. Was your father responsible?"

"He was pulling strings in the background, of course, being the Dogfather."

"And the others?"

"Going chronologically, there's Molly, a vet like my dad. And Aidan, who's in special ops in the Middle East right now, and finally, Darcy. She runs the grooming business when she's around, which isn't always. She's a tumbleweed like you."

"I love these generalizations you make about me," she mused. "I'm a germophobe. I'm appearance obsessed. Now I'm a tumbleweed. The fact is, I'm neat, I care what I look like, and I travel for business."

He angled his head in concession and a silent apology. "So you don't make generalizations about people?"

"I try not to."

"What about dogs?" He half held his breath waiting for the answer.

"I don't know anything about dogs," she said. "I've never had one, never took care of one, never..." She shifted in her seat. "I'll be honest, I don't think I've ever petted a dog."

He almost slammed on the brakes out of shock. "You've never petted a dog?"

"I told you, I'm not a dog person."

"But...but...are you even a person? Who hasn't ever petted a dog?"

"Maybe when I was little," she said, squirming a bit. "Please don't make me feel bad about it, Shane. I'm in this truck, and I'm on my way to meet a dog that might live with me. Do you know how huge that is for me?"

Maybe he didn't. Maybe he should. "This is more than just getting old Bitter Bark to buy your idea, isn't it? More than just proving something to me."

He watched her swallow. "Every once in a while," she said slowly, "I realize that I need to break a barrier. It's not easy for me. It's not natural for me. But if I can do it, I feel...better."

"Oooh." He let out a long, low sigh. "Then I'll tell you right now she's a Staffordshire terrier."

She didn't react, but that made sense. A lot of people didn't know the official names of certain dogs. "That sounds British. Like something curled at the queen's feet."

Exactly what a non-dog person would think. "You might be thinking of a corgi or Cavalier King Charles. Actually, Daisy's a little different."

"In what way?"

"You'll see." He reached the front gates of Waterford and made the turn into the big drive. When he parked the car, he put his hand on her shoulder. "For what it's worth, Chloe, I like a woman who can break a barrier."

"I'm not doing this for you," she said. "I'm doing this for me. And Daisy."

He let that hit his heart. Hard. Damn. Now he *really* liked her.

Chapter Seven

Chloe looked at Waterford Farm through the eyes of a tourism expert, and it was a dream. The property just got prettier and prettier. From the classic entrance that led to a winding paved road lined with oak and maple trees, right up to a lovely buttercream-colored farm-style house with a row of charming dormers and green shutters on every window. The whole place had a quintessential Southern magic that made her want to swing on a glider with a glass of sweet tea.

"You do run tours through here, I hope," she said to Shane as they parked in a wide circular drive that already had a collection of trucks, cars, and one particularly mangy yellow Jeep.

"Not usually. Clients come to check the place out all the time, and we get a lot of professional trainers, therapy trainers, and law enforcement."

They walked around a huge grassy area to the back, where she could see that the house was built on a slight rise, overlooking acres dotted with clapboard buildings, that looked like they might be kennels, classrooms, and a small veterinarian office. Beyond the circle of buildings were more grassy areas with several dogs wandering about, some taking commands from people she assumed were trainers, some lying in the sun by themselves.

The entire facility was surrounded by rolling hills, woods, trails, and a large pond that sparkled in the sunshine.

"Shane," she said, unable to hide the awe in her voice. "This is absolutely beautiful."

"Thanks." He looked around, as if seeing it through her eyes. "It's home, of course, because I grew up here. But it also represents so much hard work and sweat equity. Sometimes I forget how damn nice the place is."

"You could make it a real travel destination."

"Not sure that's what we want to do, but I'll let you take that up with my dad. You know." He gave her a playful elbow. "The old guy."

"I prefer to think of him as the Dogfather," she replied. "And I really hope he loves the idea."

"He might, the way you present it. Anyway"—he gestured toward the central penned in area—"this is our main training ground," he said. "All the dogs on-site spend some time here every day, or in one of the smaller pens. And over there are the kennels, where all the dogs, no matter why they're here, live, eat, and sleep. Want to go meet Daisy?"

"Sure." But she slowed her step as they headed to the kennels. "Shane, what if she senses that I'm not, you know, a dog person? They can pick that up, right?"

He shrugged. "Dogs are super sensitive, and they'll smell fear or any kind of trepidation."

"Should I be afraid of her?"

"God, no." He put an arm around her, pulling her closer to a place that was warm, strong, and solid, leading her forward. "I would never give you a dog that might hurt you. I talked to my brother about it last night, and he agrees that Daisy needs to be in a home and yours is perfect. You even have a fenced-in backyard."

She nodded, giving in to the comfort of his voice and strong body.

"How many dogs are usually here at one time?" she asked as they passed the training pen.

"It varies. We give training classes for individuals with dogs, and we also bring in classes of people who want certification to become trainers. And we have special programs for therapy dogs. If all those are in full swing, we could have thirty or more dogs boarding here or coming through for day classes. Liam's law enforcement dogs come with police officers and sheriff's deputies for training, and he always has one or two German shepherds he's training for high-protection duty. Plus the rescues."

As they reached the entrance to the kennels, the door popped open, and a tan and white dog came bounding out right at them, making Chloe leap back in shock.

"Down, Lola!" Shane ordered the dog, who immediately fell to her haunches and looked up at him, all obedience.

"Lola!" Another man called from inside the kennel, coming out with a woman with shoulder-length red hair, the two of them laughing at something. "Hey,

Shane," the man said. "Jessie and I were checking on Daisy. I hope this is her foster mom, 'cause she's itching to get out of that kennel."

The man gave Chloe a wide smile that nearly matched Shane's. He had deep-blue eyes and long black hair that fell over the collar of his shirt, but the stamp of brotherhood was easy to see.

"Liam or Garrett?" she guessed.

"I'm Garrett." He shook her hand, then gestured to the woman next to him. "This is Jessie Curtis, my fiancée."

"Hi, Garrett, Jessie. I'm Chloe Somerset and...." She smiled at the dog who was still sitting, waiting for a command. "I take it that this isn't Daisy?" Which was too bad, because this dog looked so sweet and...clean.

"Oh, no," Jessie said. "This is Lola. She's all mine." At the sound of her name, the dog stood and gave her full attention to Jessie. "That's right. All mine." Jessie bent over and hugged the dog's head, adding a kiss. *Full contact, lips on fur.*

Oh, that might be a barrier too far.

"Daisy's inside," Garrett said. "And I really appreciate you taking her for a while. She'd be fine here, of course, but she's been a well-loved house dog owned by a woman who knows what she's doing. Problem is, Daisy doesn't want to sleep in a cage. I suspect she'll be jumping in your bed with you before long."

Chloe managed not to let her eyes pop in shock, but Shane laughed. "I don't think Chloe's going to be sharing her bed with Daisy," he said.

Garrett's eyes flickered at Shane, and immediately

Chloe knew how he was taking that comment—like her *bed sharing* was going to be with Shane.

"I'm not..." She put up a hand. "I'm not going to be sharing my bed."

Garrett laughed. "That's what they all say."

Did he mean Shane's women or dog sitters?

"She's super sweet," Jessie said, probably picking up on Chloe's discomfort. "And I'm sure she'll be very happy in a dog bed next to yours." Then she laughed guiltily. "Though I can't stop Lola from climbing in when there's a storm."

Before Chloe could react, Shane put a hand on her back and guided her past them. "Come on, I'll take you back," Shane said. "It's time to end the suspense and meet her."

She didn't know exactly what suspense he meant, but she let him usher her inside a maze of white-walled and gated doggie abodes, all brightly lit by skylights and windows. The halls echoed with all different kinds of barks, but the area was wide and cheery. It didn't smell bad, and it was remarkably clean.

So she relaxed a little.

"It was really important to us that the kennels be a great place for the dogs," Shane said, as if he sensed her mood shift.

"I did expect something more like a prison."

"Everyone does, but that's one of the many things that makes Waterford so special."

She paused along the way to smile at different dogs who greeted her, each one unique enough to hold her attention. "A Dalmatian," she said, proud she recognized at least one breed, even if it was from a Disney movie.

"That's Spot."

She laughed. "Seriously?"

"Liam named him, and I tell you, the guy has zero imagination. Spot's in training to be a therapy dog for stressed-out students at Vestal Valley College during exam week."

She leaned in toward Spot, who instantly came over and attempted to lick her jeans. "Oh." She backed away, making Shane laugh.

Next was something small and white and insanely cute. "Who's this?"

"Gumby. Her owner is training here and staying in our dorm for a few weeks to take intensive classes."

"People really do that? They live here to learn how to train their dogs?"

"Some do. Listen, people are nuts about their dogs, Chloe. That's why your idea for the town is so smart."

She really relaxed then. "You really think so?"

"I honestly do." He angled his head toward her. "And you look like you're feeling a little better about having a dog."

She looked down at Gumby, who gazed up with adoring brown eyes and waved her fluffy little tail furiously. "A little," she confessed. "That one right there looks downright pettable."

"Don't go crazy now." He grinned at her. "And I better warn you, Daisy is a little less precious. But still great."

He guided her a little farther, pausing at a kennel with a yellow dog like the one they'd seen in the park, then a sweet hound-type with floppy ears, then they turned the corner to a row of larger kennels.

In the first one, a dog lay in the corner, looking up from a two-toned face with intense brown eyes rimmed with the slightest bit of pink.

"Meet Daisy."

She stood and slowly came to the gate with a few loud, deep, deafening barks.

Chloe stared at the dog, taking in the power of her small but muscular body, looking a little like a fighter with an intense gaze. Her eyes…those eyes were so distinct.

Wait, she knew that breed. Had seen stories on the news. Heard people talking. Saw it from behind fences with Beware of Dog signs.

And then she realized what she was looking at. This dog was a pit bull. On instinct, she took a step back, hitting the hard muscle of Shane's chest. He put his hands on her shoulders, as if steadying her. As if he'd known she'd need some support.

She just closed her eyes and let her head drop back against the man behind her.

"Shane," she whispered his name, the back of her head still pressed against his chest, the curves of her body against his torso.

But that wasn't a sigh of arousal or desire or surrender. Maybe she knew more about dogs than he was giving her credit for.

"I don't think I can do this," she added.

He squeezed her shoulders. "You don't even know her yet."

"I know…"

Don't say it, Chloe. Please don't say it and be like everyone else.

"Enough," she finished. "I thought you said she was a Staff…something."

Daisy barked again, and Chloe flinched as if the noise terrified her. But Shane knew she only wanted to be let out. "She is a Staffordshire terrier."

"I was expecting…Toto."

He let go of her, inching her to the side to get to Daisy. "Hey, girl, it's time to show off for Chloe. You ready?"

She barked and gave a friendly wag of the tail.

"Sit." Instantly, she obeyed, and Shane unlatched her gate. "Stay." She didn't move, not so much as an eyelid.

Walking inside, he could practically taste Chloe's fear. To show her how unfounded that was, he got down on his knees and leaned his head down, making himself completely vulnerable to the dog, who still wouldn't move until told.

"C'mere, Daisy. Give me some love."

She took a step toward Shane and nuzzled his neck. Shane bent over completely and let Daisy lick him thoroughly. Then, she got to the floor, turned over, and spread it all out for him.

Nothing but love.

He glanced up at Chloe, hoping for some warmth, some reaction, some softening. Who could resist a dog spread-eagle on her back?

Chloe stared, a mix of horror and disbelief in her eyes.

"Chloe, she's the sweetest, most obedient dog you'll ever meet."

She swallowed visibly. "Shane, she's a pit bull."

His chest tightened on Daisy a little as a familiar resentment rose up in him, and he tried to remember she knew nothing about dogs and that people could be idiots when it came to this breed. Who knew that better than he did?

"I don't have that experience with dogs. Especially a dog like that."

"Like what?" Even Daisy startled at the sharpness in his voice, and he comforted her with a slow, steady stroke.

"Shane." Chloe let out a frustrated sigh. "You know what I mean. They're...famous. *Infamous*. I've heard that they can be...dangerous."

Couldn't she see this dog was no more dangerous than a stuffed animal? "That's like judging a person by the color of their skin," he shot back, giving in to the low-grade anger bubbling up in him. "Do you do that?"

She paled and closed her eyes. "Of course not."

"Well, this is no different. People make assumptions, wrong assumptions, because of things they heard that have very little basis in reality. This is known as a nanny dog. Does that tell you something about the breed?"

She didn't answer but took a few steadying breaths. "You know I'm a novice," she finally said.

"Which is why this dog is the right one." Slowly, he stood, getting the leash that hung on the wall. "She responds to every command. She's friendly, sweet, easygoing, and hasn't done anything to earn your mistrust except be hung with a handle that gets a lot of bad press."

"But she is a pit bull?"

"Pit bull is a loosely used term that experts disagree on," he said, clicking the leash onto Daisy's collar. "There's a lot of confusion between an actual breed and a dog type. A pit bull is a *type* of dog, and obviously, it's a type that has negative connotations. Staffordshire terrier or American bull terrier are *breeds*. When properly socialized and trained, not inbred and not trained by morons to be fighters, they are some of the friendliest dogs in the world. They're famous for how loyal they are, good with kids, and absolutely brimming with enthusiasm. Which, I see, you are not."

"I'm sorry," she whispered. "I'm sorry I've disappointed you."

The apology gutted him, mostly because he didn't want to hear it right that minute. And because she was right—she *had* disappointed him, and obviously, he didn't have the class to hide it.

As he brought Daisy out of the kennel, Chloe backed away, giving the dog a wide berth. "She's not going to attack you," he said quietly. "For God's sake, give her a chance to prove what she is."

She bit her lip, eyes on the dog, silent.

"I'm walking her, if you want to come. But if you don't, I understand." He didn't wait for her to answer, heading around the corner to the kennel door, letting Daisy happily lead.

As he reached the sunlight, Chloe caught up to him.

"So is this some kind of test?" she demanded.

"If it was, you failed."

"No, Shane, *you* failed."

At the accusation, he spun to her, a little surprised to see her color was high and her dark eyes gleamed with anger of her own. She was angry? After judging a dog based on nothing but conjecture and assumptions and stuff she didn't know?

"How's that?" he asked.

"You could have warned me. You could have given me the little breed-and-type lesson in advance. I told you this isn't easy for me."

"And I told you that you don't have to take her. I'm going to walk her and…"

"And cool yourself off," she finished for him.

He tamped down a fiery response, because he knew, deep in his gut, she was right. "Maybe you're not the only one trying to prove something," he finally said. "It really frosts me when people automatically assume this type of dog is a killer. People who abuse them are monsters, not the dogs. Believe me, I know that."

She took a slow step closer, but as she did, two therapy dogs in training came toward them, with Allison, a Waterford staff member, behind them. Instantly, Daisy reacted, pulling on the leash and giving one loud bark of warning.

Allison gave a command to her dogs, who slowed and kept their gazes straight ahead, undaunted by the new arrival. They received pets and praise, but Daisy's bark grew louder, along with the pressure on the leash.

"Hey, Shane," Allison said as she and her dogs walked by, barely looking at Daisy or Chloe. Allison was focused on her charges, ready for them to react, and the dogs knew there'd be a reward if they didn't.

Daisy followed them with her eyes and another insistent warning bark.

"What's wrong with her?" Chloe asked.

The barking stopped the minute the therapy dogs disappeared.

"Nothing. She barks at other dogs, but that doesn't mean she'll attack. She's a good girl."

As if to prove his point, Daisy sat and looked up at him, her eyes saying what her mouth couldn't: *Please stop talking and take me on a walk.*

Chloe reached out her hand, tentative and slow, making Shane look at her in surprise.

"Give me the leash," she said softly.

"Are you sure?"

She took a slow, deep breath, as if trying to keep from saying *yes*, which they both knew would be a lie. "I'll try."

He handed her the end of the leash, and as she took it, he closed his hand over hers. "Sorry to act like a jerk about it," he said softly. "Prejudice against pits is a hot button for me."

"Obviously."

She took control of the leash, and Daisy pulled a little, starting to walk, a tad impatient with all the human yammering. "Oh." Chloe let herself be pulled a little, then jerked the leash reflexively.

Immediately, Daisy turned with a look of dismay, uncertain of what she'd done wrong.

"See?" Shane said. "They don't come any sweeter."

"It's okay, Daisy," she said, lifting her other hand as if waving at the dog would make her point. "Just walk, girl. Walk." She looked up at him. "Is that the right command to use?"

His heart squeezed a little at her determination to do this, even though she really didn't want to. "If you walk, she will. Like this." He took Chloe's hand and started them both toward some open grass away from the training area.

He could feel how tense she was, her fingers stiff in his hand, her shoulders square, her gaze locked on the dog a few feet in front of them as if Daisy could turn at any second and attack.

"It's hard for me to understand what that must be like to have never been around any dogs," he admitted. "I haven't spent a day in thirty-six years without a dog in my life. Usually way more than one."

Daisy started to pull to the left, off the path. "Where is she...what is she..."

"She needs to pee."

"Oh."

"Or poop."

"Poop? You mean...now?"

He fought a laugh. "This is not something you can command a dog to do or not. She's going to go the minute she gets outside, most likely twice a day."

She swallowed hard. "Okay. What do we do about that?"

"Let her. And then pick it up."

She blinked in horror, making him laugh.

"If we didn't pick it up, Waterford would be swimming in the stuff."

"Pick...it..." She turned to Daisy, who was already in a squatting position. "Up?" Her voice cracked.

"We have stations everywhere. See?" He pointed to a small green can with a bag dispenser about fifteen feet away, tucked between two trees. "And look what's on the shelf there?" He pointed to the large container of hand sanitizer. "Chloe's happy juice."

She barely smiled, sneaking a peek at Daisy, who'd finished her work and started toward the dispenser, already knowing the drill at Waterford.

"Come on, you can do it."

"I can, but I *won't*."

"I swear you get so used to it, you don't even think about it."

"If you make me pick that up, I don't think I'll ever think about anything else as long as I live, which won't be long."

He laughed, relieved that her humor was back at least. "I'll do the first one."

"You'll do *every* one."

Still laughing, he went and grabbed a bag, cleaned up the mess in one move that he'd done so many times in his life, he didn't think to explain how, knotted the recyclable plastic, tossed it, and made a show of pumping a gallon of hand sanitizer into his palms.

"Should I drink a little?" he asked, rubbing his hands together.

"Just tell me that's the last time."

"On this walk."

He could have sworn she swayed, but didn't have time to take note because, now that she was feeling lighter, Daisy picked up the pace and trotted toward the beaten path and grass that led to the lake.

Chloe strode fast to keep up, clinging to the leash as if it were a lifeline, marching on with her long dark hair swinging, her arm extended so far he could have sworn Daisy could pull it out of the socket.

For a moment, Shane stood there and watched, his gaze moving from one beautiful girl to the other.

Maybe he was trying to prove a point with her. Maybe Daisy and Chloe had just become his personal project.

He thought about telling her why, but then she'd never take the dog.

Chapter Eight

The man was tireless.

And so was his dog.

Chloe sat cross-legged in the grass, occasionally closing her eyes and lifting her face to the hot North Carolina summer sun. She couldn't remember the last time she sat outside, other than next to the pool at her Miami apartment on a rare day off. She certainly couldn't remember the last time she sat in grass, but for some reason, folding down on the soft bed of green seemed natural out here. Not natural for her, but it felt good.

She heard Shane hoot and Daisy bark, the sound making her peek from behind closed lids to catch him running like he was on a football field, the dog chasing him feverishly. He stopped, fell, and Daisy jumped on him, covering his face with her tongue and paws.

Lucky dog.

Yeah, as if she'd behave that way with man or beast. Was Shane responsible for the madness of sitting in the grass, walking a dog, and thinking about doing things that normally made her...walk away from a man?

He might think he was a dog whisperer, but Shane's gift might be something altogether different. And all Chloe knew was that she wanted to be around him to get more of it.

And it wasn't only how he looked.

Although, he looked good. She stole another look, catching him running and rolling with the dog, the tight T-shirt clinging to damp, defined muscles.

From somewhere—they probably had hidden toy stations all over this place—he produced a bright green tennis ball that he held in the air. Daisy stared at the ball with what was probably the same expression Chloe wore right that moment staring at Shane. The dog waited way more patiently than Chloe would if she were on her knees in front of him. Daisy didn't move until she was told she could, then she shot off after the ball, snagging it with her teeth and wagging her tail at her accomplishment as she trotted back to Shane for more.

There was nothing intimidating about that dog.

Maybe that was Shane's magic. He got creatures to do things they might not otherwise do. So that was one good reason to take the dog—it guaranteed more time with Shane, which guaranteed more…broken barriers.

She swallowed and thought of one barrier she might actually consider breaking. Sex.

She let out a sigh at the thought, dropping her head back again and closing her eyes. Sex had never gone *well* for her, but with a man like Shane? Despite the sun, a shiver danced over her. She could imagine it, imagine *him*.

Something warm blew on the skin of her arm, and a loud breath—

"Oh!" Her eyes popped open, and she came face-to-two-toned-face with Daisy, panting six inches from her.

"We decided you were thinking too hard." Shane was on the other side, looming over her, blocking the sun.

"That scared me."

"You were moaning."

"I wasn't…" She collected herself and lifted her hands off the grass, straightening her back.

Daisy barked, and Chloe jumped, gasping again.

"She wants you to acknowledge her," he said, slowly folding down to sit next to her. "You need to recognize her."

She turned to the dog, still feeling the puffs of her warm breath, her pink tongue hanging out, her half-brown, half-white face oddly symmetrical and appealing to look at. "She's going to lick me, isn't she?"

"She's cooling off," he explained. "That's why her tongue is out. She's going to stare you to death if you don't give her a little attention, though."

"Hi, Daisy," she said, giving a little wave.

Shane laughed softly. "You know she won't hurt you, right?"

"Yes, of course. I…just…" For a long moment, she held eye contact with the dog, seeing her own reflection in the dark eyes. And something else. Something like…emotion. "Does she feel things like that? Like what other people think?"

"I believe dogs have souls," he said. "Because they have feelings. Shame, anger, love. Lots of love." He leaned a little closer. "They need love more than anything."

She sighed and lifted her hand, slowly laying it on the dog's head. "Hey, Daisy," she whispered. "How are you?"

Almost immediately, the dog got down on her belly, turning her head one way and then the other.

"She wants a neck scratch," Shane explained. "Dig your nails in a little, and she'll be yours forever."

She let her fingers go deeper in the soft, short coat, surprised at the lovely texture of the fur and the hard muscles underneath.

Daisy lifted her head and looked up adoringly at Chloe.

"Not forever," Chloe said. "I can't do forever."

"Oh, no. Marie would kill me," Shane said. "I called her this morning to make sure she was cool with this idea, and she loved it, but warned me that she'll cut my heart out with a blunt knife if someone wants to take Daisy from her. And she wants to be texted pictures every day."

"I can take pictures of her," Chloe said, surprised at how much she liked the feel of the dog. She felt warm, solid, and clean. "It's like being handed a baby and having no idea what to do."

Shane stretched out on the other side of Daisy, taking off his baseball cap so that Chloe could see tiny beads of sweat on his forehead. His chest rose and fell as he caught a breath and laughed as Daisy collapsed between them. "Lucky for you, I train people how to handle dogs for a living. Couple of lessons on the basics, and you and Daisy will be great together. Is that all you were whimpering about?"

"I wasn't whimpering."

He made a face like he didn't buy her denial, so

she turned her attention back to Daisy and the neck scratch. Otherwise, she'd just stare at him and study every individual bead of sweat and imagine petting him instead of the dog.

"I was making my pro and con list for taking Daisy," she finally said.

"There's no con."

"Poop."

"Look, you have a yard. Let it go and don't pick it up. Dissolves in the rain and fertilizes the grass."

She looked skyward. "My, you really know how to talk to a girl."

"What other cons?"

"The whole 'bed in storms' thing. I can't sleep with her, Shane."

All of a sudden, Daisy sat up and shook off, making Chloe quickly draw back her hand at the force of that. Then she repositioned herself closer to Shane, who was on his side, his head propped up on one hand. She snuggled against him and lay down with a sigh.

Chloe had to laugh. "She understood that, didn't she?"

"Yep." He ran his large hands over Daisy's side, stroking her over and over. "And she answered by showing you who she really wants to sleep with." He squinted up at her, grinning. "Can you blame her?"

No. "But what if I don't let her in my bed? Will she jump up in the middle of the night?"

"You can close your door and let her sit outside your bedroom and listen to her cry."

"Which would be cruel."

He leaned to whisper in Daisy's ear. "Great news, doggo. She *does* have a heart."

Chloe kicked his shin with her sneakered foot. "Stop it. Don't make her dislike me."

"What else is on your stupid con list?"

"Can I go out without her?"

"As long as I'm with you." He winked. "Just kidding. But it's not a bad idea. Dinner tonight?"

Why the hell did the casual invitation make her heart dance a little? Because it was a date. And a date would mean...another kiss. And another kiss would mean trouble. Fortunately, she was ready.

"Actually, I have plans with Andrea Rivers," she said. "But not if I should stay home with Daisy," she added quickly.

"Architect Andi?" He seemed amused. "You two could raise some eyebrows...and other things. Where will you be? I'll come and make sure no one bothers you."

She smiled at the *other things*. "No one will bother us. We're having dinner together. But if I take Daisy home today, can I go out tonight? Is that okay?"

"Of course," he assured her. "You can leave Daisy for hours as long as you make sure she has food and water and hits the backyard before you leave. Her breed doesn't do well alone for long stretches, but I tired her ass out. She'll sleep on your sofa all night."

She angled her head and gave him a death stare.

"Or your floor." He laughed softly. "Until you leave. Don't worry, very low shedding with Staffies."

"Shedding. I hadn't even thought of that."

"Then don't." He dropped the hand holding his head and patted her leg. "Stick with the pros, not the cons."

Like the fact that having Daisy meant seeing more

of Shane. That was still her favorite pro. "Well, I suppose she makes the house more secure, too," she said instead.

He scratched his head, thinking about that one. "I hate to break your closely guarded preconceptions, but Staffies don't make such superb guard dogs unless your house is being robbed by another dog. They'll bark, but then be pleased to sit on the sofa with your intruder and watch the football game."

She eyed the dog, her heart shifting a little at the way Daisy snoozed in the sun, her broad back rising and falling contentedly. She didn't look like she could hurt, well, a mouse. "I did misjudge her, Shane. I'm sorry."

He looked up at her from his prone position on the grass. "You misjudged me, too."

"No, I..." Then she remembered meeting him. "I thought you were a back-bar fix-it guy."

"And still you gave me a little tongue."

She tapped his arm, almost toppling his head. "Don't remind me."

"Why not? I thought about it for days and jumped all over the opportunity to see you again." He leaned forward, his chest covering Daisy. "I wanted a second chance since I failed so hard the first time."

"Failed? I *kissed* you."

"And then ran off like Cinderella without leaving a shoe, last name, or phone number. I had no way of finding you."

Why that gave her a little thrill, she couldn't say. But it did. A not so little thrill.

"Billy mocked me mercilessly the third time I asked him if you'd come in again, and I actually hung out near the Bitter Bark Bed & Breakfast on the off chance I'd see you."

She felt her mouth open in surprise. "Really?"

"No reason to lie, Chloe. I liked you. I wanted to see you again." He plucked a blade of grass, looked at it for a second, and put it between his teeth. "I wanted to kiss you again."

"Not after you put grass in your mouth."

"Grass is clean."

"At a *dog training facility*?"

"Shit." He spit it out and wiped his mouth. "There. Clean as before."

She rolled her eyes, fighting a smile knowing that she *would* kiss him despite the egregious hygiene. He was that cute. That close. That kissable.

"Why are you so freaky about germs, anyway?" he asked.

"Not *just* germs," she said. "All dirt in general is the enemy. So is clutter, disorder, anything unkempt, messy, or out of place."

"So I was right about the underwear rolls?"

She gave him a slow smile. "My panty drawer is a thing of symmetric beauty."

He fell on his back with a grunt. "Not sure if that's the sexiest thing I've ever heard or the scariest."

"It's the truest. I like my life orderly."

"Why? Disorderly is so much more fun."

"Fun for you maybe, but I told you, I was a sick child." Sick from the time she was born until the day she left her hot mess of a mother when she turned eighteen.

"Did you have something specific?"

"I had everything. Every allergy known to man, every virus within a ten-mile radius, every cold, flu, headache, and illness you could get, I had it."

He eyed her, spending a long time on her face, then even longer on her body. "You sure look healthy now."

"I am," she said proudly. "I had allergy shots in my twenties, so I've got allergies under control. And I haven't taken an antibiotic or so much as a sip of cold medicine in ten years. But having been sick that long and that often made me super germ-conscious, and my neatness is who I am, so sorry if that bothers you."

"Doesn't bother me," he said. "And I understand it now. Doesn't actually explain the underwear drawer, though."

"You can't stay away from that, can you?"

"I admit I'm captivated by the idea. Will you show it to me?"

She laughed. "If you stop teasing me about being a neat freak."

"Lie down."

She blinked at the order. "What?"

"I want to see if you can do it. Lie down on the grass like I am."

Looking down at the grass, she considered it.

"You really can't do it."

"I can," she said. "I'm not sure I want to."

He ran his hand over the grass. "It's cool. Soft. Green. Natural. Daisy and I love it. Lie down, Chloe."

The invitation sent another one of those shivers over her again and an ache in her chest. She wanted to lie down. Wanted to line her body up with his and just be a normal person hanging out in the grass on a lovely summer day.

She swallowed, the familiar, unnamed fear trickling through her.

Oh, no. It had a name. Doreen Somerset, ruiner of normalcy.

"Sure," she said, stretching out her legs and slowly bringing her upper body to the ground. She rested her elbow on the grass, then relaxed a little, turning to face him and Daisy. "See? Lying."

"Yes, you are." He reached over Daisy, but she popped up and trotted away, leaving nothing but space between them. Space Chloe suddenly wanted closed. "I've never seen something so simple cause so much pain."

"I'm not in pain," she replied.

"Then why are you frowning?"

She forced the furrow out of her brow. "Stop it," she said. Because if he kept digging deeper, she'd probably admit more, and then he'd know her issues were deeper than dirt and way, way more complicated.

"I like teasing you," he said softly, leaning a little closer. "You're pretty when you laugh."

She opened her mouth to respond, but her breath caught in her throat. A response so low and real and feminine rolled through her, surprising her with its power. "You really are a...whisperer."

"I am," he said with that undercurrent of cockiness that was both annoying and attractive. "I get creatures of all kinds to change."

"You do?"

"Mmm." He nodded. "Takes a little patience and persistence, but you know what the trick is?"

"I think I'm about to find out."

He leaned a little closer. "Letting them know who has control."

She tried to swallow, but her throat was bone-dry.

Speaking of complicated issues. "I don't lose control," she said, holding his gaze to make her point. "Not in life, not at work, not with men, and not in my underwear drawer. I always have control."

"Yeah, yeah, yeah." His mouth curled in a smile. "You know the other trick?"

"What?"

"A reward they can't resist." He let his gaze move from her eyes to her mouth, settling there long enough so that she knew exactly what that reward would be. And, damn, it would be good.

The sweet smell of the grass and summer air disappeared. Even the pressure of the ground under her and the summer sun on her shoulders and face lightened.

It was like every one of her senses was focused on him.

"Did you forget the grass in my mouth yet?" he asked.

"No."

"So I can't kiss you?"

"I didn't say that."

He touched her lips with his, as light as air at first, like he was giving her time to get used to the idea, then he slid his hand around her neck, the heat and strength of his long fingers suddenly as intense as the kiss.

Her breath hitched again as he added pressure, easing her back a bit, letting their tongues touch as he tunneled deeper into her hair. He tasted pretty damn good for a guy who'd just had grass in his mouth. Delicious, in fact.

He broke the kiss first, inching back. When Chloe opened her eyes, she was surprised to see his closed for a second, then he met her gaze.

"I swore I wasn't going to kiss you until I knew for sure," he said.

"Knew what?"

"If you were going to take Daisy. I can't kiss a person who doesn't like dogs. It's against my personal code of ethics."

She smiled. "You had no problem in the bar the other night."

"I plead ignorance and overwhelming desire. Are you taking her?"

"If you'll agree to give me a little training first."

"On kissing or dogs?"

"Both."

"Then you have come to the right place. And the right man." He kissed her lightly on the mouth and pushed up. "Let's hit the training pen."

She looked up at him, probably not able to hide her disappointment that training took precedence over kissing.

He reached his hand out. "You could always break your date with Andi Rivers and go out with me tonight."

"Nope." Not a chance she'd ditch a new girlfriend for a guy. Not even this guy. "Train me, Shane Kilcannon."

"Just a warning, Chloe. You really don't want to give me a challenge unless you're ready to see me meet it."

One more shiver danced over her as she took his hand. "I'm ready." She hoped.

Chapter Nine

When Shane left her house, Chloe stood very still in the living room and watched Daisy continue to sniff the place out.

Every once in a while, she'd stop, highly interested in something, and Chloe would brace for...an accident.

But she was fine and eventually settled next to a small pile of dog toys Shane had brought along. He'd piled them up in the middle of the living room, stored some dog food, set up the bowls, and left a bag of treats.

And asked again if she'd reconsider her dinner plans.

But Chloe was more sure than ever that she needed a girls' night out and some time to talk to someone who wasn't a Kilcannon. She'd met so many of them today! Liam, the tall, quiet former marine who commanded attention from dogs and people. And Molly, a bubbly, hilarious veterinarian who took no grief from no one, along with Darcy, the youngest in the family, who had an irrepressible charm that reminded Chloe of Shane.

Garrett and Jessie had joined them, and the whole afternoon turned into a day of laughter and barking and...fun. Chloe couldn't remember the last time she'd had such a good time, in the heart of a big family who obviously loved each other—and teased mercilessly.

But now she needed a shower—or two—to get ready for her dinner with Andi Rivers.

"You stay here," she said to Daisy, who looked up with a tilt to her head and a question in her eyes. Then she remembered her training. The command, the name, the eyes, the treat.

Oh, the treats were in the kitchen. "Hang on," she muttered, but the dog followed her right into the one room where she really didn't want her.

"Really?" she asked. "Couldn't you stay out there, in the living room? On the floor, not the sofa."

Daisy walked by her and went right to the cabinet under the sink, barking at it.

Oh God. Another mouse?

The dog turned and looked up at her, barking again, then scratching at the cabinet door, a little frantic. Chloe had gotten so wrapped up at Waterford, she'd forgotten about sealing the hole Shane had found.

"Is something in there, Daisy?" Her voice cracked.

Daisy barked and scratched some more.

"Okay. Here goes." Cringing, she inched the cabinet door open, and Daisy muscled her way in, fearless. She knocked over the 409. Some sponges came flying out when her back paw hit them. All Chloe could see was Daisy's tail thwapping back and forth, and then she popped out, with something squirming in her mouth.

Chloe shrieked in horror, terrified Daisy would drop it in front of her. On instinct, Chloe pivoted to the sliding glass door and threw it open, and Daisy ran out with her victim.

Chloe watched in terror as Daisy ran to the back corner and started digging. Then the mouse disappeared into the dirt and Daisy turned and trotted back toward the house, looking pretty damn happy with herself.

"My hero," Chloe whispered as she came back in. "But do not, under any circumstances, expect me to kiss you."

Chloe got the water bowl and put it in front of the dog encouraging her to drink. Daisy slurped noisily and, after a minute, Chloe headed for the hottest, soapiest, longest shower she could imagine.

An hour later, Chloe walked into an Italian restaurant on the square called Ricardo's and spotted Andi waiting in a booth, her caramel-blond hair spilling over a gorgeous cobalt top that made her eyes an even deeper shade of blue.

"Thank God, it's not called Bitter Bark Pizza," Chloe said after they shared a quick hug in greeting. "I was starting to think that every single business in this town was called Bitter Bark Something."

Andi laughed. "Only here in Bitter Bark Village, which is the official name for this part of downtown, only nobody uses it. The 'Bitter Bark everywhere' was by design—and not my design, I might add. I only helped on the architectural team. That was all the first Mayor Wilkins's work."

"My uncle Frank," Chloe reminded her. "How did you get involved?"

"Kind of a long story, but I took an internship and entry-level job with Bruce Williams, the architect in charge of the Bitter Bark project, after I got my degree and accreditation from Boston University."

"Boston?" Chloe drew back. "And you came to Bitter Bark, North Carolina? Are you from around here?"

She shook her head. "Massachusetts born and raised. And I hadn't planned to come here, but then…" She smiled wistfully. "I hadn't planned on getting pregnant a few months before I was fully accredited."

"You have a baby?" Chloe asked, the news coming out of left field. "But didn't…" Didn't Shane tell her Andi and Liam used to date? She frowned. "I'm confused."

"He's not exactly a baby anymore. Christian is six and starting first grade in the fall. I've been a single mom from the beginning, well, sort of." She flipped open the menu, averting her gaze for a moment. "It's a little complicated."

A "sort of" single mom? Definitely sounded complicated. And, having been raised by one, intriguing to Chloe. But that didn't sound like an invitation to probe. "Oh, okay."

Andi gave her a warm look. "But maybe with some wine I can share?"

Chloe smiled. "Definitely with some wine. I'm walking, not driving, tonight."

"Me, too."

They ordered pinot grigio and, while they waited for the wine, chatted about the vote and the gentrification of Bushrod Square that Andi had been involved in from the day she arrived in this town.

"It came at the perfect time for me," she said. "Bruce is based in Raleigh, but he got the Bitter Bark job and opened up an office here and needed someone to run it. I had great qualifications and some work experience, more than he was getting from other applicants. I needed to work somewhere that would be flexible for me as a single mom, and running a one-person/one-project office is ideal."

"A *sort of* single mom?" Chloe reminded her.

She sighed. "My ex and I went to school together and both interned at an architectural firm in Boston. We landed jobs in Europe, with our firm. And then I got pregnant with Christian and Jeff didn't want to go to Europe with a newborn."

The waiter came and poured wine, giving them a chance to taste it, order, and get back to Andi's story.

"But Christian's father went to Europe?" Chloe guessed.

"Without blinking an eye," Andi replied. "The opportunity was huge and Jeff wasn't about to give up working in Europe for..." She let out an exhale. "Anyway, we broke up."

"Oh, that's a shame." Chloe took a sip and already felt comfortable enough around Andi to ask more. "Is that when you dated Liam Kilcannon?"

A little color rose in her cheeks. "You heard that already?"

"I spent all day at Waterford with Shane."

It was Andi's turn to look surprised. "Well, well, well. You have more to share than I do."

Chloe shrugged. "Not too much to share, but what happened with Liam?"

"Jeff came back," she said. "Christian was four. I'd just started dating Liam. Maybe a month or so. And wham, incoming from Munich. Jeff quit the company and said he missed me and wanted to be a father to Christian."

After he ditched her when she was pregnant? Chloe didn't say anything, but nodded and let Andi finish.

"I had to give him a chance," she said. "For Christian, who adored him."

"But it didn't work out?"

She shifted in her seat. "We lived together, but..." She closed her eyes. "He was killed in a car accident about a year after he got back."

"Oh, Andi." She reached over and put her hand on the other woman's, a rush of sympathy washing over her. "I can't imagine what that must have been like."

"Hard. Even harder for Christian than me," she said, her voice thick. "He'd really gotten attached to Jeff. I was...not sure about our relationship. We never even talked about marriage, but stayed together for Christian while Jeff looked for another job. But Christian *adored* him. And after Jeff died, Christian started having nightmares and, for a while, he hardly talked. He's still an incredibly shy little boy, ever since Jeff died."

"Oh." Chloe closed her eyes. "What a shame. For both of you."

"We're fine. We're a team, and I've sworn off all men until my boy is raised. But I have plenty in my life. In addition to work, I'm teaching an adult-ed class on European architecture at the local college, and I've become immersed in this town," Andi told her.

"You like it?"

"I love living here, love raising my son here, and absolutely love my job." Andi scooted closer, her smile back in place. "Which would be even better if you succeed with this dog idea."

"Oh, I hope I do."

"Is that why you were at Waterford? For a possible town event?"

"And to get a dog. I've agreed to dog-sit an adorable little girl named Daisy. Shane asked me and…"

"Who can say no to a Kilcannon?" Andi asked wryly.

"Apparently, you."

Andi laughed and lifted her glass in a friendly toast. "Here's to Kilcannon men. There really are few quite like them. Have you met Liam?"

"I did, this afternoon. Met a lot of them, as a matter of fact. Molly and Darcy, and Garrett, with his fiancée, Jessie. Dr. Kilcannon wasn't there, though I'd met him at the first advisory committee meeting."

"How about Gramma Finnie?"

"They talked about her, but she was out at a church thing. Does she really blog?" Chloe asked. "And tweet?"

"Like a machine." Andi laughed. "I bet you had a good time."

That was an understatement. "The whole family is terrific, and Waterford is gorgeous."

"And Shane?" Andi prodded.

"Shane is…also gorgeous," she admitted, making them both laugh. "He seems to have a power to get me to do things I wouldn't normally do."

Andi answered that with a raised eyebrow.

"Like take in a dog," Chloe added, to clarify exactly what she meant.

The waiter delivered dinner and, before they ate, Chloe lifted her glass again. "To Better Bark," she said.

"To new friends," Andi replied. "I certainly could use some around here."

"Happy to oblige, but you know I'm on temporary duty."

"I'll take what I can get. And brava to you, Chloe Somerset. I absolutely think it's a genius idea to make this town the dog-friendliest town in America."

They chatted easily through dinner, sharing some more personal history and talking a lot about the pluses and minuses of being thirtysomething single workaholics, although Andi's challenges as a single mom were so much different.

In fact, she'd checked her phone multiple times for updates from the sitter. On the last one, she grinned. "Christian is officially asleep," she announced with a relieved exhale. "And I'm not quite ready to end my rare night out. Bushrod's?"

"Is that a bar?"

"It's *the* bar, at least the one not filled with college students. You'll know it as Bitter Bark Bar, of course, but it was Bushrod's for a hundred years before that, and some things do die a slow death around here."

"I do know that place," Chloe said. "Had a glass of wine there the other night." And her first Shane Kilcannon kiss. "But it didn't seem like anything was 'hopping' there."

"Saturdays there's a DJ and a good crowd. You up for it?"

117

She checked her watch, thinking of Daisy alone at home. But she'd been gone only an hour and a half, and she was having too much fun. "Absolutely."

"If I have to watch Garrett and Jessie kiss one more time, I might start throwing back shots to put me out of my misery." Shane gave Liam a challenging look. "You with me, Bro?"

Liam shrugged and gestured to his ear, like it was too loud to hear anything.

It wasn't, but Liam would use any excuse not to talk. Plus, he hated this place. They'd gone out to dinner with Garrett and Jessie and talked plenty about the time they'd spent with Chloe today, then a beer at Bushrod's seemed to be the natural way to call it a night. Liam agreed, but kept one eye on the door most of the night, as if planning a quick escape.

"Hey," Shane said, wanting to get some kind of communication out of his brother. "Did I tell you Chloe is having dinner with Andi Rivers tonight?"

Liam heard that. Shane saw the big guy react by sitting a little straighter and narrowing his gaze on the front door. "No, she's not."

"Sorry, but she is."

"Not right this minute," Liam said. "Because they just walked in."

Shane turned immediately, but heard Liam's soft grunt as he mumbled, "Damn, she looks good."

"Yes, she does," Shane agreed. Liam probably meant the pretty blonde, Andi, but Shane's attention was riveted on the sexy brunette scanning the bar scene. Oh man, she slayed it in a deep-red top and glossy lipstick that he wanted to lick until it was gone.

"Wouldn't expect her in here tonight," he mused. A bar this crowded? Surely she'd have to bathe in hand sanitizer afterward.

"You want to stay now, I guess," Liam said.

"Hell, yeah. Don't you?"

Liam shifted uncomfortably. "I dunno."

"Suit yourself, big guy. I'm going to buy some ladies a drink before anyone else does. Can I bring them back here or not?"

Liam looked up, indecision in his gaze. "Sure. Bring 'em over here."

"Will you still be here?"

Liam almost smiled. "No promises."

With that, Shane headed straight to the bar, keeping an eye on the blonde and the brunette, who made it exactly seven seconds before some joker tried to talk to them.

Andi gave the guy a noncommittal glance and tried to get closer to the bar, so the bonehead started chatting up Chloe, getting right in her face. And maybe letting some spit fly, based on the way she backed up with every word. Shane moved in closer.

"My name's Doug Johnson," the guy said. "Haven't seen you around here before."

His intro and lame pickup were fully audible and followed by a nervous cough that he covered with his hand. And then he stuck that same hand out for a shake that, of course, made Chloe freeze and inch back, right into Shane's waiting arms.

He closed his hands over her shoulders, making her jump.

Roxanne St. Claire

"Bad night to leave your hazmat suit at home," he whispered in her ear.

Instantly, he felt those narrow shoulders relax a little, like she felt safe in his touch.

The other man looked up at him, a little dismayed by the interruption.

"Sorry, Doug. She's spoken for." Without waiting for a reaction, he turned her around, a little sucker-punched by how pretty she was in her evening makeup and how happy she looked to see him. "Unless you're interested in the coughing Johnson."

She laughed softly. "Thanks for the save."

"Buy you a drink?" He looked over her head and caught Andi's eye. "Liam's over in the corner by the window, and we have extra seats if you want to join us there," he said to both of them.

Even in the dark light of the bar, he could see a little bit of color drain from Andi's pale skin. "Oh, I...I don't know." She gave Chloe a questioning glance, silently communicating the way women did in situations like this, covering for each other if coverage was needed.

"Whatever you prefer, Andi."

Andi thought for a moment, still holding Chloe's gaze, then she nodded. "Sure. I'll meet you over there."

"A drink?" Shane asked her.

"Whatever Chloe's having," she said, slipping away.

Taking Chloe's hand, Shane maneuvered through the crowd to the bar to get drinks.

"Dry white with a side of fingerprints?" he asked, getting rewarded with an easy laugh.

"That'll work, thanks."

He ordered drinks and turned her again, this time so the crowd was behind her and she had nowhere to look but at him. "Nice surprise," he said.

"Small town." She tried for total nonchalance, but he could see the gleam in her eyes. She was as happy to see him as he was to see her.

"How's Daisy?"

She took a slow breath. "You mean my mouse catcher?"

His jaw dropped. "She got one?"

"Before my very eyes."

"And you survived that?"

"Better than the mouse currently buried—by Daisy—in the backyard."

He gave a little fist pump. "That's my girl." Then leaned forward to touch his forehead to hers. "Both of them."

And he felt her quiver ever so slightly at the endearment. "It went a long way to making me like her even more."

"Did you lock up your shoes?"

Her mouth opened into a pretty, glossy O. "I forgot!"

"She has plenty of chew toys," he assured her as the drinks came. Chloe took the wines, and he took fresh beers. "Come on, follow me."

He wove through the crowd, heading to the long table near the window, where Liam and Andi were sitting catty-corner from each other, talking. *Both of them.*

So that was the trick to get Liam to move his mouth. And *laughing.* Holy shit, Andi had the *stuff.*

"Oh, thank you," Andi said when Chloe gave her the drink.

"Thank Shane," she replied, sitting down and lifting her glass toward Liam. "Nice to see you again, Liam."

He nodded with a typical Liam smile that barely lifted his lips.

"Did Chloe tell you she's boarding a Waterford dog?" Shane asked Andi. "And that we worked her in the training area all afternoon?"

"She told me a little," Andi said.

"Tonight, after I got back, we had to leash-train puppies," Shane said, knowing the entertaining story would break any ice. "God, I wish you could have seen that," he said to Chloe.

He caught a look between Liam and Andi that he didn't understand, but wanted to keep the conversation going so his brother had a chance with this woman he'd always liked.

Shane launched into a description of the puppy fail they'd had, making everyone laugh, and flirting shamelessly with Chloe while he told it. But not so much that he didn't notice more of those looks passing between his brother and the blonde. Definite looks. Maybe a few sparks lighting things up, too.

Until Andi pulled out her phone and sighed. "Oh, the text I've been dreading."

"Everything all right?" Liam asked her.

"My sitter is wondering when I'm coming home." She looked at Chloe, and Shane felt a thud of disappointment that was mirrored in the look on Liam's face. "I didn't expect our dinner would turn into a night out, and I told her I'd be home by ten."

"Totally understand," Chloe said, reaching for her purse as Shane spun through all the possible ways to avoid her leaving, starting—and ending—with Liam taking Andi home.

But Shane didn't want to put his brother on the spot.

"No, you don't have to leave," Andi said to Chloe. "You're having fun. My house is on the other side of the square. I'll be home in ten minutes."

Aw, come on, Liam.

"I wouldn't think of letting you leave alone," Chloe said.

"Please, you don't have a six-year-old, and it's Saturday night. Enjoy—"

"I'll take you home." Liam leaned forward. "Let me walk you home."

Now we're talking, big man.

Andi looked a little surprised, but only a little. "Okay, that would be great." This time, the spark was in her eyes.

"Are you sure?" Chloe asked.

"Only if you have someone to take you home," Andi said.

Shane held up his hand. "I got this."

"Then I'm sure." Andi turned to Liam and gave a smile he hoped Liam recognized for what it was: interest. "Let's go."

Shane watched his brother put his hand on Andi's back and lead her out the front door, then shifted his gaze to Chloe. "You have no idea what a breakthrough we just witnessed."

"Liam and Andi?"

"And Liam saying ten whole words. And laughing."

"Stop," she said, poking him easily. "He talks plenty. You should quit giving him such a hard time."

"Where's the fun in that?" The music shifted down in key and rhythm. "Oh man, that's our cue," Shane said, pushing back his chair and reaching for Chloe's hand.

"You want to leave?" she asked, confused.

"I want to dance." He pulled her up, not giving her a chance to argue. He slid an arm around her and led her to the edge of the dance floor, seeing Garrett and Jessie already dancing close.

Gramma Finnie would call this a luck of the Irish night, for sure.

He wrapped both arms around her waist and pulled her all the way against him, a little surprised at how eager he was to get her right where he could feel her whole body.

Angling his head so they fit perfectly, he swayed them both to the slow pulse of the music, loving the way the bar light made her hair shine like wet ink over her shoulders.

"Did you have fun today?" he asked.

She leaned back to look up at him. "I had an amazing day," she admitted.

"Really?"

"I kissed a boy. I got a dog. I met a big family. And now I'm dancing."

He eyed her suspiciously. "That's all it takes to have an amazing day? 'Cause I could blow that out of the water before the sun comes up."

"I have no doubt you could."

He lowered his face to hers, but before he kissed her, she rested her head in the crook of his shoulder, which was more intimate somehow. "Want me to?" he asked.

She didn't answer but sighed into his kiss, swaying with the music. She tightened her arms around him, which he took as a very good sign that the Kilcannon luck was going to continue all night long.

Except, somewhere deep in his gut, he already knew he wanted more than one night with her.

Chapter Ten

Well before midnight and already thinking about Daisy, even though Shane assured her she'd be fine, Chloe was ready for Shane to walk her home. The glow of a great night, a few more slow dances, a lot of laughs, and just the right amount of wine to be relaxed warmed Chloe as they walked hand in hand through the square.

On the way home, she got a text from Andi thanking her for understanding that she wanted to leave and checking to make sure Chloe had gotten home okay.

"I guess that means she's not with Liam," Shane said, sounding a little disappointed.

"You thought he'd stay?" she asked, texting back a reply.

"I don't know. I'd like him to get that itch scratched."

She turned to him. "That itch *scratched*?"

"No, no, I don't mean, no," he backpedaled. "It's just that Andi makes Liam...itchy. He's crazy about her, not that you could tell, but I know him better than anyone."

"She's had a tough time, but she did tell me she's sworn off men."

"She wasn't looking at him like she'd sworn off anything."

She slowed her step and eyed him. "Really? You picked all that up while you were describing the puppy pileup on Liam's back?"

"I can read people." He eased her closer. "Like I can read that you really want to kiss me again and you're thinking about when and where that's going to happen."

"Your confidence is a thing to behold, Shane Kilcannon. What insecurities is it covering?"

"Insecurities?" He sounded like he couldn't even say the word. "What are these insecurities you speak of?"

"Nobody has as much bravado as you if they are one hundred percent secure. I think a lot of it's an act. You're competitive, especially with Liam. I saw it with the dogs today, and even at the bar."

"I'm competitive, no doubt about it. I'm second in a long line, and I think that makes me try harder to beat big, bad Liam." Still holding her hand, he slid his arm all the way around her. "And I like that you're giving me so much thought, Perfect Chloe. You may not realize it or like it, but that's a shower of compliments all over my poor, insecure heart."

She laughed as they turned on her street, but she stopped at the sight of her very dark and deserted-looking bungalow. "Oh my God, I forgot to leave a light on! Oh, I'm a terrible dog mother."

"She'll forgive you," he assured her, hustling them

closer. "Just love on her and take her out to do her business." At her look, he added, "Or I will. Tonight, anyway. Come on."

As soon as they reached the driveway, Daisy started barking at the front window.

"Poor thing alone in the dark," Chloe said, furious with herself and the oversight.

Shane pulled out his phone and tapped the flashlight, and that made more guilt press down on Chloe. "Hey, you're a rookie and forgiven. She's a dog and will forget about it five seconds after the light is on and there's a treat in her mouth."

"Still, she's in a new place." They walked up the three steps to the front porch. "And all alone and—"

"Whoa, watch your step." Shane grabbed her hard enough to jerk her back and prevent her from going one more inch.

"Why, what..." She stared at the worn wooden planks at their feet. "Is that what I think it is?"

He leaned closer and sniffed. "Yup."

"She got out!" Panic took her voice up an octave, more worried about the dog than the defilement to the porch. "How could she have gotten out?"

"No, I don't think so." He shook his head. "Because she wouldn't have gotten back inside. Are you sure she wasn't out here before you left?"

"Not once. We were in the house and in the back. I haven't been out here at all." She could barely hear herself talk or think over Daisy's now frantic barking.

"I'll take care of it," he said, steering her gingerly around the pile. "Let's get her calmed down."

Rage bubbled up inside Chloe's chest. "I don't get this. A dog came to my front door and...did that?"

Her stomach gripped at the many levels of violation she felt.

"That's not right."

"You can say that again." She unlocked the door and opened it, instantly on the receiving end of a wild frenzy of barking, panting, and pawing.

"Daisy! Sit! Sit, girl." Shane got a hand on the dog's collar as Chloe turned the light on the entryway table, spilling a golden glow into the pitch-black house.

In a second, Daisy was quiet as Shane rubbed her head and let her bathe his face. "Thanks, dog. You've killed any chance of a good-night kiss," he joked.

But Chloe didn't laugh. She was still too upset about the front porch.

Standing, Shane put a comforting hand on her shoulder. "Take her out to the back, and I'll deal with this, okay?"

She nodded. "Do dogs do that?" she asked. "Do they roam residential streets and leave their calling cards on people's porches?"

He looked hard at her, and she braced herself for a lecture on how only bad dogs did, and not all dogs were bad, and if she was going to make this a dog-friendly town, then she damn well better get used to—

"No," he said simply. "They do not."

She blinked at him. "Then someone *put it there*?"

"I don't know, but take her out back. I'll clean it up."

She was on the back patio a few minutes later, rubbing her bare arms, watching Daisy romp around the grass. Shane stepped out, holding up his hands, surgeon style.

"All clean," he assured her.

"What do you make of that, Shane?"

He lifted a shoulder, slowly shaking his head. "I don't know. The only thing I can think is someone was ticked off at you for leaving a dog in the dark and wanted to send a message."

Her eyes popped. "How about leaving a nasty note taped to the door?"

"Shhh." He pulled her into him, folding his arms around her like he did on the dance floor and getting the same warm reaction in her body when the two of them molded together. "Did Daisy licking me kill any possibility of a kiss? I swear I washed my face."

She looked up at him, the moonlight highlighting the angles of his face and the familiar scent of her lemon kitchen soap all over his cheeks. The consideration that showed touched her. She let her eyes close and angled her head.

"I'm feeling reckless," she whispered.

He gave a soft laugh that was lost when his lips covered hers, as smooth and warm to the touch as she'd imagined. He opened his mouth and eased her even closer, somehow making the kiss a full-body event, letting their chests meet and hips touch and thighs press.

With the softest groan from deep in his chest, he turned his head, took another angle, and let their lips find the sweet spot of contact. For a moment, Chloe couldn't do anything but feel, completely lost to the tender, delicious warmth that rolled through her.

A little dizzy, she managed to break the kiss, opening her eyes to meet the dark arousal in his.

"Daisy's watching," she managed to joke, not sure at all how—or if—she was going to stop this.

"Hate to break it to you, but Daisy's digging to China at the moment, and she couldn't care less what we're doing."

She turned to look over her shoulder and, sure enough, the dog was rooting in some soft dirt with raw determination. "Oh. She's going to be filthy."

"Better keep her out of your bed, then..." He caressed her back, his possessive, hot hands moving up and then back down, until they rested on the rise of her backside. "Which means there's more room for me."

Smiling, she managed to shake her head. "You're too much."

"You don't know that yet. I could be..." He dipped his hands. "Just right."

She let her head drop back with a soft moan, and he moved right in to place soft kisses on her exposed neck. Chills covered every inch of her body, and her knees literally felt like they could buckle.

"Garrett and Jessie are waiting for you at the bar. Isn't Jessie the DD tonight?"

"I can text him and get myself home...tomorrow."

Temptation, as raw and real and unfamiliar as any of the things she'd felt that day, wended its way through her body, settling somewhere low and primal in her belly.

It thrilled and terrified her. "I think you better go," she said, as much to herself as to him. "I think that's a good idea."

"Really? 'Cause I think that might be the stupidest idea yet."

She kind of agreed, but knew from experience that this wasn't the kind of "mess" she could handle very well.

"I can't," she said. She didn't tell him what she couldn't do, because Shane Kilcannon would take that as a personal challenge he couldn't possibly lose.

"You can, but you won't," he replied. "Which is totally acceptable and understandable. If I know why."

"Because…" She spun through all the reasons that wouldn't sound like she was scared of another mess. "You're on the advisory committee."

He snorted with disdain. "Pretty sure there are no bylaws against sex with committee members."

Sex. It was all so messy. And frustrating. And…no. "It would ruin our friendship," she tried.

That made him smile. "Could make us the best of friends."

He'd have an answer for any excuse she threw at him, except the truth. But there was no way she'd get into that now. He'd be here all night psychoanalyzing her and…no. She didn't have to give him a reason not to have sex.

She looked up at him. "It's time to leave, Shane."

"Got it." He instantly nodded and stepped back. "But will you come to Waterford tomorrow for Sunday dinner?"

Her eyebrows raised. "Sunday dinner?"

"It's a weekly event you don't want to miss. We also do Wednesday nights as a family, but that's not quite as sacred, or as fun. On Sunday, Dad cooks, booze flows, insults fly, and fun is had across four generations of Kilcannons."

She almost couldn't breathe it sounded so

wonderful, and so completely foreign. "Yes, sure. That sounds like a blast."

"I'll pick you up around one." He lowered his face and kissed her again. "Wear jeans, and you can help me clean the kennels."

She laughed. "You sure know how to make me weak in the knees, Shane Kilcannon."

"You know I do." Hugging her tighter, he took one more kiss.

"Thank you for being my personal sanitation specialist tonight."

"Hey, there's more where that came from." He eyed Daisy, who'd given up on her hole and rested on the grass, watching them. "I could wash her down for you."

She put her hands on his chest, which was so broad and solid, she had to fight the urge to rest her head on it. All night. "I'll see you tomorrow, Shane."

He kissed her forehead one more time and let her walk him to the front door, with Daisy on their heels. As soon as he was gone, the dog heaved a sigh and let out the saddest little whine.

"Same, sister." She snapped her fingers and headed to her bedroom. "Come on. Let's go to…the floor."

"Go to the farthest corner and…be fast about it." Chloe pointed to the edge of the fenced-in yard and looked hard at Daisy, praying she understood. "And then…wash your paws."

The answer was one loud, serious bark, then the dog darted over to one of the tennis balls she'd carried out to the patio, snagging it in her teeth and carting it back to Chloe.

"You want to play fetch?"

She lifted her head and offered the slobbery ball.

"Oh, Daisy, I'm so not a fetch player."

She came closer, then dropped the ball at Chloe's feet, her meaning and needs crystal clear. And so much guilt in the eyes.

On a sigh, Chloe reached down and used her nails to pick up the ball by the well-chewed threads.

"Here we go," she said. "Fetch," she whispered, giving the ball a hard toss to the far end of the yard, making Daisy turn and run like her very life depended on beating the ball to its destination. "And while you're there, do your, uh, business," she called.

The doorbell rang, startling Chloe. She wasn't expecting Shane for a few hours to take her to Waterford, so who was here on a Sunday morning? Daisy was on her way back with the ball, but Chloe held her hand up.

"Stay."

Instantly, the dog stopped and sat down.

"Wow, you are a good girl. And I would probably come right over there and hug and kiss you, but..." She pointed to the house. "Doorbell. So, you play here with the ball."

Sighing at how inane she sounded, she walked back into the kitchen, washed her hands, then glanced down at her sleep pants and T-shirt, wondering again if her guest was Shane. Maybe he couldn't wait until this afternoon, a thought that gave her an absolutely uncalled-for thrill.

She peered at the tiny window in the front door,

not seeing a man at all, but immediately recognizing the soft ashy waves of her aunt. She opened the door without hesitation.

"Hi, Aunt Blanche," she said, unlatching the screen door. "This is a nice surprise."

"I hope it is." She smoothed a pale blue linen dress, worry in eyes the same color. "I just came from church and thought I better tell you that word of what you're planning to do is out already."

"Really? Well, it is a small town," she acknowledged, opening the door wider. "Come on in. Would you like some coffee?"

"I'd love—" A noisy bark from outside stopped her words and movement. "You have a dog, Chloe?"

"Oh, I should have told you," Chloe said. "Is it a problem? I know the lady who lived here had a dog."

"Not a problem," Blanche assured her. "Yes, Rose took Ziggy with her, but it wouldn't be an issue. I'm surprised, that's all."

"That makes two of us," Chloe said on a laugh, leading Blanche into the kitchen.

Daisy was on the patio, barking at the sliding glass door. When she wasn't licking it. There really wasn't enough 409 on the planet for this situation.

"Shane convinced me it would be a great idea to help show the town I love dogs. So don't you think that's—"

She turned to see Blanche staring in shock at the dog. "It's a pit bull," she said.

"Well, technically," she said, surprised at the kick those words gave her. "That's a type of dog, not a breed. Daisy is a Staffordshire terrier."

"Call it what you want, but a pit bull can be a scary dog."

She tried to remind herself she'd said the same thing yesterday. "She's not scary, Aunt Blanche. She's an absolute doll. And if people see that, it will go a long way to taking away any worries about dangerous dogs."

Daisy wasn't helping her case by letting out a series of deep, loud barks that Chloe knew by now was just her voice, not anything fierce.

Blanche backed up as if the dog were going to crash through the glass and attack.

"Oh, no, you have her all wrong. Look." Chloe pushed the slider open, and Blanche let out a fearful gasp.

"Be careful!"

Without thinking, Chloe dropped down and slid both arms around the dog, determined to show her aunt how sweet Daisy was. "She's a good dog." And that was met with one huge, wet, loving tongue that slapped onto Chloe's cheek and took a swipe that missed her lips by centimeters.

And she lived. Barely.

"Oh, oh," Blanche stammered. "My, she is friendly."

Chloe wanted to recoil and wipe and take a quick hand sani bath, but that would make Daisy look bad. "She's super sweet. Right, Daisy girl?" She gave her head a good rub, and Daisy got so excited at the affection that she popped up on her hind legs, gave another gooey jaw lick, and slammed her front paws on Chloe's shoulders, almost knocking her over.

"I really didn't know you were *such* a dog lover."

Neither did I. "Come and meet Aunt Blanche." Chloe managed to stand and get Daisy's collar. "Stay. Stay."

Of course, she did, plopping down and looking up at the new arrival with nothing but love and hope for more affection in her eyes.

"So, she's not at all dangerous?" Blanche asked, visibly relaxing.

"Not in the least," Chloe said, slowly letting go of the collar.

Blanche bent over. "Hello, Daisy."

Sensing the trepidation, Daisy walked slowly to Blanche, barked a few times, then went right by her to a chew toy she'd left on the kitchen floor. Blanche watched her for a moment, then sat down at the small kitchen table, letting out a sigh as if the dog encounter had made her adrenaline spike.

"You have a dog, Blanche, right?" Chloe asked as she went to the sink to nonchalantly wash her hands and maybe wipe some slobber from her cheek.

"Yes, I have a standard poodle," her aunt replied. "I love dogs. But I'm scared of pit bulls."

That's like judging a person by the color of their skin.

She was tempted to throw Shane's line at Blanche, but it had hurt her to be accused of prejudice, and she had no reason to make her aunt feel bad. "No need to be scared of Daisy," she said instead, pouring some coffee from the pot she'd made not long ago. "Now tell me how bad our security leak is in town hall."

"Oh, honey. Three people talked to me at church today, and they don't even work in town. Word is out."

Chloe brought coffee for both of them and sat across from her. "That's not good," she said. "I don't want the town council to make up its mind before I've had a chance to go in there and wow them."

"And they will," Blanche agreed. "So I'd like to call an emergency council meeting this week, maybe as soon as Tuesday or Wednesday."

"Okay," Chloe said. "I was planning to really fine-tune that presentation for a bigger crowd, and I'll get that done tomorrow."

"And you should take any time before that to make some friends, too," Blanche said. "I'm going to send you a list of who's on the town council and where they work, or where their spouses or kids work. Your idea is fantastic, but you're also selling yourself in a town like this."

She smiled. "Shane said the same thing."

Blanche's brow lifted. "I heard you were dancin' mighty close to Shane Kilcannon last night."

Chloe felt her eyes pop wide in shock, making Blanche chuckle.

"Changing the name of the town wasn't the only thing folks were talking about at church," Blanche said with a teasing smile.

"Wha...we...I...." Chloe had to laugh at her own inability to form a defense. "I ran into him at Bushrod's."

Blanche gave a pretend toast with her mug. "Listen to you, knowing what the locals call the Bitter Bark Bar."

"I'm trying," she assured Blanche. "And I'll do my best this week to stop into every place I can. Should I presell my idea? Talk about it openly?"

"Hard to say." Blanche frowned, gnawing on her lower lip and slowly turning toward where Daisy lay. When Daisy felt Blanche's gaze, she stood up and trotted over and practically begged for a little love. "But maybe you don't have to do any talking," Blanche said, reaching out to scratch the brown patch on Daisy's head. "Daisy can do it for you."

Chloe smiled. "How's that?"

"If people in this town could see this dog wandering into stores and shops, looking like she could be dangerous, but acting like a sweet little puppy? You're going to go a long way to alleviating issues and fears."

Chloe sat up, thinking about how Shane had said she needed a partner. "You don't think someone at the Bitter Bark Bakery would recoil if I walked in with Daisy?"

Blanche looked hard at her. "That's the whole point, honey. In five minutes, they'd see she's sweet and harmless. Of course, you'd have her on a leash and she'd obey your every command."

"She'd obey Shane's every command," Chloe said. "I'm still learning."

"Then bring Shane," Blanche said with a playful gleam in her eye. "From what I heard in church, that won't be a hardship."

"Don't people pray at church?"

"And we 'fellowship,' which means a lot of discussion about who was dancing with whom at Bushrod's."

Chloe laughed and rolled her eyes. "I'll talk to Shane and see if he thinks it's a good idea. I wouldn't want Daisy to do something that would blow up in my face."

As if she understood, Daisy dropped to the ground at Chloe's feet and rolled over, practically begging for a belly rub and making Blanche laugh heartily.

"Like tear people's hearts out with her cuteness?" Blanche asked. "I know this town, Chloe. Daisy could be our secret weapon to winning the Better Bark battle."

Chloe couldn't help it. She bent over and stroked the smooth belly exposed in front of her. Daisy's head rolled from side to side, and Chloe could have sworn she was smiling.

"Careful you don't make her pee," Blanche said.

Chloe jerked her hand back with a gasp, and Blanche laughed again, then her smile faded. "This is very good for you, Chloe."

"Good?" She looked up from the dog and met the blue eyes of a woman who'd sometimes been a real mother to her. Not often, because Mom hadn't liked when Aunt Bland, as she'd called her older sister, would swoop into Little Fork and announce she was taking Chloe on a "special goddaughter weekend."

"Good that you can, you know, let go." Blanche angled her head. "It doesn't make you like your mother if you don't have complete control of everything."

Chloe swallowed at Blanche's rare mention of Mom. She'd never criticize her sister, but she knew why Chloe clung to control. She'd seen the mess. The filth. The trash of life with a hoarder.

"Trust me, Aunt Blanche, control has been slipping away since I set foot in Bitter Bark."

"And how do you feel about that?"

"A little thrilled. And terrified."

Blanche nodded and gave Chloe's hand an encouraging pat. "That's normal, dear."

Good. Because normal was all Chloe wanted to be in the whole world.

Chapter Eleven

Take Daisy in and out of businesses all over Bitter Bark? Shane slowly shook his head when Chloe told him this plan on the way to Waterford.

"You think it's a terrible idea?" she asked.

"It's so brilliant, I can't believe I didn't think of it myself."

She laughed. "That would be high praise for any idea."

"I did suggest she be your partner, but I was thinking some walks in the park, maybe stop and talk to some people. But, yeah, you take her into shops and restaurants. We'll know who's going to fight it and who's on our side."

"Our *side*." She reached over and put her hand on his arm. "Thanks for being on mine."

"How could I not?" Easily, he reminded himself for the tenth time that morning. He was digging himself deeper every minute with this woman, and like a crazed dog with a hole, he couldn't stop. Sex wasn't guaranteed. And messing with her, like he wanted to at first, had started…messing with him. "The whole idea of a dog-friendly town can only help

Waterford," he added, as if that were his excuse for staying so close to her.

"Well, it's good to have the support of the whole Kilcannon family."

"Uh, not so fast. You still haven't met Gramma Finnie."

She blinked at him. "You don't think your grandmother will like the idea? I understand she's an institution around here."

"An institution in Bitter Bark and an Internet sensation with a blog and Twitter account that make her an official old Irish lady celebrity."

"That's right, so I really do want to present the idea to her today."

"Unless she knows already," he said. "If you were the talk of the ten-thirty service at the Presbyterian church, then you were probably on the lips as much as communion at the Catholic Mass. Gramma Finnie'll tell us."

She nodded, thinking about that. "If the idea is good for Waterford, why wouldn't your grandmother like it?"

He pulled his truck into the drive and didn't see any other cars, so they were first. "She tells a story— well, she tells a lot of stories, so brace yourself. She also speaks in Irish proverbs and with a pretty thick brogue."

"Okay. What's the story?"

He laughed a little, thinking of the thousand or so times he'd heard it. "I'm sure she'll tell you one of many variations she has," he said. "But the short version is that when she and my grandfather came here from Ireland in the fifties, they drove into Bitter

Bark, saw the sign, and the setter du jour—Kilcannons always have one—started howling off-key. Gramma called it a 'bitter bark' and decided it meant they'd found their forever home."

"Oh, that's so sweet."

He chuckled. "The first hundred times you hear it, yeah."

He parked and climbed out, and Daisy jumped up and barked, but stayed in the truck bed.

"And you think that emotional tie to the town's name would be a reason she'd be opposed to changing it?" Chloe asked as she got out of the passenger side.

"It's possible."

"Wait, wait." Chloe came sprinting around the truck to where he was. "Let me tell Daisy to get out of the truck," she requested. "I want her to listen to me."

"Okay. Hit it." He pulled down the tailgate.

"Do I need a treat?"

"Probably not. Remember, eyes, command, then name, maybe snap your fingers, if you like. Reward her with a big hug and kiss."

She threw him a look.

"Okay, a little hug and pretend kiss."

She stood right in front of Daisy and locked gazes. "Daisy. Down." She snapped, and the dog jumped out, barked once, and looked only a little bit more proud of herself than Chloe did.

"Reward," he reminded her.

She took a breath and bent over, awkwardly rubbing Daisy's head. "Good girl," she murmured, then wiped her hand on her crisp, *ironed* khaki shorts.

"My little dog whisperer," he teased, giving Chloe's hair a playful rub like he would a favorite pet.

Keeping it light, as he'd promised himself last night when he went to bed aching for what he hadn't had. He wanted to be around her, but if she needed things to be platonic, fine.

Maybe better even, considering the way she managed to get under his skin and he didn't seem to knock so much as an eyelash out of place for her.

"Hardly a dog whisperer," she said. "But we did okay, right, Daisy? She slept on that dog bed in my room and, wow, does this dog snore."

"Better watch out, Chloe. Next thing you know, she'll be eating off your plate."

She gave a throaty laugh, the sound somehow playful and sexy at the same time. "That would be my line in the sand. Unless..." She gave him a questioning look. "Would that win your grandmother's heart?"

"Like I said, she could go either way," he said. "Gramma Finnie is a stubborn old Irish woman with a lifelong connection to this town. Just give her a chance to get to know you." He put an arm around her and pulled her close to encourage her and also because he couldn't keep his freaking hands off her. "She's going to like you."

"How do you know?"

"Because I do." Oh man, he was killing it with the *keep it light* technique. Too bad. He tucked her closer, nestling his nose in her hair to inhale the fresh fragrance of it and whisper the rest. "Should never have left you last night," he confessed.

He felt her shudder at the admission. "Shane, you're going to complicate things."

"I like complicated."

She slowed her step. "And when I disappear and go to Roatán?"

"That's where you're off to next? Some two-bit Caribbean island?"

"Might not be two-bit when I'm done."

"Fine, fine. I'll take what I can get," he said, not nearly as casually as he'd have liked. "Couple of days. Couple of weeks. Couple of…nights."

She looked hard at him, her gaze as serious as he'd ever seen her. "Let's get the town council vote first."

"That's what it's going to take?" He drew back, feigning shock. "Chloe Somerset, is there no end to your bribery and corruption?"

"I'm not bribing you," she said, elbowing him. "I'm setting a timeline."

"By telling me I can sleep with you if I influence everyone on the town council to vote in favor of Better Bark?" He crossed his arms and shook his head. "That is bribery."

A soft flush darkened her cheeks. "I didn't say that."

"You didn't *not* say that." Holding on to that, and her, he led her into the side kitchen door, pausing for a second before he opened it, bracing for what he knew was going to hit his heart.

"Shane?" Chloe asked, slowing her step when he did. "Are you okay?"

How could he answer that? How could he tell her that every single time he opened this door and walked into this house, the familiar and unwelcome smack of grief almost knocked him over? Not outside on the farm, not anywhere else, and not usually when he had to run into Dad's office or get something from the house.

But Sunday dinners without Mom? It usually took a few minutes and a Bloody Mary to bury emotions that threatened to ruin the day.

"Fine," he told her, pushing the thoughts away with the same ease that he breathed every day. "Just want to be sure you know that my dad gives the housekeeper the day off, so it's more about the company than the food."

"That's fine," she said. "I'm happy to be here."

"Yeah, me, too," he lied. "I'm happy you're here." But that wasn't a lie. Not in the least.

A minute later they were in the kitchen, greeting Dad, getting Daisy acclimated, and settling in on the empty barstools in front of the kitchen island where Dad was cooking.

"It smells delicious," Chloe said, looking around. "And this is a beautiful home."

"Thanks to my dearly departed wife," Dad said, setting down the chef's knife he was using to chop carrots.

That didn't take long, Shane thought.

"I grew up in this home," Dad continued. "And this kitchen was little more than a corner in the house, though it functioned. After Annie and I had a few kids, and we took over ownership, my parents moved to town and my wife got the remodeling bug and never stopped fixing up this or gutting that. Took down all the walls and added this fancy granite." He gave an expansive gesture. "She was the real cook, though."

Shane heard the hitch in his father's voice, reminding him that he wasn't the only one who missed Mom on Sundays. And that reminded him that if a man doesn't let himself get too far gone in love, he never has to have his throat close up when he thinks about her.

"Did you make Bloodies, Dad?" Shane asked, pushing away from the island.

"In a pitcher in the fridge." He added a wink to Chloe. "Sunday Bloody Marys are another tradition."

"We're Irish," Shane said. "Drinking is a tradition."

"Traditions are nice," she mused, resting her chin on her palm.

"Did you have them in your family when you were growing up?" Dad asked.

As Shane brought the pitcher from the refrigerator, he stole a glance at Chloe and could have sworn she paled. "Not too terribly many," she said. "I was raised by a single mother, and we just kind of got by."

"And now you live in Miami, right?" Dad looked pleased with himself. "See? I was paying attention at my first meeting of that committee."

"Amazing," Shane said, coming around the island to stand next to his father and steal two celery stalks for their drinks. "Considering you spent that meeting trying to figure out a way for Liam to take your place next to Andi Rivers."

Dad chuckled, knife in action again, knowing he was busted for his matchmaking ways. "I've always liked that young woman."

"I like her, too," Chloe said. "I had dinner with her last night."

"And then..." Shane leaned into his father. "Andi left Bushrod's on the arm of your oldest son."

Dad stopped chopping, and his eyes grew wide. "Really."

"All without your help," Shane teased.

"Well, he was here in the kennels before the sun came up, working with Jag and, whoa, he was in a foul mood," Dad said. "Liam, not Jag."

"How could you tell that from his normal mood?" Shane joked, but deep inside, his gut wrenched for his brother. Foul mood meant no dice with Andi, and Liam really liked her. He'd barely looked at another woman since Andi broke up with him and it had to be two years now.

"So maybe I made the right decision not sending Liam to the committee," his father mused, looking deliberately from Shane to Chloe.

Shane rolled his eyes. "This one's all me, Pops. Although the Dogfather will no doubt take credit."

Chloe laughed. "I heard about that nickname."

"Irish style," he joked, eyeing them both. "And you two make a fine couple."

"Oh, we're not..." Now she was uncomfortable, shifting on the stool.

"Chloe's a temporary addition to our town," Shane said, helping her out. "But I'm happy to help her win the *Better* Bark cause."

"Ah, yes, the name change," Dad said, lifting his dark brows. "What an idea, young lady."

"Do you like it?" she asked.

"Very much," he assured her. "A family that can travel with their dog is a happy family indeed."

"That's what I was thinking and why it makes so much sense from a tourism standpoint."

"When's the council meeting?" Dad asked. "I'll want to call in a few favors."

"Call them in fast," Shane said. "They moved it up to Tuesday or Wednesday of this week."

"Any advice for me?" Chloe asked.

Dad thought about that, scraping his chopped veggies into a large pan. "It's a big council," he said. "Maybe thirteen on it now? They'll all love you."

"We're hoping they love Daisy," Chloe said. "My aunt thinks I should be taking her into local businesses around the square to meet people and make them fall in love."

Dad looked up, nodding. "Good idea. She's a great dog."

"And she could go a long way to dispelling some really stupid preconceptions," Shane added.

Dad gave him a sharp look, but just then, Molly's twelve-year-old daughter, Pru, came in. Chloe turned to greet them, but Dad leaned closer to Shane. "You can't change the world's opinion, Son," he said under his breath.

He didn't get a chance to argue that as the whirlwind that was Prudence Kilcannon blew deeper into the kitchen, swirling around Chloe. "Oh, you must be the tourism lady. Mom and I were talking about you on the way home from church. And your big doggie idea."

"Chloe, this is my niece, Pru," Shane said. "And if you want to get on my grandmother's good side, this is your girl."

"Hi, Pru," Chloe said.

"Oh, everyone's right," Pru said, openly assessing the new arrival. "You *do* look like Vanessa on *The Bachelor*."

"I do?"

Molly and Darcy blew in next, delivering hugs, hellos, and generally increasing the noise level.

"So why didn't anyone call Darcy and me to tell me there was a Kilcannon drink fest at Bushrod's last night?" Molly demanded with a playful fist on Shane's chest.

"It wasn't a drink fest," Shane said.

"And word is there was kissing." Darcy put her hands on her hips and looked from Shane to Chloe, who started laughing.

"Who was kissing?" Dad asked, frustrated that he didn't know this tidbit.

Molly poured a Bloody Mary from the pitcher into a glass Shane handed her in a move they'd done so many times, it felt choreographed. "Who *wasn't* kissing would be a better question." Molly took her own celery stick for the drink and pointed it to Dad. "In fact, our very own Liam—"

"Left with Andi Rivers," he finished for her. "Don't even have to go to church to get that gossip."

On his other side, Darcy elbowed him. "You shoulda gone, Dad. Molly said Cassandra Michaels was there."

"There and looking good," Molly added. "She dressed to impress *somebody* and it wasn't Father John, based on the number of times she looked back at Gram and me."

Dad shot her a deadly look. "That'll be enough of that," he said gruffly, turning from the island and heading into the pantry, far enough away to end the conversation.

"Enough of what?" Liam asked, coming in from the living room, rolling up a sleeve of his white dress shirt.

"Did you go to church, too?" Shane asked, not

quite able to keep the disbelief out of his voice. Raised as Catholic as any Irish brood, most of the Kilcannon kids hadn't stepped inside St. Cecilia's since the day of Mom's funeral. Molly took Pru sometimes in her effort to be a better mom, and Darcy drove Gramma but rarely stayed for the service. Shane, Garrett, and Liam never went.

"I did," Liam said, starting on the other sleeve.

Except never say never.

"Things so bad with Jag's training you have to pray for him now?" Shane teased.

Liam ignored him. "Hello, Chloe, how are you?"

"I'm good, Liam. Thanks for walking Andi home last night."

Molly and Pru shared a look and Darcy plopped both elbows on the island and stared at her oldest brother. "Spill it, big guy."

"Shut it, little girl," he fired back.

Darcy just grinned and flipped her long, blond hair, a wicked smile on a face too beautiful for its own good.

"Oh, Liam," Dad said, coming back in. "I heard you saw Andi last night."

Everyone laughed, but Liam just closed his eyes and shook his head, stepping closer to Chloe who was perched on her barstool taking in all the verbal volley like she was on the main court at Wimbledon.

"Hope you're ready for a Kilcannon Sunday dinner."

"I'm starving," she said.

"Don't think that's what he means," Molly quipped.

"I can handle it," Chloe assured them, then laughed. "I think."

That cracked them all up and took the heat off Liam, and then Garrett and Jessie came in with Lola, and the party was in full swing. A house full of dogs, drinks, and lively discussions.

Shane was quiet, though, taking it all in.

Maybe it was the first kick of Dad's supercharged Bloody Mary. Maybe it was the family teasing or just Shane's leftover libido that was still taunting him, but as he watched Chloe navigate the always bubbling waters of the Kilcannon family, something felt a little out of sorts in his chest.

Was it just the way her dark eyes sparking in a way that reflected all the energy in the room? Or was it just that he wasn't fighting that low-grade anger that bubbled up when he was in this house? And why wasn't he? Something was different today.

"Don't you think so, Shane?" Chloe asked, putting her hand over his.

Damn, he'd missed the question.

"Don't you think that change will be great for everyone?" she added.

"Oh, yeah, definitely." He turned his hand and threaded his fingers through hers, not caring that Molly, Pru, Darcy, and Dad were zeroing in on the gesture. He wanted to thank her for the distraction and the relief from a pain that had been around so long, it was part of him.

"All right, all right, I'm here."

Every sound in the room instantly stopped, and all heads turned toward the living room. Around the corner came Gram, eighty-six years old, barely an inch over five feet, and just as mighty as ever.

"I thought you wanted me to pick you up in half an

hour, Gram," Darcy said, instantly popping over to put her arm around their grandmother's tiny frame.

"I got a ride," she said, looking hard at Dad. "Cassandra Michaels of all people."

"Imagine that," Dad said dryly.

Gramma came all the way into the kitchen and scanned them all with blue eyes behind rimless bifocals. She walked right up to her, crossed her skinny little arms, and stared Chloe down. "Are you the lass who wants to change the name of this town?"

Chloe visibly swallowed. "Yes."

"Let's take a walk, then. I have a story to tell you. It happened in the year of our Lord nineteen hundred and—"

"Fifty-four!" Every single Kilcannon in the room said it in unison.

Chloe blinked. "Okay."

"Brace yourself," Shane whispered. "You might be getting the long version."

Molly picked up Chloe's half-finished Bloody Mary and stuck it in her hand. "Here. You'll need this."

Everyone cracked up except Chloe. She just took a big, deep gulp.

"They said you were a pretty one," Gramma Finnie said, her Irish lilt as lovely as her sky-blue eyes and surprisingly creamy skin for a woman closer to ninety than eighty. "But then, I wouldn't expect Shane to go for anything less. Rachel was a beauty, too."

Rachel? First she'd heard of a Rachel. "Sounds like

they've said a lot of things," Chloe replied as they left the back patio, keeping her steps slow so she could maintain the older woman's deliberate stride.

"It was a wonder Father John could preach a sermon today without mentioning you, lass. Seems like most other folks could talk of nothing else."

Chloe had to laugh. "I think I've invaded all the churches in Bitter Bark this morning. So much for the confidentiality of the Tourism Advisory Committee."

"Welcome to Bitter Bark and the news according to Jeannie Slattery."

"So she's the leak," Chloe mused.

"I'm sure she's leakin' plenty when she climbs out of Mitch Easterbrook's bed."

Chloe coughed a shocked laugh. "I thought I sensed a little something between those two."

"What's between them is little for sure with that man."

A laugh bubbled up, along with a memory. "That sounds like something my mother would have said," she quipped. But Doreen Somerset's caustic humor had also been cruel. Somehow, Chloe didn't think Finnie Kilcannon had a cruel bone in her little body. "And good information to have in my back pocket."

"Oh, I'm a fountain of information and, in case you haven't heard, I'm Irish. Born there, you know. But the best part of my life started when Seamus and I pulled an old clunker off the highway for gas, and Corky, my setter, read the name of the town and started to howl like a sick puppy." Finnie elbowed her. "You can tell Shane you got the short*ish* version. The long one always includes the fact that Seamus had to go to the bathroom so bad, I didn't think we'd make it to the gas station." She chuckled. "I like that version."

Chloe smiled and put a hand on the woman's narrow shoulder. "I'm honored to hear any version of this story, Gramma Finnie. It's history and I don't want to mess with that. I'm trying to change the future, not negate the past."

"I like the dog idea," Finnie said with a dry laugh. "Obviously. And I see that you want to lose the bitter, not the bark."

"Of course, we can make Bitter Bark dog-friendly, and if we get businesses to agree and the committees to do events, that will help. It doesn't have to be a permanent change, but in my experience, you have to package something and make it obvious. That's the difference between moderate improvement and huge success."

"I heard that about you, too."

"That...being..."

"You're a persuasive one." A smile threatened. "Good trait for a woman to have."

She felt a little sigh of relief slip out. "I believe in what I'm trying to convince the town to do," she said. "I'm sure you know that when you believe in something, it's easy to persuade others to join your side."

"It won't be easy." Finnie steered her off the path, away from the wide areas where a few dogs were running around with one person, toward the shade of the overhang of another building with a shingle that read Kilcannon Veterinarian. There was a bench that was probably for clients to wait with their dogs, and Finnie gestured to it, ready to sit. "This is as far as I want to go."

Chloe sat next to her, crossing her hands on her lap, sensing that this wasn't the time for small talk or idle conversation. Gramma looked up at her, searching her face as if looking intently for something. A flaw? The truth? Chloe didn't know, but she didn't look away.

"I hear you kissed my grandson at Bushrod's last night."

Chloe laughed softly and shook her head. "What did this town talk about at church before I showed up?"

"The undertaker and the redhead," she answered without hesitation. "Shane's a fine lad, don't you think?"

"Yes, I do. As evidenced by the well-documented kiss on the dance floor."

"Damn fine-looking," Gramma added.

"Gorgeous, really."

"Smart as a whip, you know."

"Georgetown Law," Chloe said. "Obviously very intelligent."

"He makes me laugh more than any one of my grandchildren," she added. "He's got a heart for animals, of course, and there isn't a thing he wouldn't do for me if I asked."

Chloe nodded. "He is an all-around great guy."

Gramma lifted a white brow. "Is he a good kisser?"

She dropped her face into her hands, not sure whether to laugh or cry. "Yes. One of the best ever."

Gramma's expression was pure satisfaction as she leaned back with a grunt as if to say, *I knew it!* "Course, he is Irish. Seamus could kiss my panties off faster than I could down a glass of whiskey."

"So good kissing is a family trait?" Chloe joked.

Gramma just smiled and looked straight ahead, a little lost for a moment, maybe thinking about Seamus's panty-stealing kisses. "If I support this idea of yours, it will help you. I'm small but mighty in this town. And on the Internet."

"I understand that, and I would only want you to do what makes you happy and comfortable."

She inhaled slowly. "I need to know why."

"Why? The idea? Well, I've done this kind of thing for other tourism councils. A big idea that people rally around can really make a difference and will honestly bring a lot of money into the town."

"But why do you want to do it?" she pressed. "To add this success story to your fancy résumé? To impress my grandson? Why does it matter to you, a young woman who lives somewhere else?"

"Blanche Wilkins is my aunt," she replied without hesitation. "Her husband, Frank, put his heart and reputation on the line with the first phase of the gentrification of Bushrod Square."

"Frank was a good man," Gramma said. "A little better in the mayoring department than his widow, I'm afraid."

"Maybe, but I have the ability to help her, and she's my family." Chloe leaned a little closer. "She's my only family," she added. "My mother is gone and my father died when I was a baby. I have no siblings. And Blanche didn't have children. My whole life, she's been a…a special aunt. My godmother, actually. I want to help her."

Gramma Finnie turned, stunning Chloe with moisture-filled eyes. "You and Blanche? That's it?

That's a small circle of strength. That's what Irish say a family is, you know."

She wouldn't know. She had no idea. "Yours certainly is," Chloe said.

The old woman studied her for a long, long time, thoughts brewing in those blue eyes that were still swimming with tears. "All right, then. I know all I need to know. Family matters to you. Even if you don't have much of one." She stood, putting a hand on Chloe's thigh to get a push up. "Then we should try and do something to help yours."

She looked up. "Does this mean you'll support the name change?"

She gave a sly grin. "A name change is exactly what I'll be supportin', lass."

Chapter Twelve

The emergency meeting of the town council to vote on the consideration of a name change got scheduled for Wednesday morning. But that had given Shane and Chloe two full days to take Daisy in and out of many of the shops that ran the perimeter of Bushrod Square.

And every time a person fell for Daisy—like the bookstore owner who ended up on the floor with her and the florist who tucked daisies in her collar—they not only won important hearts in town, but Shane's own heart felt lighter.

He didn't know what he loved more, converting the world to pit bull lovers or watching Chloe become more and more comfortable with touching and petting Daisy. The more she fell for the dog…the more he fell for her.

They learned early on that most of the time, they needed to buy something, so every few hours, they'd go back to Chloe's house to give Daisy a break and unload their purchases.

Together, they were the proud owners of more stationery, baked goods, T-shirts, socks, teacups, craft beer, candy, fresh produce, a box of nails with a hammer, and body butter than either of them could ever use. Although, that last one? Shane was pretty sure he could come up with something creative.

Tonight. This afternoon. *Soon.*

But Chloe had to present today to the town council and to what he knew would be a sizable audience of non-voting, but very interested, townspeople. Every one of their Daisy Drop-ins, as she called the visits they'd made for the last two days, had helped the cause.

There wasn't universal support for the name change, but if the popular vote were taken today and not just the council vote, Shane was pretty sure he'd soon be living in a town called Better Bark.

Daisy had indeed been a secret weapon. In fact, right now she was pacing the brick sidewalks of Bushrod Square as if she expected to be taken into a local business and fussed over.

"Not today, girl," Shane told her as he settled on a park bench and took a few more pictures of her to text to Marie, since he'd been keeping her informed about Daisy's PR job. "Chloe's doing her special Chloe thing."

Chloe had left a key to her house hidden for him and asked him to stop by and take Daisy out while she was presenting to the town council, since she had no idea how long she'd be. As soon as he got the dog, he knew he wanted to be the first person she talked to when she left that presentation.

He wanted her to win this for so many reasons. He was all in on the idea, of course, having spent days with her learning how her business worked. No nights, though. He'd left her house three—no, four—times in a row with no more than a lot of long kisses. Anything more and her wall went up and she grew cool and distant.

"Hello, Shane."

He turned, pushing up the beak of his ball cap to get a better look at the man walking toward him. Even with the sun in his eyes, he recognized the wide girth of Dave Ashland, the real estate broker he'd last seen at the Tourism Advisory Committee meeting. "Dave."

Daisy got up as Dave got closer, making the man slow his step a little. "That a Waterford rescue?" he asked.

"Not a rescue," he replied. "We're watching her for a friend who's laid up for a while, and she's living with Chloe Somerset."

At the mention of Chloe's name, Dave glanced toward town hall. "Heard they called an emergency meeting of the council to vote on her big idea."

"I'm surprised you're not there," Shane said, surreptitiously holding tight to Daisy's leash as Dave came over and sat down on the bench. She trotted closer and sniffed, and Dave gave a shaky smile, inching his legs away.

"I heard all I needed to hear at the last one." He was still staring warily at Daisy. "Got bit by one once," he said. "Looked a lot like this."

Shane eased Daisy closer and gave her a look, which was all she needed to sit. "I got bit once, too," he said.

"Really?" Dave seemed surprised. "That pit bull breed?"

"She's a Staffordshire terrier."

Dave gave a dubious look. "Right."

Shane resisted a *screw you* response, knowing that having the man see Daisy in action—or not, as the case might be—would be a lot more effective than telling the big, fat blowhard that one bad experience didn't define the breed.

"Sure would be nice to get that tourism stuff passed and do some more tenants down here for my client, James Fisker," Dave mused, shielding his eyes from the sun as he looked toward town hall. He was about the same age as Shane's father, but this man had lived life a lot harder.

"Yes, it would be nice," Shane agreed, not really interested in chatting, but not wanting to be rude.

"In fact, I talked to him today and told him big things were going to be happening for this town."

"Could be. I'm waiting to find out how her presentation went."

He gave Shane a bit of a side-eye, as if that connection surprised him a little. "Yeah, that dog idea sure would be a boon for Waterford Farm, I guess."

"Waterford is pretty much packed to dog capacity, to be honest. But we're going to be happy to help out with some of the events that get planned."

Just then, the front doors of the town hall building opened, pulling Shane's attention.

"If they get planned," Dave murmured, but Shane barely heard him because Chloe stepped into the sunlight, in a white dress that fit her curves without being too tight and fell above her knees, showing her pretty, long legs.

Perfect.

"I gotta go," he said, standing up.

Dave followed his gaze. "Pretty and smart, that one."

"Sure is." He gave Daisy's leash a tug. "Come on, girl. Let's go find out how it went."

Dave stood, too, putting a hand on Shane's arm. "Mind if I offer a word of advice, Son?"

Shane tried not to appear completely impatient, but he didn't want Chloe taking off before he reached her since she didn't know he was waiting. "Sure."

"Keep a good eye on her."

"I know," he said. "Pretty and smart. I am, don't—"

"That's not what I mean."

Shane felt his brows draw together, more at the slightly ominous tone than the statement. "Then what do you mean?"

Dave looked from side to side as if Bushrod Square were teeming with spies. "Folks will want to stop this, and she's going to be a bit of a...what's the expression? A lightning rod."

"I imagine there will be a contingent opposed to changing the town's name," Shane said, choosing his words carefully.

"Pretty strong contingent, backed by Mitch and Jeannie, two of the most well-connected people in town. They're going to do everything they can to stop it. Just sayin'."

Shane nodded. "We can—she can—handle it."

"Okay, then, you let me know how things are going. Let me know what your plans are, maybe who tells you they're for it or against. I can help, quietly, in the background."

Shane considered that and the amount of power this man had with his close connection to one of the town's largest landowners, even if Fisker had moved away. He still wielded power, and it was good to have Ashland on their side.

"Thanks," Shane said, his eye on Chloe, who paused on the steps to take out her phone. "Good to know you're supporting it."

In his pocket, Shane's phone vibrated with a text, and he reached for it, using it as an excuse to end the conversation. "Got a call, Dave."

"Of course. You take care, Shane." Dave headed off in the same direction he'd come as Shane read the text. And smiled.

Did you get Daisy? Is she okay? BTW, meeting was awesome! Can't wait to tell you.

He didn't know what he liked more—that she cared enough about Daisy to ask about her first, not even an afterthought or that she cared enough about him to want to share.

He thumbed back *Look across the street.*

"Good news, Daisy," he whispered as he hit send. "She likes us both."

In a second, she read her phone, looked up, searched the park, and lifted her arm in a happy wave when she spotted him. She'd skipped the tight ponytail today, and when she scampered down the steps like she was floating on air, her long hair swung over her shoulders like a chocolate-colored waterfall. And all he wanted to do was drown in it.

"Good thing, too," he added. "'Cause I like her. A lot."

Daisy barked as soon as she saw Chloe coming toward them.

Guess they both liked her a lot.

For the briefest second, Chloe almost couldn't take a breath she was so darn happy to see him. To see *them*.

This was the icing on a Very Good Day cake, Chloe thought as she navigated the stone stairs in heels and made her way across the street to the square. By the time she got there, Daisy had broken into a run, pulling the leash Shane held.

"Whoa, whoa, girl." Shane held her back before she jumped on Chloe. "Woman is in white, *again*, head to toe."

"I'm going to have to change to a more dog-friendly wardrobe," she joked. "I'm so glad you're here."

He gave her a huge smile while Daisy barked and barked. "You're going to have to greet her."

"Of course." She reached down and stroked Daisy's head, giving a good scratch behind her ears, because Daisy loved that. "I have good news for you, Miss Daisy."

"They voted already?" Shane rounded the dog and put an arm around Chloe, the move completely natural. Just like the shiver it sent through her when he pulled her in for a hug.

"They're deliberating and then voting, and Blanche thought it was good for me to be gone during all that, but Shane…" She bit her lip and looked up at him, knowing her whole face must be lit up with the afterglow of an incredible presentation. "It was so good! I think I nailed it."

"Way to go!" He pulled her all the way in and bent down to kiss her. Just a celebratory peck, but the feeling of his mouth on hers never got old. It was never *just* anything but amazing. "I had no doubt you would rock the house."

"There were so many people, too. The town council, which has thirteen voting members, plus my aunt, Blanche, but she doesn't vote. And for some reason, there was an audience."

"Word got out."

"It sure did," she agreed. "Another twenty or more people, but at least eight people asked me where Daisy was."

"You could have taken her!" he exclaimed. "Why didn't we think of that?"

"It's okay. It wasn't the right place for her and, you know, all that applause when I was done might have scared her." She slid her arm around his waist as they walked.

"Nothing scares her, or you."

She looked up at him. "Plenty scares me and you know it." Like sex. Sex scared her, and surely he'd figured that out by now.

"One barrier at a time, Chloe."

She gave him a grateful smile, too happy with her work and the day to think about anything else. Even something she'd been thinking about morning, noon, and night since she'd met him. Especially at night, when Daisy's snoring kept her awake and thoughts of Shane kept her…uncomfortable.

"So, tell me everything," he said, obviously not mired in a 'should I or shouldn't I' scenario like she was. "What was the vibe when you presented the idea?"

"Well, some people whined about permits and licenses and specifics like that, but I felt the momentum was on my side all the way, for sure."

"So what happens next?" he asked.

"Lunch, I hope. I'm starving."

She looked up at Shane, drinking in the lines of his face, his hazel eyes returning her gaze, the ball cap making him look ridiculously masculine and handsome and kissable.

"What?" he asked, obviously sensing her staring at him.

"Nothing, it's just…you look cute."

He laughed and pulled her closer. "You are flirting so hard, Perfect Chloe."

"And you are flirting right back, Dirty Shame."

He pulled Daisy's leash and brought her to a complete stop at the intersection while they waited for cars to pass. "You want me to kiss you right here in the middle of the street in Bitter Bark?"

She inched forward. "Better Bark, and yes."

He met her halfway, putting his lips on hers.

"Uh, the light's changed, you two."

They broke apart at the sound of a woman behind them, turning together to offer an apology.

"Oh, hello, Rachel."

"Rachel Marcus?" Chloe remembered the woman immediately, one of the town council members, a very attractive interior designer who owned an antique shop. "I thought you were still in the meeting."

She gave a wistful smile, her dark brown gaze

drifting straight to Shane and staying there. "My mind was made up, so I slipped out to run an errand." She swallowed visibly. "How are you, Shane?"

Oh, this was the beauty Rachel that Gramma Finnie had mentioned. Every womanly radar Chloe had went on an instant low-grade Ex Alert.

"I'm good, Rach. I forgot you were on the town council this year. I guess you two have met, then." There was the slightest hint of awkward in his voice to confirm Chloe's guess.

"We sure have," Rachel said, the enthusiasm a tad forced. "I didn't realize you knew each other that well."

Well enough to kiss on the street. She didn't say it, but Chloe could read the rest of the sentence, and maybe a hint of sadness, as the woman brushed a light brown lock away from a lovely face.

"Thank you for your support in the meeting," Chloe said, remembering that Rachel had asked several very intelligent questions, and when a small debate broke out, she'd clearly been in favor of the name change.

"Thank you for a delightful new idea." As if she simply couldn't resist, her attention slipped back to Shane. "I guess I understand the inspiration now."

"Oh, no, not me. This was all Chloe's idea. I was on the advisory committee."

"So, you've only recently met?" she asked, trying for polite and interested, but Chloe was a woman, too. The hitch in the voice, the little bit of defeat in her shoulders, even the way she looked at Chloe—as if she was trying to figure out *what does she have that I don't?*—it was all there.

"I'm taking care of one of the Waterford dogs," Chloe said, somehow wanting to alleviate the sting of seeing an ex, or maybe a crush, kissing another woman on the street.

Rachel looked down at Daisy. "She's a beauty." Without hesitation, she lowered herself to meet Daisy's face, giving her a friendly, fearless scratch and, of course, getting a juicy tongue bath on her hand as a thank-you. Rachel laughed and didn't flinch, of course.

She rose slowly, her game face back on now that the dog had given her a chance to recover from the unexpected encounter. "You do love a Staffy, Shane. That much hasn't changed."

"No, that will never change." He gave her a warm, kind, but definitely a *sorry things didn't work out* smile and got exactly the same thing in return.

"Well, I better get moving, or I won't be back in time for the big vote," she said brightly. "I'm sure you'll get exactly what you want, Chloe."

Was there double meaning in that? "I really hope to have the full support of the council," she replied smoothly. "And thank you again."

"Well." Rachel gave a *you never know* shrug. "I haven't voted yet. Oh, there's the light again. Let's cross this time."

They did and said goodbye quickly on the other side, then took a few steps toward the sandwich shop in silence.

"I'm sure she'll give you her vote," he finally said.

"You think? Maybe she changed her mind after seeing you kiss me."

He opened his mouth to argue, then shut it again. "She's not a vindictive person."

"But she is an ex?"

He nodded. "Two years ago. A month or two. No biggie."

Bet it was a "biggie" to Rachel. She wanted to ask more, but he steered them toward the outside tables. "We're not eating in the square?"

"Not today. Daisy has to work."

She laughed, knowing from the past two days that Daisy loved having a job, and her job was making people adore her. They sat right in the middle of a group of about eight tables, getting a few interested—and some not so thrilled—looks from other patrons.

"You sit here with her, and I'll get lunch. Make friends."

"Are you sure you shouldn't sit here and talk to people? You handle her so well."

"You handle her perfectly, and they're not just voting for dogs, Chloe, they're voting for you." He pushed her chair in from behind and planted the lightest kiss on her head. "Salad with ranch and ten extra napkins, right?"

She laughed and nodded.

"Knock 'em dead, baby."

In keeping with a darn near perfect day, Daisy was a dream. She settled right in at Chloe's feet, looked around, then rested her head. Not a bark, snarl, or moment of worry. Two people at the next table commented on her behavior, and one added, "For that breed," to his compliment.

No wonder Shane was so sick of hearing that.

Chloe made small talk, used her hand sani, and checked her phone, then looked up when Shane came back with lunch. Daisy didn't move, but watched him carefully.

"She was like this the whole time you were gone," Chloe informed him.

"Of course. Our girl is as perfect as you are." *Our girl.* Her heart turned over on that one. He winked and handed her a handful of napkins. "And, as always, in white."

"It's my favorite color."

"I noticed. It's actually the absence of color."

"And the absence of dirt," she replied.

"So no pesky molecules of uncleanliness can hide on you."

"Just the way I like it."

He put an elbow on the table, studying her. "Have you ever gotten really absolutely filthy dirty?"

"I was a waitress one summer in college, and I got pretty grimy by the end of the night."

He fought a laugh. "I mean really, truly dirty. Like outdoor dirt. Real filth."

"Why would I want to?"

"For one thing, it might fix your phobia."

She snapped the lid of the container, cracking it a little too hard. "I do *not* have a phobia. I have a healthy, clean, sanitary lifestyle. And..." She leaned forward. "I'm living with a dog."

He shook his head. "It's not healthy," he mumbled, opening his sandwich.

She picked around the salad to find the red onions, but there were none.

"Had them hold the onions," he said.

Sighing, she opened the dressing container. "I bet you made a terrific boyfriend," she mused.

One brow launched north as he held a sandwich poised at his mouth. "What brought that on? Rachel?"

"The onions. You're thoughtful. And Rachel."

He shrugged. "Big family. You get the hang of being nice. It's a survival skill."

"I think you're just *nice*." She stabbed a cucumber, thinking. "Was she brokenhearted?"

After swallowing a bite, he wiped his mouth with a napkin, then looked down at Daisy. "I knew we'd go there," he whispered to the dog. "You're supposed to be a distraction."

"I'm going to take a wild guess and say you broke up with her."

"Why would you make that assumption?"

Because he was gorgeous, a great catch, and *nice*. "She had a little tinge of, I don't know, sadness? Regret? The one that got away-ness?"

He put the sandwich down and opened a bag of chips. "It was mutual," he finally said.

"Really?"

"Don't you think it's possible she dumped me?"

"No."

He angled his head. "I think there's a compliment in those two letters."

"Just stating a fact. And she was way more ruffled by the sight of you than you were of her."

He considered that, eating some more, not talking. Then he said, "She wanted to get serious."

"And you don't *do* serious."

He looked long and hard at her, as if he was trying to decide how honest to be. "I don't believe in...all that," he finally said. "I mean, I know it happens to some people, and that's great, but I honestly think that whole live happily ever after forever and ever thing is a myth."

For some reason, his words made her chest tight. "Gosh, if someone like you who was raised in a happy home with healthy parents and a totally lovely family doesn't believe in it, what hope is there for the rest of us?"

"You can have hope, I just don't like mine to be ripped to shreds. It feels too much like losing, which is something I don't like to do."

"So when you think you might lose something, you don't try?"

He shifted a little in his seat and looked down at Daisy, who snoozed on the ground between them. "Maybe," he admitted softly.

"Is that what happened with Rachel?" she asked. "You decided it wasn't worth trying on the off chance you would fail?"

"Look, Rachel wasn't right for me. But, it's not an 'off chance' of failure. It's a one-in-a-zillion chance of success. I don't take bets I'm bound to lose."

"Why do you hate losing so much?"

"Why do you hate dirt so much?" he fired back.

She had her reasons, and it hadn't taken a shrink to figure them out. Not that she'd ever go to a shrink, because only crazy people did that, and she wasn't—

Her phone hummed with a text. Turning it over, she saw the name Blanche Wilkins and some beautiful words on the screen: *VICTORY! We won by 8-5!*

With a soft gasp, she held the phone to him to let him read it.

"You know what that means, Chloe?"

"We are one step closer to changing the name of this town and making it the dog-friendliest place in America?"

"That and…we have to celebrate the win." He winked and took her hand. "And if there's one thing I know how to do, it's celebrate a win."

She laughed. "I'm sure you don't know what a consolation prize even feels like."

He pulled her hand to his lips and pressed a kiss. "Of course I don't. But I know exactly how we're going to celebrate this one. There's only one rule."

She looked at him, waiting.

"Don't wear white."

"Why not?"

His smile was slow and sexy and sinful. "Because you're going to get very, very dirty."

She couldn't move. She couldn't breathe. She couldn't wait.

Chapter Thirteen

Shane poured the last gallon of gas and wiped some sweat from his brow, considering if he should take a shower before Chloe arrived. That would be a complete waste of time, but he was filthy from working in the kennels, running some hands-on training and now, at the height of the day's heat, filling tanks in the storage shed. Absolutely filthy.

Well, that's what today was all about.

"Shane, you in here, Son?"

"In the back, Dad." He came out from behind a row of dirt bikes to see his father wandering into the shed. "S'up?"

"You've been busy today," he said. "I've been wanting to talk to you, but every time I look for you, you're surrounded by trainees."

"New class started today," he reminded his father. "But I'm done working now. What did you need?"

"Just wanted to tell you I heard that things went Chloe's way yesterday."

"Yeah." He grinned and gestured to the ATV next to him. "We're going to celebrate the Waterford way."

Dad nodded. "Good day for a ride. Although, I wouldn't take her as the four-wheeling type."

Shane cocked his head. "She wasn't the dog type, either." And he liked helping her break her little barriers. He liked it a lot.

Dad leaned against a workbench, crossing his arms, that expression of expectation he wore when he really wanted to talk about something. "Town's buzzing already."

"I imagine it is."

"I got a call from Ned Chandler at the *Banner* a while ago. Has he reached you yet?"

Shane shrugged. "I haven't answered my phone and ignored voice mails and texts." Except for the exchange with Chloe to set up today's "surprise" celebration. And remind her to wear jeans and boots.

"Well, he will. He was in his 'I'm a hardened former *New York Times* reporter' mode."

"Who is now the editor of the *Bitter Bark Banner*," Shane noted. "How the mighty have fallen."

"He might say the same thing about you."

"Wait a second while I try to care." He stopped, thought for a moment, then shook his head. "Nope. Still don't care."

Dad smiled, but it didn't reach his eyes. "He's running an editorial a day, starting today and going until the popular vote in a week. He's looking for every possible reason from the hundred-and-fifty-year-old incorporation bylaws to interviews with people from other towns who've lost tourism after a name change—"

"He can find them?"

"He says he can," Dad replied. "My point is he's going to get very nasty."

"What does he care what we call the town?" Shane asked. "He's lived here two years."

"He's a reporter with a bone and some actual news. A cause. He's going to go after every angle, and I wanted to warn you."

"Thanks," he said. "Unlike my younger brother Garrett, I'm not afraid of the media."

"But look how well that worked out for him."

Shane grinned. "I guess if I wanted to marry Ned Chandler, I could follow in Garrett's footsteps."

Dad didn't smile. "I'm trying to protect you, and Chloe. You have a personal relationship with the woman spearheading the project. That will come out."

"I'm pretty sure—speaking as a citizen, not an attorney, now—that there isn't a law against two single people dating. Maybe he can scare one up in the bylaws from 1870 or whenever."

"He'll make you look bad."

"For going out with a beautiful, intelligent, personable woman who has come to town with a brilliant idea to do the very thing we hired her to do? I fail to see how that makes me look anything but on top of my game. Unless Ned's jealous."

Dad nodded slowly, obviously aware he'd lost whatever argument he'd come in here to make.

"But it's good to know," Shane added, because he felt like he'd been fighting with Dad too much lately. "I'll talk to him if he calls. I'll wrap his ass in legalese." He grinned and pulled out his phone. "Come to think of it, that sounds like fun. I think I'll call him first."

But he was distracted by the text that had come in ten minutes ago. *On my way.*

And how ridiculously happy that made him.

"You do like her," Dad mused.

He looked up from the phone. "You read minds now?"

"Expressions. Body language. And I know my children very, very well."

He conceded with a shrug. "Nothing to hide. I like her a lot."

"But she isn't…permanent."

"I'm well aware she comes with an expiration date and lives in Miami." He turned to put the gas can away.

"Which is why she's perfect for you."

He whipped around, that feeling of being tweaked by the Dogfather firing some fury up his spine. "She's perfect for someone looking for perfection. I'm not."

"Then what are you looking for?"

"I don't know, Dad, but if I tell you, I'm afraid you'll line up some candidates and shove me at them."

"Does that scare you?"

"Not as much as conversations like this." He put a hand on his father's shoulder, not surprised to feel that it still had good muscle tone and size but very surprised at how angry Dad could make him when he was only trying to help. "I appreciate your concern, but you know how I feel."

Dad heaved a sigh. "Annie would know exactly what to say to you right now."

The words punched, and a lump he hadn't felt for a long time grew in his throat. "But she's not here, Dad," he said on a harsh whisper. "She's gone."

Damn that lump. It hurt now. And so did the look on Dad's face. "And I don't ever want to feel the way you do right now. Ever, you know?"

Dad's lips lifted in a slight smile, and his eyes welled enough to sucker-punch Shane with guilt.

"It really is better to have loved and lost than never to have loved at all," Dad said.

Shane opened his mouth to make a crack about how unoriginal that was, then closed it. He knew better than to tease a dog he loved.

"Thanks for that advice," he managed.

Dad got the message and started to back away, then stopped. "You know, spending your life alone is merely a different way of losing the game."

Shane stared at him, fighting the emotions bubbling up, clenching his jaw to keep from barking at this man who only meant well.

Then Dad nodded. "You have a good time today. Should be nice and messy after that rain last night."

"Messy is what I'm going for."

"Love is messy."

He burst out laughing and gave his father a nudge. "You've officially lost your mind, Pops."

He wasn't interested in love. But sex? Yeah. He was really interested in that. In fact, that was all he was interested in. That might disappoint his dad, but it was a fact.

Shane was as dirty as the day she'd met him. Might even have been wearing the same T-shirt that, even if it had gone through the laundry, needed to see the inside of a washer again. He wore soft, worn jeans, the ever-present ball cap, and a smile that did really stupid things to Chloe's heart as he strode across the driveway to greet her.

He held up his hands as he got closer. "You probably don't want to touch me."

And that's where he would be wrong. She didn't want to do anything *but* touch him, and the neediness of that was starting to wear her down, steal her sleep, and make her think about giving up this fight.

"I'll take a chance." She splayed her fingers on his chest for the sheer pleasure of enjoying the cut of his muscles, but was surprised by something else—the fast and furious beat of his heart.

Because of her? Judging from the dirt, sweat, and way his chest heaved, he'd probably just run around that training pen with a dog.

"Did you decide to leave Daisy?" he asked, checking out the backseat of her rental car.

"Yes. It's such a beautiful day, and she was so happy roaming the backyard. I left toys, food, water, and locked the gate. I knew if she was here, she'd be in the kennel, and she hates that."

He smiled. "She has you wrapped around her paw."

"She's working really hard to do exactly that."

"I know exactly how she feels." He closed his fingers over hers, leaning back to take a slow look up and down and up her, lingering on the gray T-shirt she wore and the dark jeans and boots. "Are these clothes you don't care about?"

"I don't understand that concept," she said. "I care about all my clothes."

"Can they get, uh, a little dirty?"

"Yes." She gave him a flirtatious smile. "You said you had something unclean in mind."

His grin was slow and a little evil. "Actually, it's filthy."

Heat singed every nerve ending. "Dirty Shame."

Taking off the ball cap, he leaned over and kissed her, somehow managing not to let their bodies touch, no matter how much she wanted them to. "Perfect Chloe." He kissed her again, then inched back. "Let's go get...dirty."

She tried to breathe, but the air got caught in her lungs. "Okay, let me get my bag."

"You don't need your bag."

Her bag had everything she needed in it. Phone. Wallet. Lipstick. *Condoms.* "Are you sure?"

"One hundred percent. I have everything we need."

Trusting him, she took his hand. "So where to?"

"It's a bit of a walk, but worth it."

He led her around the far back of the facility, pointing out various training places, including a huge area of nothing but...trash.

"The rubble pile," he explained.

"Lovely."

"It's where Liam spends all his time in K-9 training, sniffing out bombs, drugs, and other evils hidden in garbage. Don't you really like him even more now?"

"Considering that he trains dogs that save lives and stop crime, yeah." She leaned into him. "I think your brother is awesome."

He took the bait. "I train dogs that save lives. I don't just train civilians and other trainers, you know.

I work with the therapy dogs, too, you know. I sent a poodle out of here last week whose job is now to visit pediatric cancer patients in Charlotte."

"Aww." She put her hand over her mouth to hold back the burst of emotion and affection simply imagining something like that. "That's so touching. You're changing lives."

"It *is* life changing," he agreed. "*My* life. And I've trained dogs for kids with autism, for nursing-home visits, and even had a Husky here last year who can now sense when his owner's blood-sugar level is low."

"That's remarkable," she said. "How do you do it?"

"We have two incredible dog behaviorists on staff, and I've learned so much from them. I've taken classes, and a lot of it is my gut instinct."

She could hear the passion in his voice, and the joy. "It's great when you love what you do for a living, isn't it?"

"You do, right?"

"I do," she said. "Wouldn't mind a little less travel, but that's the job." He led her deeper into the trees, something making his eyes twinkle. "We're, um, going into the woods?"

"Do the woods scare you, Little Red Riding Hood?"

"Maybe." She laughed, keeping pace with him, but looking down. "Oh, there are mud puddles." She took a huge side step to avoid one, cracking him up.

"Ah, baby, it's going to get much worse. Or better, depending on your perspective." He guided her through the break in the trees and stopped, gesturing grandly. "Welcome to Mud Road."

Her mouth fell open as she looked down the five-foot cliff over a big pool of mud the color of a giant cup of overly creamed coffee. In the middle was one great big splattered yellow vehicle, propped on fat, meaty tires in six inches of brown muck. On it were two helmets, gloves, and jackets.

"You can't be serious."

"You are looking at the elite-level ATV mud path that Kilcannon kids have been digging, fixing, and riding on for thirty years."

"On that thing?"

He chuckled. "That's an ATV. All-terrain vehicle. A 2-up, so there's plenty of room for you to ride safely behind me. I'm going to take a wild guess that you have never been muddin'."

She gave a nervous laugh.

"You're starting on one of the best courses in North Carolina, if not the world. It goes a half a mile that way." He pointed off to the distance, where there were more trees and fields and mud.

So much mud.

"We'll hit the next property," he continued, leaving no time or room for arguments. "But that's the Goffersons, and they don't care, so we ride through their woods, then worm through the creek and way up some hills to the lookout, where the views are in-freaking-credible, then some more woods, but it's all trailed, I promise. Then down a killer incline, but you'll be a pro by then, or I'll take you down the chicken-shit route that Molly takes, then around there, and back here. Sound good?"

"Sounds...I think I'll take the chicken-shit route. On foot."

"Come on, Chloe." He took her hand and tugged her into him. "Two miles of slippery, gooey, filthy, dirty…" He kissed her mouth. "Fun."

"This wasn't what I expected," she said slowly, eyeing the ATV and trying to imagine herself on it.

"You thought maybe I had a romantic bed set up with champagne and satin sheets under the sunshine?"

"Clean sheets."

He laughed. "I thought you liked to break those barriers. Muddin' is definitely a barrier."

"A barrier too far," she murmured, staring at the machine and mud a little longer.

"It's entirely up to you," he said. "If you don't want to go, we can take a nice walk along the path and—"

"I want to go," she said, surprised at the surge of feeling the admission gave her. No, not really surprised at that. It was more that he could do this to her, and for her. "I do," she assured him.

He gave a slow smile. "Oh, I hear the sound of barriers breaking, Chloe Somerset." He took her hand and guided her down the cliff and, of course, she stumbled right into a huge hole that soaked her jeans in mud up to her knee.

"There," he said, helping her right herself. "Your mud virginity is gone. Let's get you up on Old Yeller. All our ATVs are named after famous dogs."

"Of course they are."

He put the helmet over her head and helped her into a thin jacket that had to be more for staying dry than warm, since it was at least eighty in the sun. "Remember to try to keep your mouth closed," he said. "'Cause, mud."

She closed her eyes. "Mud."

"And bugs," he added with a grin.

She let him hoist her up and settle into the little backrest, pressing her feet on the raised floorboards and sliding the leather gloves over her hands. With his helmet on, he climbed up and situated himself in front of her.

Which was so not how she'd been fantasizing about getting him between her legs.

He fired up the engine and yelled, "Hang on, honey!"

And the next thing she knew, the world was flying by in a slow blur, a rainbow of blues and greens. And brown. Plenty of slippery, sticky, splattery mud.

The front wheel dipped into a hole, and she squealed and automatically wrapped her arms around his waist, squeezing tight.

Then he gunned it, sending a rooster tail of muck all over her leg and arm, and then they took off with a wet, wicked rumble that she could feel right through her whole body.

It was fast, filthy, and frightening. She could taste the dirt, feel every bump in her teeth, and her heart hammered so fast it could have broken a rib.

And she'd never had so much fun in her entire life.

With a whoosh of air and a splatter of mud, something changed. Something in her whole being felt free and utterly out of control, and all she could do was hang on and let the thrill zip through her.

Chapter Fourteen

S hane took them to the highest point on Waterford Farm, the place they called the lookout. He had, possibly a hundred times in his life, stopped here with Garrett, Liam, and Aidan after a hard six or seven rounds on Mud Road to chill and relive every minute of fun.

In the spring and summer, they'd be covered with mud, as he and Chloe were now. Vibrating from the engine, tired, sweaty, sore, and exhilarated.

He was all those things as he climbed off and unclipped his helmet, then helped her do the same thing. Her whole body was quivering, so he knew she felt all of that, and more. Well, the screams of delight, the whoops of fun, and the desperate clinging to his waist kind of gave it away.

"You liked it," he said as he got her on the ground.

She yanked off the helmet, still catching her breath, her dark hair spilling all over her shoulders as it came out of a loosely held ponytail. "I...did not like it." She closed her eyes, and he made a face, not expecting her to—

"I *loved* it." She grabbed his head and pulled

him in for a hot, demanding kiss, like putting an exclamation point on her elation.

"Whoa, yeah." He pulled off his gloves and tossed them, threading his hands into her hair to intensify the mouth-to-mouth. "I knew you would."

It was like she couldn't contain all the new feelings, and that all translated into more kissing, her hands all over his chest, which was, she might not have noticed, drenched in mud.

"Oooh. I like Dirty Chloe," he murmured.

She pulled him down to the ground, which required zero effort, and in a second, they were on a mix of grass and dirt, with him on the bottom and her on top, both of them frantic in the need to kiss and touch and finally give in to the electricity that had been arcing since the day they'd met.

She fumbled with the zipper of his jacket, a little desperate to get to what was underneath. Laughing, he rolled them over and took the jacket off, then unzipped hers and helped her out of it. Half sitting, half lying, they both took a second to catch their breath and stare at each other.

"How's it feel to be this filthy?" he asked on a whisper.

"It feels…liberating. Different. Normal."

"Does that mean you like it?"

"I like…" She reached for his head to drag him down. "This."

He kissed her again, slower this time, taking a moment to taste her and smell the wind and dirt and air of home all over her. She moaned softly as he dragged his hand from her throat down, down, down over her body. She moved under him, arching her back in a silent invitation to touch more.

"You taste like dirt," she murmured into a kiss.

"Good, huh?"

"Delicious." She delved her tongue into his mouth and touched his chest with the same appreciation he was using on her.

Somebody had officially lost control. *Finally*.

Their legs wrapped around each other, and they rolled again, Chloe crying out a little when a stone dug into her back.

"It's okay," she assured him, pulling him back. "It's okay."

He laughed at her exuberance. "You know, this place is called the lookout, not the *make* out," he said.

She took a deep breath and turned her head one way, then the other. "Okay. I looked." Then she reached up and grabbed him for another kiss. "Make out."

Happily, he obliged. And found new places to kiss under her ear and down her throat, tasting salt and grit and skin and Chloe. "You really did like that ride," he joked in between kisses.

"You knew I would." She found a few places of her own to kiss, sending fire through his veins and way too much blood southbound. "You planned this."

"Not this." He eased a finger under a lacy bra, making her shudder at the contact. "I did not plan..." Lowering his head, he put his mouth over her bra, already reaching behind her to get the thing off.

"Shane."

"Mmm?"

"We're doing this?"

He lifted his head. "We're doing something."

She didn't speak, holding his gaze as he slowly dragged his hand from the back to the front, under the bra, closing his palm over the curve of a sweet breast, her nipple budding in his hand.

Her jaw loosened as she fought for a breath. "That's really...nice."

"No kidding. Let me taste." He dipped down and kissed the skin, suckling her while she rocked under him. He fought for control, instinctively knowing she'd need things to be as slow as he could stand to make them.

"You made me leave my bag," she said.

He lifted his head, thrown by the statement that made no sense in his blood-starved brain.

"I brought condoms."

And that made him smile. "You sly dog." And then he remembered his wallet was in the ATV shed. "And way smarter than I am."

"We can't—"

"I know, I know," he assured her. "But we can..." He moved his hand over her belly, thumbing the button of her jeans. "Play."

A flash of warning in her eyes stopped him from opening the jeans.

"Too dirty for you?" he guessed. "Too many germs if I..." He inched a finger below the waistband. "Touch you." He lowered his head to whisper. "And make you lose control in a very, very good way?"

He felt her shake her head and barely whisper, "Oh, no, I couldn't."

He kissed her ear and leaned up again. "Just let me give you pleasure."

"I can't," she said, adding a meaningful look. "Like, literally."

He couldn't have heard that right. She said she brought condoms, so surely she could, but… "Do you mean… Is an orgasm against your rules or something?"

She bit her lip. "It doesn't happen for me. I mean it has…alone."

"Oh. *Oh*." He shook his head. "This is not right."

She laughed now, closing her eyes. "I knew you'd take it as the ultimate Shane Kilcannon must-win challenge."

"Hell yeah," he insisted. "Right here, right now, sweetheart."

Her laugh faded. "You can't."

He gave her his best *you gotta be kidding me* look. "You're not even going to let me try?"

"I…"

He didn't wait for her lame response, dipping his mouth to hers to quiet her with a kiss. She didn't argue, but kissed him back, letting him take his sweet time, letting him roam her bare breasts and heat her whole body to a point where all she could do was sigh when he unzipped her jeans.

He needed only to touch her. Just a gentle, easy, perfectly placed finger…

She gasped when he found that place, closed her eyes, and bit her lip.

"Look at me, Chloe," he urged. "Look at me."

She slowly opened her lids, her eyes so dark with arousal he couldn't tell the iris from the pupil. It was all deep and dark and locked on him.

"Relax," he whispered. "Let me touch you. Like this. And this. And…"

She lifted her hips, letting him deeper inside her. "Shane...oh, Shane."

"There." He had her now. Had her. Held her, kissed her, found her sweetest spot and whispered her name and all he could do to her in her ears until she reached up and dug her nails into his shoulders.

"Let go, Chloe. Let go and let me have you."

With a whimper, he watched her unravel, clinging to him, rocking against his hand, her body vibrating as he eased her over the edge to satisfaction. She bit her lip, closed her eyes, and melted into a breathless release.

"Now you've learned the most important lesson of all," he finally whispered.

"How to lose control in broad daylight when covered in dirt?"

He laughed softly. "Never, ever give me a challenge."

She managed to open one eye, turn her head, and peek at him. "You made it seem effortless."

"I'm really trying not to gloat, but it's difficult not to."

"You deserve to gloat. You got me riding in mud and basking in the afterglow all in one afternoon."

He leaned over and kissed her, brushing some hair from her cheeks. "Not to diminish my expertise or anything, but you were basically wired to explode any second."

"All this time with you, I guess."

He fell back with a thud. "And she wonders why I'm a cocky son of a bitch."

"You're not a son of a bitch," she said, pulling him back to her. "You're wonderful, and you make me feel...normal."

"If normal is perfect, then yeah. Good enough to eat next time."

Her eyes widened.

"Aaaannd I crossed the line," he teased. "Sorry."

"Sex is so…messy."

"I hate to break it to you, Chloe, but we are literally lying on dirt and grass, covered in mud, and probably being feasted on by a critter or two. You haven't died of the mess."

"Not yet. Tomorrow I could be in the ER."

He lifted up. "Really? That's what you're worried about? That you'll get sick?"

She didn't answer for a long time. But she had something to say, he could tell. So he waited, still, close, patient. The way he would with a broken dog who was about to put two and two together and figure out what got rewarded.

"You know I told you I lived with my mother, alone, growing up."

He nodded.

"She was crazy." At his look, she shook her head. "Like, literally not right. She was a filthy, messy, disorganized, distracted…pig. My home growing up was a sea of boxes that should have been thrown away, clothes that were never in place, magazines, papers, mail, stupid things she found that she wouldn't let go of…lamps, pictures, *crap*." Her voice cracked with anger. "It was so unfair. So awful. Such a flagrant way of telling me she didn't love me. And I was sick. Allergic to dust, which was like snow in my house, and mites and molds and paper and…you name it."

"It's unthinkable to live like that," he said, stroking

her arm in a way that gave sympathy, but he knew it wasn't enough. "Where was your father?"

"They never married, but my dad worked in a coal mine and died in an accident when I was a baby. Our only family was my aunt. A couple times a year, my aunt Blanche would come to town and take me away. She was my godmother and, believe me, Cinderella didn't do any better. My mom was very protective and really didn't like Blanche, but she lost the battle. My aunt would take me to a pretty hotel, and we'd shop and go out to dinner. We didn't talk about my home life or my mom. We still don't, really, but she knew how hard it was to grow up like that."

"And that's what made you a neat freak."

She turned to him. "Please don't say that. Don't imply that I'm not normal, because it's my greatest fear that I'm going to turn out like her."

He stroked her cheek, regretting the comment. "I'm sorry," he whispered. "How'd you manage to get out of there? How'd you find a way to study and get to college and build a career?" All of that must have taken one helluva lot of willpower and discipline, especially without the help and love from parents that he had always taken for granted.

She shrugged. "I had my sanctuary, my room, so clean you could eat off the floor, and I did occasionally when I couldn't bear the kitchen. And I was smart, got good grades. I didn't have a social life, because friends would mean I'd have to bring them to my house, and I would never do that. I got scholarships and took off after high school for Lexington and UK and never went home except for very brief visits and her funeral."

"How did she die?" he asked.

"She got an infection after a routine surgery, which, I'm sorry, was probably her own fault."

"So it didn't crush you when she died?"

"I spent my life mad at my mother," she admitted. "When she died, I was twenty-five. I was finally able to let go of some of that hate. It's a slow process, because I was well and truly formed by then, including my, um, habitual tidiness."

"So different from when my mother died," he whispered, vaguely aware that he slid her T-shirt back down and tucked her closer to him. "That's when I got—what did you call me? Cynical?"

She turned to him, searching his face. "I bet she wouldn't have wanted that."

"No, she wouldn't have," he said, feeling a punch of guilt. "But I can't change."

"Really? You can change other people—make them fall for dogs and ride in mud and get all kinds of messy—but you can't change yourself? Maybe you haven't met the right person to make you…what's the opposite of cynical?"

"Trusting? Secure? Hopeful?"

"Are you any of those things?" she asked.

"Not since she died," he said softly. "You were full of hate, but I was full of love. And it all evaporated when she left us. I still haven't forgiven her."

She inched up. "Forgiven her? For having a heart attack at fifty-five?"

He turned away, but she took his chin and made her face him. "Yeah, I'm mad about it," he admitted.

She stared at him, her impossibly deep brown eyes glinting with gold in the sun, with sympathy and warmth and a promise of something he…something he wanted and couldn't even articulate.

And it wasn't sex. At least, not only sex.

A cold, crazy sweat stung the back of his neck.

"Well, that's all kinds of wrong," she said, sitting up all the way.

"Yeah, I guess it is," he admitted, knowing that wouldn't change a thing.

After a moment, she reached behind her and hooked her bra, then stood, slowly zipping up her jeans. He didn't move because he didn't even understand what he was feeling.

Chloe.

What if she was the right one? What if she was the one-in-a-zillion person for him? What if—

"Will you let me drive the ATV back?"

He blinked at her, the change of subject throwing him—and relieving him a little, too. "Can you?" *Can you change me back, Chloe?*

"If you don't mind going really, really slow."

But the problem was, he was falling really, really fast.

Chapter Fifteen

Chloe's whole body was still humming when Shane pulled his truck onto her street. Humming from the wild rides, the intimacy, the secrets they'd shared, and the emotions that had churned up with as much force as mud under the ATV tires. But all that buzz went silent and cold at the sight of Aunt Blanche in the driveway looking wild-eyed and desperate.

"Oh my God, what's wrong?" She dove to climb out the minute Shane stopped the truck. "What's the—"

"Daisy is gone! She's running around the neighborhood, and I can't find her!" Blanche exclaimed. "I've had ten phone calls in the last hour."

"Gone?" Chloe whipped around to Shane. "I locked the gate," she insisted, turning from side to side as if Daisy might come bounding out from behind a bush.

Blanche looked like she was fighting tears, then she stepped back and blinked at Chloe's mud-stained clothes, but didn't say anything.

"Where was she last seen?" Chloe asked, reaching for her aunt as the severity of the situation rolled through her. "Close to here? On this street? How far did she get? Oh God." She put her hand to her mouth and stifled a scream of pure fear and frustration. "She'd never hurt anyone, Blanche, if that's what you're thinking."

"Oh, I know, honey. I've told that to everyone who's called, but…" She closed her eyes. "We have to find her."

Yes, they did.

Chloe caught sight of Shane running to the back of the house, heading for the gate, which she *knew* she'd locked. "Who saw her last? Who's called you?"

Blanche let out a breath. "Who hasn't? It was people from this neighborhood mostly." She pointed down the street. "Cindy Mayfield, who lives down there with her mother. The couple across the street with two kids. Someone called from their car, too, from two streets east." She grabbed Chloe's arm. "He didn't say his name but told me pit bulls should be shot."

Chloe swayed like *she'd* been shot. "I'll head that way. Tell Shane where I went."

Blanche nodded.

"I swear I locked her in," Chloe added.

"I know, but she got out."

Impossible, Chloe thought, but didn't take time to argue. Instead, she bolted in the direction of the sightings, calling Daisy's name and peering between houses, around bushes, down the side street.

Please, God. Please bring her back. Please let her be safe. Please let her be safe.

She heard footsteps behind her, glancing over her shoulder to see Shane catching up, a phone at his ear.

"Just get here fast, Liam. If Garrett's free, get him, too. Molly and Darcy. We don't know how long she's been gone or how far she got. We have to spread out."

He caught up to her as he put the phone away.

"I locked the gate," she said again, her voice cracking as tears threatened. "I swear I locked the gate."

"I know you did. The lock was broken. Someone did this on purpose."

She froze and sucked in a breath. "No." Then ice-cold terror spilled through her veins. "Oh, Shane, if someone hurts her, I'll kill them with my bare hands."

"Only after I do it with mine." He gave her a nudge. "You go that way. To the back of every house and look around. I'll go this way. I left Blanche at your house with treats in the driveway. Hurry. Don't let her get far."

She nodded and ran toward the next house. "Daisy!" Nothing. She ran around the back, up the other side, and into the next yard. No Daisy. No Daisy. *No Daisy.*

How could this be?

On the third house, she barely made it halfway to the back when a side door opened, and an older man in a robe stepped out, scowling at her. "I lost my dog," she explained. "Have you seen a little brown and white terrier?"

"Pit bull!" he barked. "He was right here, and I called the police and the mayor. If we had a dog catcher, I'da called them, too."

"She's not…" Never mind. It wasn't worth it. "How long ago and did you see which way she went?"

He pointed to the next house. "Through the back. Maybe twenty minutes."

"Thank you. I'm sorry." She took off, calling for Daisy again and again, her voice rising with a frantic sense of panic with each empty yard she examined. She'd lost track of Shane, of time, of anything but the need to find Daisy.

Who would do that? Who would break a lock and let a dog out?

Someone who hated her idea? The answer was so obvious, she stumbled a little at the thought, but shoved it down, needing concentration and energy to find that dog. Someone would hurt Daisy to hurt her?

"Daisy!"

She whipped around at the sound of another woman's voice, spotting a Waterford Farm truck with the windows down, Molly in the driver seat, Darcy next to her, calling for the dog.

"Anything?" Molly called when she spotted Chloe.

Chloe shook her head. "I'm checking yards."

"Stay on it, we've got this street, and Garrett's one road over. Liam's on his way."

She nodded, almost too overwhelmed with gratitude to even thank them, then she heard a loud, high-pitched whistle that she knew had to have something to do with this. Was that Shane? Was Daisy hurt? Had she been hit by a car or...*oh God*.

Fighting tears, she ran back to the street, still checking around every tree and bush, hearing the whistle again. A truck came around the corner and honked at her, and this time she saw Liam at the wheel.

"Shane's got her," he called to Chloe. "Hop in."

She almost collapsed with relief, running to the truck and yanking the door to hoist herself up. "Is she okay?"

"I don't know, I just got the text that he has her." He looked sharply at her. "What about you? Are you okay?"

"Just a little freaked out." Blowing out a breath, she tried to pull it together. "Someone did this to her. To me. Someone broke the lock on the back gate."

He grunted. "See? This is why I hate people."

"Vote against the idea, for Pete's sake," she mumbled. "Don't risk a dog's life."

Liam threw her another glance, his dark eyes a perfect reflection of the intensity that seemed to hum through him all the time.

"I mean, is it worth it?" she asked, too worked up to hold back her frustrations. "Daisy could have been hit by a car or lost forever or..." She put her face in her hands, wanting to wipe out all the possibilities. "Oh God, that poor dog."

"Look," Liam said, gesturing ahead. "Shane's got her. She's in good hands. You both are."

She could practically taste the adrenaline that dumped through her. "Oh, she's safe. I was so scared. So scared."

"So was my brother."

Even from the distance, she could see how pale Shane was. "He loves that dog," she said.

"He loves all pits. Ever since Zeus took a chomp out of him when he was a kid, he's been on a mission to save every dog and convert the world to the love of pitties."

"Zeus?" Had he ever mentioned a dog named Zeus? "Shane's been bitten?"

Liam cringed like he wanted to kick himself. "I assumed you've seen the scar."

No, she hadn't. And she had a feeling he had more than one scar he hadn't shared. She didn't have time to ask more—not that she'd get it from Liam— because he pulled up to the driveway. Chloe scrambled out and ran to Shane who cradled Daisy in his arms.

"Is she all right?" she asked, automatically reaching for Daisy.

"By the look of her, she's been digging more holes than Easterbrook the Undertaker." He brushed a layer of grime from her paw. "A little scared. Not hurt. Misses you."

"Oh, Daisy." She wrapped her arms around the dog and pulled her close, getting a huge lap of the tongue right over her face and mouth and eyes and, yep, the mouth again.

"What I wouldn't give for a camera right now," Shane said softly.

She could only imagine that picture. Chloe caked in dirt, hair knotted, cheeks streaked by mud and dog saliva, makeup smeared to a dark shadow under her eyes.

"Come on, let's take her in and I'll bathe her for you," Shane offered.

She swallowed, aware of a buzzing in her blood that she didn't understand or recognize. "Would you mind if I did it myself?"

He smiled. "She's really got you now."

Someone had. She clung a little tighter to Daisy's

muscular middle, stroking the head that rested on her shoulder as she looked at Shane. He had that expression on his face again, the one she'd seen at the lookout, the one that reached into her chest and threatened to rip her heart out.

The one that made her think…he really cared. And what would she do? Pack up and move away and live alone and avoid the mess of love, that's what.

She needed to think. Needed to clean. Needed to organize all her crazy—no, not crazy!—thoughts and feelings, and if he walked in that house, they'd end up all tangled up in a new kind of mess.

"Would you mind if I did that alone?" she asked softly.

For a second, he looked shell-shocked. Then, "Chloe, someone purposely broke the gate to let that dog out. I don't want you here alone."

"I'll be fine. I'll lock the doors. I have Daisy and…it's what I want."

She saw the disappointment register. "It's not what I want."

"I know, but…" She looked down at Daisy. "I think I've broken enough barriers for today."

"You know there's one thing you can't control, Chloe." When she looked up at him, he whispered, "It's your feelings."

She swallowed and nodded. "Hey, I know," she agreed, taking Daisy from him to hold her in her arms like a baby. "I've gone ahead and fallen for a dog."

He gave a whisper of a smile. "I'll leave my truck for you and go with Liam," he said, pulling out his keys. "It's good to have it in the driveway. Doesn't look like you're alone."

"Thank you."

"Call me after you get yourself and Daisy all cleaned up. You two can come to my house. Whenever you want. If you want. For as long as you want."

As long as she wanted had never been very long. Why would this be different? He'd just have a new woman to be mad at, another reason to be cynical and not hopeful.

"'Kay," she murmured. "Thanks." Still lugging the dog in her arms, she turned toward the house and started walking.

"Chloe, wait."

Closing her eyes, she froze. Torn. Dying for him but absolutely needing to push him away. Why? Why? What made her think *that* was normal?

"You forgot your bag," he said, coming up next to her and sliding it on her shoulder. Then he leaned right into her ear to whisper, "You sure you're okay?"

No, damn it. She was not okay. She was a mess, inside and out. Mostly inside. "Yeah, of course. Just a little overwhelmed by the day."

"Call me?"

"I promise." She slipped away, unlocked the front door, and stepped inside without looking back. Because she might do something stupid like beg him to come back to her and kiss him and shower with him and make love to him and then...what a mess.

Still lugging Daisy, she went to her bathroom, closed and locked the door, then twisted the shower knob. Finally, she set the dog on the floor as she stripped off the mud-covered clothes and shoes, aware of those brown eyes locked on her.

She didn't speak, because her voice would crack and tears would flow. Naked, she stepped into the tub and started to close the shower curtain. But before she closed it, Daisy put her paws on the side of the tub and looked up, her desire as clear as if she spoke English.

Wordlessly, Chloe hoisted her up and set her in the bottom of the tub.

That was it. She lost it.

As the tears bubbled up, she slid down the cool tile and landed under the spray, the shower water sluicing over her, making rivulets of brown and gray as the mud washed off. Daisy wedged herself between Chloe and the side of the tub.

Well, here she was. In a bathtub with a dog, having sent the sexiest man who'd ever wanted her away. The very definition of *not* normal.

Stroking the dog's head, Chloe started to hum a song her mother used to sing and let the shower wash away her sadness.

Chapter Sixteen

"What the hell, Shane?" Liam sounded purely disgusted with him. "Blow the damn whistle!"

Shane peered across the massive training field, barely hearing what his brother said but knowing he'd screwed up the training. Liam had shot a Thunder 100 launcher, Jag was at his perfect balance between still and interested, and when the dog hit the marker, Shane was supposed to blow the whistle to teach Jag to stop on a dime.

Now the dog was confused, and Liam was rightfully ticked off.

"Launch the retriever again, and I'll nail it."

"Never mind." Liam folded to get on Jag's level, giving the regal German shepherd some love, but not too much, Shane noted as he walked toward them. Couldn't reward Jag since Shane screwed up.

"Sorry," Shane muttered as he got closer, scooping up the marker in the middle of the field as he passed it. "Distracted."

"And I thought that was Jag's problem." Liam squinted up at him, one hand still on Jag's head. "I had him right there, on that hairy edge between desire and control, which isn't easy to achieve."

"Really? 'Cause I feel like I'm living there these days," Shane admitted, dropping down on the grass to get face-to-face with Jag. "Sorry," he repeated, this time to Jag, rubbing his knuckles over the thick black and tan fur. "You deserve better, Jag. We all do."

Liam snorted softly.

"What?" Shane demanded. "What was that supposed to mean? I don't speak in grunts, Brother."

"You think you deserve better than Chloe?"

"Who said anything about Chloe?"

Liam lifted his dark brows like he knew everything. "She's all you think about."

And clearly he knew a lot, if not everything. Shane had always respected his brother for that. "Since when do you know what I'm thinking about?"

Liam shook his head, his attention back on Jag. "What do you say we take a break, big guy?"

"You talk to dogs more than people, you know."

Liam angled his head. "I like them more."

"Even me? Never mind." Shane started laughing. "I already know the answer to that."

"That's your problem, Shane," Liam said softly. He always spoke low, when he talked at all, which made whatever he was about to say seem ten times more important than it probably was.

"What is my problem?"

"You think you know all the answers."

"Well, when it comes to women, I'm pretty sure me and Jag here *both* know more than you."

Liam ignored the dig. "Why don't you tell me

what's eating you? She won't have sex with you? Isn't that usually your end game?"

"Isn't that everyone's end game?" he fired back.

"Not mine." Liam stroked Jag's coat, his big hands always a good touch on any dog. In seconds, Jag got the message she was off duty and folded for a rest. "Although if it was, I wouldn't have come home alone the other night."

"Big fail with Andi?"

"We're not talking about Andi," Liam replied, shutting the door firmly in a voice Shane recognized as final.

Shane whistled out a slow sigh. "So what if it wasn't my end game?"

Liam gave him a doubtful side-eye.

"She's going to leave, of course. She lives in Miami. She'll leave. Not that I care, but…"

"Oh, you care. You care so much you can't blow a whistle on time."

Shane gave his own grunt of disgust. "So what if I do care? It can't last. Nothing really good can last."

Liam angled his head and scowled at him. "How can you say that? Look at Mom and Dad."

"Precisely. Look at Mom and Dad. Dad's entire world gone in a heartbeat. Literally."

"So you think Dad shouldn't have married Mom because they only had, what, thirty-six years and six kids together? What the hell do you want?"

He used to be able to answer that question easily: sex. He always wanted only sex from a woman, right? It was a game—one he easily won. And then along came Chloe and all her perfection, and he wanted…more. "I'm mad at her," he murmured.

"At Chloe? For sending you off yesterday after you found Daisy? She obviously needed to decompress after that ordeal. I could see that from twenty feet away."

Shane swallowed, hating what he was about to say. Hating the sting behind his eyelids even more. "I'm mad at Mom."

Liam gawked at him. "I really hope I didn't hear that right."

"She was my rock, Liam. She was so solid. So right there. I don't care if that makes me sound...foolish. I loved that woman, and I want her to meet the person I fall in...I care about." He tried to laugh but it came out strangled. "I trust her judgment more than Dad's."

"You trust mine?"

"On German shepherds."

Liam almost smiled. "I don't know Chloe that well, obviously, but I saw a woman who was genuinely upset about the well-being of a dog yesterday. She was crying over Daisy. I know what Mom would say about that."

"What?" Shane asked, a little surprised at how much his whole body tensed waiting for Liam's answer. "You can trust someone who loves dogs?"

"She always said, 'You don't know what's really good until you try a little of it.'"

He frowned. "I think she was talking about, you know, broccoli."

"Or relationships."

No, Shane didn't think so at all. Would Mom like Chloe? Or would she think she was a neurotic clean freak who ironed her shorts and ran from dog poop?

God, he wished he knew. Which was why, right now, he was mad at her for leaving him. For leaving them all.

And not just right now. If he was perfectly honest, he'd been pissed off for three years since his cell phone rang and all he could hear was Dad crying on the other end. He didn't even know how mad he was until recently.

What the hell?

"And why haven't you told Chloe about Zeus?" Liam asked, yanking him back to the conversation. "I thought that was your big move when you talk about your dog attack and show that scar on your hip that conveniently requires you to lower your pants."

He hadn't told her because he'd yet to lower his pants. And because he liked her so much he'd have to tell her the truth. And that would be…a barrier too far, as Chloe would say.

"How'd you know I haven't told her?"

"She was surprised when I mentioned it."

"Five minutes alone with her and you tell her about Zeus." He gave his brother a vile look. "That's a low blow."

He grinned. "Now you'll have to show her the scar. You can thank me by getting off your ass and paying at least as much attention to training as Jag."

"'Kay." He pushed up and grabbed the launcher. "You going to tell me what happened with Andi the other night?"

"No."

"Or why you went to church?"

"No."

"Why do I even bother with you?" Shane asked.

Liam gave a rare grin and signaled Shane to go to the marker.

Chloe brushed some crumbs from her fingers, dropped another raspberry on the floor next to Daisy, and picked up her phone when it buzzed with a call, getting the usual reaction when she read the caller ID. Would her heart ever *not* kick up a notch at the sight or sound or possibility of Shane Kilcannon?

"Where are you?" he asked without saying hello first, his voice deep and sexy and exactly what she wanted to hear after the long, lonely night.

"I'm sitting in the Bitter Bark Bakery eating the most delicious buttery croissant. Where are you?"

"Where's Daisy?"

"At my feet. And don't get mad at me, but did you know she loves raspberries?"

He laughed softly. "Continuing Daisy Drop-ins without me?"

"Guilty as charged, Counselor," she said. "I decided to go back to the places where they loved her the most and start talking to customers, too. We stopped at the bookstore, and Jackie got down on all fours again. Max, the guy who owns the florist, gave us a full daisy chain, which my girl is currently wearing around her neck. And now we are at the bakery, and Linda May gave me a tiny bowl of raspberries, which I'm feeding her one at a time."

"Out of your *hand*?"

"Shane. Be real."

He laughed softly. "So no damage from yesterday?"

"None to Daisy's reputation, but…"

"But what?" He sounded genuinely concerned, and she bit back a smile before making the admission, not entirely sure how he'd take it.

"I, um, I slept with a dog on my bed."

Dead silence, then, "Don't move," he said. "And get me one of Linda May's blueberry muffins. I gotta hear about this."

Less than fifteen minutes later, the Bitter Bark Bakery door chime rang as Shane came in, wearing a Waterford Farm T-shirt and jeans. He might have a little dog dirt on him, but he looked good to Chloe.

It had been a long night of emotional battle, but the sun came up on a new day, and Chloe wasn't ready to give up on *Better* Bark or the wonderful man she'd met here.

When he came to her table by the window, Daisy stood and barked, earning a quick look from a couple at another table, but they smiled as if they'd already been charmed by her.

"You should have told me you were going out," he said, pulling out the wrought-iron chair next to her. He reached down to scratch Daisy, lifting the chain of knotted flowers. "You weren't kidding. Why didn't you call me or come over?"

"I knew you were busy at work." She handed him a muffin wrapped in wax paper, a cup of steaming coffee, and a tiny bottle of hand sanitizer. "And I really decided I couldn't stay imprisoned for one more minute."

"Imprisoned?" He squeezed the sani into his palm, probably just to make her happy.

"Don't you think that was the point of someone letting Daisy out? To make sure I stay in the house with her?"

He considered that as he took his first bite and a few crumbs of that sugary coating rained down all over his T-shirt, making her itch to wipe it off.

"Possibly," he said after he chewed. "Or someone wanted Daisy to scare people. Who knows, but I'm certain it was a deliberate act to sabotage your plans for the town and get the vote against you."

"I know that," she said. "Which is why I'm here and ready to tackle all the places we haven't been with her yet and return to some we have."

"Alone?" He seemed genuinely hurt.

She looked down for a moment, gathering her thoughts, then back at him. "I know, but…"

"You got scared."

So, so scared. "Shane, I'm not going to stay here. You know that. I know that. So, whatever we do together, that's always going to be in the background."

He reached over the table and put his hand over hers. "Listen to me. I want to be with you while you're here. That's it. No strings, no ties, no expectations, no discussions of anything that makes you uncomfortable. We'll be together as often and as long as you like."

"It never works like that," she whispered, wishing it could. Just this once. Just this man.

"You know," he said, blowing out a breath. "A wise woman once said, 'You don't know what's really good until you try a little of it.'"

She lifted one eyebrow, surprised to think she

hadn't tried before. "What are you suggesting we try?"

"Um...I think they call it a *relationship*, but I could be wrong."

She leaned forward to whisper, "I think they call it sex."

"If that's what you want to call it, but take the relations out and you have a...ship."

"Ships sail, you know."

"I won't drown when you do," he said.

For a long moment, neither spoke, and it felt like somehow they'd silently sealed a deal. One step, one day, one barrier at a time.

"Ooh, who do we have here?" A woman's voice behind them made him turn to see Andi Rivers coming across the bakery toward them. "A little four-legged PR professional?"

Andi greeted them both with quick hugs and slipped into the empty seat at the next table, giving some love to Daisy. "I heard she caused quite a stir yesterday."

"You heard?" Chloe asked. "Is it all over town?"

"Somebody posted on that Nextdoor site—you know that local social media site that forces you to read e-mails from the very neighbors you try to ignore by wearing earbuds when you walk?"

"I'm not on it, but I'll sign up," Chloe said. "What are they saying?"

"That you have a pit bull and can't control it. And that could be a real problem if we turn Bitter Bark into Better Bark. Someone called it Biter Bark."

Shane murmured a curse, but Chloe held her hand up to stop him. "It's fine. All the more reason for me to walk her in and out of every business and all around

Bushrod Square. It takes, on average, three minutes to fall in love with Daisy."

Andi smiled down at the dog. "You had me in two, Daisy."

"So, I'll be marching through town for the next week, talking about my idea and events, and Daisy will win this thing for me."

"Daisy…and Shane." He leaned forward and put his hand over hers. "Like a ship. Sailing together. For a while. Until one leaves."

Or sinks.

"I think I've missed something," Andi said with a laugh. "But I have to tell you what I've been hearing around town, just so you know."

"Spill," Chloe said.

She leaned in and lowered her voice. "Jeannie Slattery has made it her business to tell every single woman who comes into her spa that this idea is a travesty. Even if they like it, she yammers on about how dumb it is. And she's posted something that says, 'Dangerous Dogs on the Loose' right at the reception desk, with pictures…" She looked down at Daisy. "Of dogs that look like her."

"Oh, I should go there," Chloe said. "But I don't want to waltz into a spa and make a scene. It's not like a bakery or florist."

"Why would you go in there?" Andi asked.

"Three minutes to love Daisy and change her mind."

"Jeannie's a notorious bitch," Andi warned her.

"To customers?" Shane asked, taking out his phone to tap the screen a few times, staring at it, then putting it to his ear. "Yeah, hi. I'd like to make a special appointment for my girlfriend this afternoon."

Girlfriend? She felt Andi's leg add a tiny amount of pressure under the table and resisted the urge to look at her friend.

"Whatever you do for the works. Mani, pedi, massage, a face…thing." He gave them a silent plea for more.

"Waxing?" Andi suggested.

"Waxing?" Chloe mouthed at her, eyes wide.

"Waxing," he said into the phone. "Well, wherever she wants it."

Chloe dropped her head into her hands with a moan, but Andi cracked up.

"So would you give her the works?" Shane asked. "Everything you have. Spend…a lot. Yeah, I'll stop in later and give you my credit card. Everything deluxe. Three thirty is open? Perfect. Oh, and she has a therapy dog that needs to come, too. Thanks."

He tapped the phone and gave both women one hell of a cocky smile.

"That was impressive," Andi said.

"And smart."

"Just be sure they wax you and not the dog." He stood up, taking his coffee. "Come on, Chloe. Let's see if we can get that fall-in-love time down to a minute thirty."

She looked up at him, blinking in disbelief.

"I meant with Daisy."

"I know what you meant."

But Andi was still laughing as she walked to the counter and gave them a quick wave goodbye.

Chapter Seventeen

Shane had thought of everything, including a small yellow jacket for Daisy, which looked official enough when they arrived at the upscale two-story spa situated on a shady corner of Bushrod Square.

The receptionist, a twentysomething with lavender-tipped hair, reacted with delight to Daisy, and chatted easily while Chloe waited for her personal spa escort, which was apparently what one got when they bought "the works" at Bitter Bark Body & Mind Spa.

The appointment seemed like an elaborate and expensive way to get Daisy into this place, but it had worked, and there was no doubt Jeannie Slattery was a force to be reckoned with. She had an oversized felt board in the reception area that featured all sorts of local tidbits, health updates, and the promise of a yoga studio that was in the planning stages for the second floor of this building.

"A yoga studio?" Chloe said, reading the board. "What a great idea."

"Do you practice?" the receptionist asked.

"I was thinking about doggie yoga." She glanced to Daisy. "Would you like that?"

"That would be awesome," the girl exclaimed. "I've heard about studios that let you bring your dog in for certain classes." She added a wide smile. "You're the lady who wants to change Bitter Bark to Better Bark, aren't you?"

"I am," Chloe said, reaching over her desk to shake her hand. "Chloe Somerset. And this is Daisy."

"I'm Veronica." She stood up to peer over the desk again at the dog. "She is so adorbs," she said. "I love the idea, you know. But..."

"Not everyone does."

She looked to the back door that led to the rest of the spa. "My boss is very opposed."

"I've heard."

"Really thinks it will turn our town into a laughingstock."

"Laughing all the way to the bank," Chloe replied.

"Well, we're a people spa, so maybe Jeannie thinks we'd be left out."

Chloe lifted her brows. "Dogs need spa treatments, too," she said, just as that door opened and another young woman came out and greeted her. There was more cooing over Daisy, and the receptionist shared the doggie yoga idea, which was received with two thumbs up.

So Jeannie might not like the idea, but her staff did.

The escort led them to the back, talking about the treatments, offering champagne—which Chloe accepted—and directed her to the showers, sauna, and changing rooms.

Daisy trotted along for everything.

When Chloe had to put Daisy's leash down, the dog never strayed. She was curious, friendly, and always approachable with the few women she saw, so the plan was working so far just fine.

It continued that way through a thirty-minute facial, a manicure, pedicure and, oh, she couldn't resist, a bikini wax that hurt like a mother but made her feel so silky smooth.

That made her want to show it off to someone. *Like the man who bought it.*

By the time she was led down the hall for her last treatment, the spa was empty. It had to be close to seven, and even with the snacks and drinks, Chloe was hungry.

So Daisy had to be, too. Chloe had given her the last of the treats stuffed into her bag during the pedicure, but almost canceled the therapy massage so she could to get Daisy home for dinner.

But then she was led into a room and left completely alone, so she had to wait for the massage therapist to tell her she wanted to leave.

It only made things worse that she'd been told this was a "red velvet" treatment and the whole room was scented with cinnamon.

"Sit, Daisy," she ordered and, to her credit, she tried. But the smells were too good, and she made her way around the entire room, sniffing. Finally, after a moment, she settled down.

"Good girl," Chloe said, bending over to give her some love. "You really are a sweet angel."

And today, while lovely, might have been a waste of time. Without an encounter with Jeannie Slattery,

Chloe feared it might have been a very expensive failed experiment.

Still waiting for the therapist, Chloe walked toward the window, opening a wooden slat to peek out, looking directly at the giant tree in Bushrod Square.

"You should be undressed and ready."

Chloe jumped and turned at the woman's voice, surprised to see it was Jeannie Slattery dressed in the cool-blue scrubs that all the attendants wore.

How long had she been standing there?

"Oh, I didn't hear you."

Daisy got up and barked once at the new arrival, but Chloe held her hand out, and instantly Daisy sat, silent.

"We keep things quiet here," Jeannie said, making Chloe wonder if she was referring to the bark or the fact that she'd snuck in.

And now, Chloe couldn't leave because this was her opportunity to crack the nut that was Jeannie Slattery and show her what a great dog could be like. "You certainly have a lovely business. I'm so enjoying my treatments and..." She smiled and gestured to Daisy. "So's my furry friend."

"We save the best for last," she said, coming in and walking to the window, purposely keeping a wide berth around Daisy.

"And what is that?"

"A hydrating massage with grapeseed and olive fruit oils, and at the end, a treat unlike any other: the red velvet special."

"Sounds...delicious."

Jeannie laughed as if she had a secret, tilting the

shutter slats open even more. "Looking at the Bitter Bark tree?"

"Actually, it's a hickory, as you know."

"It's a landmark, an institution, and the heart and soul of a town that doesn't need a new name, Chloe." She snapped the shutters like an exclamation point.

"I guess we'll let the residents decide that," Chloe said.

Jeannie gestured to the table. "I'll step out while you get comfortable."

"Are you doing this massage?"

"I'm highly trained. See?" On her way out, she pointed to the wall where three certificates and diplomas hung that would support that statement.

"Okay." Well, she wanted to have an encounter with Jeannie to show her how nicely a dog could behave here. And change her mind.

She hadn't expected to do that work while flat on her stomach wearing next to nothing. She considered leaving, but Daisy was snoozing in the corner now, and this would be her only chance with Jeannie.

Dropping the robe but keeping her bra and panties on, she slid under the cool sheets, cursing this idea that had gone from playful to uncomfortable. Massages weren't her favorite thing in the world, and when given by a woman who clearly hated her? She'd be a ball of tension by the time it was over.

Jeannie came back and put on some soft new age music. She worked silently, and after a few minutes, Chloe settled with her face in the terry-wrapped hole, trying to let her muscles relax under Jeannie's surprisingly strong hands.

"So," Chloe said. "You see how nice my dog is?"

"I heard he was real nice running around and terrorizing the citizens of Bitter Bark yesterday."

Her heart dropped. "*She* didn't terrorize anyone, and someone unlocked my gate."

"Hmmm."

Or maybe she already knew that. Her whole body tensed at the hands that pressed on her back.

"I was thinking of some great ideas—"

"Miss Somerset." She sounded like a schoolteacher chiding a student. "We don't talk during treatments. It ruins the chi in the room. Please be quiet."

Well. Shut me up. Chloe sighed and let the woman do her work. The only sound other than the barely audible relaxation music was Daisy's extremely audible snoring.

Chloe gave up the fight and had nearly fallen asleep herself when something cold and wet hit her skin, a thick substance that glided on like butter, only creamier and...sweet. A cloying but familiar scent nearly choked her.

Instantly, Daisy got up and took a few steps closer, the look in her eyes not completely unlike what Chloe had seen in Shane's after a few particularly heated kisses.

"No," she said softly, giving her a stern look. "Stay, Daisy."

She could have sworn she heard Jeannie chuckle as she used some kind of trowel to slather the overpowering cream down her back, skipping the silky panties but wiping the substance all the way down her leg. It smelled rich and...*chocolate.*

Chocolate?

Chloe shot up. "What is that?" She arched her back

to look over her shoulder at a thick brown gunk that looked like…cake frosting.

Daisy barked and came closer.

"No, no, Daisy, get back!" Chloe jerked away and flashed a look to Jeannie. "Chocolate can kill dogs."

"Oh, it's not really chocolate," she said with a condescending laugh. "It's chocolate-scented body butter. It's fine."

"It's not fine." She reached around and swiped her back, the gooey substance clumping between her fingers.

"It's the deluxe treatment that your boyfriend ordered. There we go." She finished with a flourish on the bottoms of her feet. "All finished!"

With that, Jeannie backed away, grabbed a towel to wipe her hands, and gave Chloe a tight smile. "You just wait for it to soak in now. Only fifteen or twenty minutes. Relax."

Daisy barked, agitated now, the smell of chocolate overpowering.

"If that's possible," Jeannie added, throwing a look at Daisy. "There's a reason dogs aren't welcome in my sanctuary."

Screw her sanctuary. "I need a towel and a shower," Chloe said.

Jeannie totally ignored the demand, stepping outside. "Remember, the longer that body butter is on, the better you feel." Her smile widened. "If I know you, you'll love it so much you'll want to change our name to *Butter* Bark."

Without waiting for Chloe's response, she closed the door behind her. Ire shot through Chloe, but she didn't have time to seethe. She couldn't take a chance that this wasn't real chocolate.

Because Daisy was way too interested.

She sniffed her hand, and her stomach tightened. It sure smelled like chocolate.

"No, down, Daisy. Get down. No." She forgot every command, and Daisy must have sensed the panic, because now she was up on her hind legs, barking with a little more force.

"No, no! Daisy!" She jerked her feet away seconds before Daisy's tongue lapped her.

All Chloe could do was roll into a ball so Daisy couldn't get even one lick, but now the dog was worked up and frustrated and scared and hungry.

"Damn it," she muttered, grabbing at a towel on the bottom of the table to wipe herself off. It didn't feel like frosting, but she couldn't take a chance.

How was she going to get out of here without Daisy attacking her for a taste of body butter that might or might not kill her? Daisy ran around the table, knocking over a small stand on the side of the room, her ferocious-sounding bark up to Defcon 1 now.

She'd been set up for failure. Chloe *and* Daisy. And, for all she knew, that woman had this on some secret camera.

Wiping furiously at the cream, Chloe perched on the massage table and used every towel and sheet she could reach. She balled each up as it filled with body butter, then tossed it to a high counter so Daisy couldn't reach. Still, the poor dog barked incessantly, so loud that Chloe was surprised someone didn't come barging in to help.

Of course not, because this was exactly what Jeannie Slattery had planned.

Finally, with most of the frosting off her feet and legs, Chloe jumped off the massage table and gave a sharp, loud command to Daisy, unusual enough for the dog to freeze momentarily.

Grabbing the robe she'd worn in, Chloe opened the door, Daisy on her heels. And ankles. And calves. But she'd cleaned them well enough.

She found her way to the dressing room, shaking as she yanked the rubber bracelet that held her locker key. Stepping into her clothes, she swore when the linen pants stuck to the backs of her legs as though she'd rubbed down in superglue.

Very funny, Jeannie Slattery. Very freaking funny.

Daisy was back, nose under the pant leg, a low growl of desperation in her throat.

Her hands sticky, Chloe grabbed her bag and opened it to call Shane, but she caught the side of the handle and spilled everything with a clatter. Two bottles of hand sanitizer, her wallet, some pens, lipstick, a pack of tissues, loose change, her phone, the condoms and, shoot, about thirty of her business cards that had somehow gotten loose.

All over the floor of a locker room. Essentially a public bathroom.

She stared at the mess, an old familiar burn in her belly. Shame. Fear. Sickness. Anger. *Filth.*

It all bubbled up, choking her, making her hands shake so hard she had to press them together to keep from letting out a moan.

She couldn't touch any of that now!

Daisy instantly bent down and sniffed, running her tongue over a roll of breath mints.

"Daisy! No!" Her voice cracked, and the dog looked up at her, taking a step back at the harshness. "I mean, don't, girl. Don't eat any of that. We'll get you home now. We'll get you dinner."

Tears threatened as she knelt down to start to pick everything up, trying to use her fingernails. She glanced around. Didn't they keep latex gloves in this place?

Frustration rocked her so hard, she almost fell over.

Instantly, Daisy was beside her, looking up, almost...sorry.

"Oh, baby, it's not your fault." She reached around the dog's head and wrapped her in an embrace, holding on for all the support she'd never imagined she'd get from a dog. "We can't let her win. Shane would never let her win. We cannot let her win."

The tears spilled over now, and when she closed her eyes, she didn't see Jeannie Slattery and her crass red hair.

She saw Doreen Somerset in a stained blue T-shirt and the same khaki shorts she wore day after day after day because she couldn't find the rest of her clothes. She saw a mess. A big, ugly mess. She saw the woman who'd tried to suck the normal out of Chloe.

She opened her eyes and stared at the floor, gently easing Daisy away.

"We can't let her win," she repeated, lowering herself to sit on the floor. It was cold and, well, *don't think about the dirt, Chloe.* "We can't let her win."

One by one, she picked up her belongings and

didn't even bother to wash them. She dropped them into her bag. The phone. The wallet. The lipstick. The condoms.

She lifted those up and showed them to Daisy. "We can't let her win," she repeated.

She got it all but the business cards, strewn facedown on the tile. Let Jeannie clean them up.

With a push, she got up, leashed the dog and walked to the sink to wash her hands.

"She's not going to win this," she ground out, shaking off her hands, looking in the mirror and once again seeing the woman who had the power to take everything from her.

Not anymore. *Not anymore.*

"She cannot take normalcy from me," she said to her image. "She cannot."

Daisy looked up, her dark eyes clear and so intelligent, Chloe could have sworn she understood. "As long as I live in fear of a mess or afraid to lose control, I'm the one who misses out on everything. I miss out on life and love and…" *Sex.* "Shane."

Daisy barked once at the mention of his name.

"That means she's stolen everything from me. All my pleasure, all my satisfaction, all my joy, all my normalcy." She shook her head as if she could knock everything her mother had done to her out of it. "She isn't going to win that. I want a mess! I want *him*."

Vibrating all over again, for a completely different reason, she took Daisy's leash and headed out.

"Oh, the treats you're going to get, Daisy. The treats you are going to get are *incalculable*." And the treats Chloe and Shane were about to get were incalculable, too. "I can't wait."

The two of them walked out into the lobby where Jeannie and several members of her staff were waiting to close after the last customer. Jeannie was reading her phone, but Chloe strongly suspected she had the camera on in hopes of recording an attacking dog.

But Daisy stood at attention. Perfect Daisy. Not Perfect Chloe...Perfect *Daisy*.

"Thank you all so much," Chloe said, looking from one to the other. "Daisy and I had a wonderful time. I'm so inspired that I've decided to add a special event to the new Better Bark Calendar of Canine Fun. Spa day for dogs! We can set it up in the square, with massage tables and grooming stations. And everyone who brings their dog will get a special pass for services here, which will really make your business boom."

"Oh, that's so much fun!" one of the girls cried out.

"I can groom dogs," the other said.

"We'd get a ton of business if we sponsored that," Veronica agreed. "Jeannie, don't you think that would be an amazing idea?"

Jeannie just stared daggers at Chloe.

Right then, the door opened, and Shane walked in, no longer dog-training dirty but wearing a sharp button-down shirt, dress slacks, and a clean shave that made him look absolutely stunning.

Chloe couldn't resist sneaking a look at the women who openly ogled him like the eye candy he was.

"Hey," he said, the single syllable so sexy she could have sworn one of those women moaned. "How was it?"

"It was amazing, Shane. I don't know how to thank you." But she was already thinking of some pretty breathtaking ways.

Taking her outside, he curled her arm around her back so he could press her body into his. He lowered his face for a kiss, then backed up and sniffed. "You smell good enough to eat, Chloe."

"Oh, trust me. I am." She reached up and pecked his lips, but he wouldn't let her stop at that, pulling her all the way in for a proper kiss that lasted a second or two too long. "And Daisy needs to eat. Everything we can give her and her favorite treat. She's starving."

"I thought we could go out to dinner," he said. "What would you like?"

She tipped her head back, got up on her toes, and spoke against his lips. "Everything you can give me and my favorite treat."

"Which is?"

She kissed him on the lips and whispered, "You."

Chapter Eighteen

Shane knew a thing or two about women. And dogs.

And from what he could tell, these two really were starving.

Chloe filled him in on the frosting debacle as he drove her home, so, of course, he had to reach down her back and retrieve some remaining body butter to taste it. And spit it out, assuring her it was not chocolate.

As much as he wanted to turn around and go give Jeannie Slattery a piece of his mind, he knew it was Chloe who needed—and wanted—attention right now. There was an undercurrent of warmth in her voice and touch, an electricity, a determination, an emotional buzz that he couldn't quite read.

In the house, she headed straight to the back to shower off the remnants of Jeannie's mess, and he took care of Daisy, who ate twice as much as her normal amount and then collapsed on the sofa where he doubted an earthquake could get her to move.

"What went on in that place?" he asked, rubbing Daisy's head as he waited for Chloe to come out.

And waited. And waited.

Even she couldn't be in the shower that long.

A tendril of worry curled around his heart. Not that he thought she could be hurt, but something was different. It was like they'd massaged the edge off her and...

You.

Her whispered promise on the street sent a bolt of heat through him. So what the hell was he doing on this sofa?

He walked back to the bedroom, surprised to see the door open, but the room dark.

Not completely dark.

There were...candles. On the dresser. On the nightstand. On a desk. About fifteen flickering, romantic candles. And Chloe was...

"Right here." In bed. On her back, covers up to her chest, shoulders bare. Her hair spilled over the pillows, and she looked like...a dream. His dream. "Waiting for you."

He laughed and came closer. "I thought we were going to, you know, have a *ship* with no *relations*."

"I had an epiphany." She inched the covers down, coaxing him closer.

"Sounds...hot."

"Oh, it's about to be."

"Chloe, are you..." His words faded as the sheet revealed her bare breasts, golden slopes of perfection in the candlelight. "Perfect."

"I think candlelight is perfect." She inched the sheets lower, revealing her narrow waist and the sweet curve of her hips.

He came closer, looking down, his pulse thumping,

his blood rushing, his brain short-circuiting for how much he wanted her. "No. You're perfect."

"That's what you say."

"I'm always right."

Down went the covers, over her sexy hip bones and navel, lower, lower, lower.

His mouth went dry at the sleek black tuft of hair, the lean lines of her thighs, and… "Heaven."

"Hell."

He looked up at her, ready to argue that.

"I meant it was hell to have it waxed, so thanks for that."

"Thanks for…" He reached for the covers to do the rest, dragging them slowly, one inch at a time, and every inch got better and better. "This. Which is…" He started to lower himself, his hands itching to touch, his body ready.

She pointed at him. "I have a strict no-street-clothes-in-bed rule."

That made him laugh. "Of course you do. Should I hose down in hand sani before I get in? Shower? Spritz a little 409 to turn you on?"

"I'm plenty turned on." Her smile flickered. "Take your clothes off, Shane Kilcannon. Real slow, so I can memorize every move you make."

He took a deep breath and started to unbutton his shirt, a little surprised that his hands trembled slightly. Holding her gaze, he undid the buttons slowly, opening the shirt, enjoying her enjoying him. While she stared, he devoured every naked curve exposed for him, every glowing inch of sweet skin, from the column of her neck, over the rise of her breasts, down to the very slick center that he needed to be inside.

He unbuckled his belt and slowly lowered his zipper. And she actually sat up a little to see everything.

"You're enjoying this," he said.

"Immensely."

Blood hummed out of his head and heart, rushing to one place, knotting him in arousal. He stepped out of his dress pants. That left nothing but boxer briefs, which were tented and tight.

And all that got worse as he could see her hungry stare in the candlelight. He finished undressing, and her jaw loosened as she looked at him with the same heat with which he had to be looking at her. "Perfect," she whispered.

He got on the bed next to her. "That's what I want this to be for you, Chloe." He lowered himself on her, his chest against hers, his mouth on her lips. "I want this to be perfect for you."

He kissed her again, putting his heart and soul into it, holding back no matter how much he wanted to dive in and take every single thing she was offering. He wouldn't. It had to be perfect. It had to be so impeccable, so clean and sweet and safe and slow that she didn't regret one second of this decision.

He closed his eyes and fought every instinct, restraining himself as much as possible.

"Shane."

He lifted his head from the kiss to look at her.

"I'm not gonna break." She squeezed his shoulders and dragged her fingers down his back. "And you..." She grabbed his backside. "Are not going to deny me the bed-shaking, brain-rattling, sweat-inducing, six orgasm-producing sex that a guy like you was built to deliver."

He stared at her, stunned. "Six?"

"Okay, five."

"Oh, I can do six."

She started laughing. "You get my point? I want sex, Shane. Dirty…" She rocked her hips into his erection. "Messy…" She dug her nails into his ass. "Crazy…" She wrapped both legs around his thighs. "Sex."

He took a slow breath, studying her face, his chest rising, and the rest of him rising even more. "You gotta stop this right now."

"Stop? Why?"

"Because you gave me a challenge, and I…I…."

"Have to win."

He closed his eyes. "Oh yes, I do."

"Then play ball, Kilcannon."

At the tease, he shuddered a little, then relaxed all his weight on her. And let it all change. He kissed her everywhere his mouth could find, and his hands began to roam and explore, and everything he touched, he had to taste.

Her breasts. Her ribs. Her stomach. Hot lips, greedy hands, sweet moans, and a tongue that made her cry out every time he discovered somewhere new to lick.

He took ownership of every move, and all she could do was grab hair or shoulders or sheets and let him have his way.

Dizzy, lost, and both of them hanging on the hairy edge of release, she spread her legs and welcomed his mouth and gave in for number one. Two and three were with his hands, his fingers in and out and around her. Then he finally knelt over her and opened a condom packet.

During this one break, she took over, exploring him with the same desperation, touching and stroking him to absolute madness, and then lowering her head to place a kiss on him. And another. She moaned and sucked lightly, nearly making him lose his balance as pleasure rocked through him.

He held her head in one hand, his eyes closed, every sense on fire as he moaned, stroked her hair, and whispered her name over and over again, drowning in the feel of her lips on him.

She sat back and touched the corner of her mouth, looking up at him.

"A Chloe first?" he asked on a gruff whisper.

She nodded, and that made his heart crack a little more open and vulnerable.

She reached up, coaxing him to her, into her, offering a kiss as they joined in the most intimate, perfect, rhythmic connection he could remember.

All he could do was hang on and ride as the pressure and pace moved from steady to crazy to flat-out senseless. Control disappeared, and good riddance to it. She took the ride as Shane plunged in and out, on the edge of surrender.

He squeezed his eyes shut and let the raw sensations rock him as they dragged each other closer and closer to the brink. He found her mouth, held the kiss, and squeezed her whole body as he finally let go completely.

She moved with him, gasping for air, pulsing over and over until there was nothing left for them to do but lie in the warmth of the bed and each other.

He had no idea how much time passed after they'd made love. Ten minutes? An hour? Half the night? All

Shane knew was a bone-deep sense of belonging and the burn in his gut that told him he did not want her to leave. Ever.

"Tell me about it." Chloe slid her hand over Shane's hip, grazing the roped muscle near the bone, then letting her fingers settle into the round scar she'd spied at the very top of his thigh, almost in the hip crease.

He moaned a little, making it difficult for her to tell if that was a postcoital groan of satisfaction or a way to say he didn't want to talk about it.

"Liam told me."

"I know. The bastard says five words in two hours, and they happen to be about my deep, dark past."

She eased out from under him, but kept her body pressed to his, sliding a leg over his and turning him, so the left-side scar was easy for her to touch. "How deep? How dark?"

He opened his eyes, golden in the candlelight, and something else, too. A little scared. "Kind of. Very. Yeah, deep and dark."

She couldn't help sitting up an inch. "I want to know."

"I was bit by a dog when I was nine." He swallowed, the very act telling her there was so much more to it.

"And still you love dogs," she said. "That's not very deep or dark. It actually says a lot of very good things about you."

He snorted and closed his eyes. "There's nothing

that says very good things about me in this story. Starting with the fact that I have never, ever told anyone the truth. Even when they deserved to know it." He looked at her then, nothing but sincerity in his gaze. "Not any of my brothers, not my parents, not a friend, not anyone."

But would he tell her? She was vaguely aware she held her breath and waited for the answer to that, surprised at how much it mattered. Not the story, but the truth.

"Zeus was a pit, a Staffy mix who maybe had something else in there, but he was a tough little dude. He'd been bred to fight, all scarred and nasty when we got him. My dad handled him, mostly, with Liam. When he'd been trained and socialized and loved like all our fosters, my mom set out to find him a home. That's what she did before Waterford was an official facility. Mom fostered rescues and found them homes. Except for the ones she fell madly in love with," he added. "And she fell head over heels in love with Zeus. He was not going anywhere."

A longing to know Annie Kilcannon hit Chloe with an unexpected punch. At Waterford, she'd seen a few pictures scattered around the house and knew Shane's mother was the one responsible for his hazel eyes and the little bit of red that highlighted Molly's hair. She had seen from the pictures that the woman had a sweet smile, good bones, and a twinkle in her eye that made Chloe imagine she held her own in the teasing department.

But it wasn't enough. Chloe wanted to hear her voice, watch her interact with her kids, and know this woman who'd raised a brood of impressive men and women.

"I knew Staffies could have issues with other dogs," Shane continued. "Even at nine I knew that. I knew we'd been very slowly introducing Zeus to others. But he didn't know them all. We had another foster at the time named Rojo, a sweetheart of an Aussie shepherd. Wouldn't hurt a fly. So one day, it was my day to clean the kennels and fill the food bowls before school. They weren't anything elaborate like they are now, but five or six big cages that my dad built under a shelter. Still, we each had mornings we had to work, and I took Rojo with me."

His words slowed as she imagined he went back in time.

"It was cold," he said. "Early December, and I was not happy about having to go out there at seven in the morning. Neither was Rojo. I mean, really, Chloe, I was cranky."

He stopped talking completely and sighed. She waited, silent, gliding her finger over the scar that was exactly the shape of a dog's mouth, the bumps on his skin easy to feel, the imperfections obvious on such a perfect body.

"I did everything wrong," he said. "Zeus got anxious and pawed at his food bowl, spilling it everywhere. I yelled at him for the mess, I let Rojo at his cage door to bark at him, I..." He clenched his teeth. "I taunted him. I took out my frustration on him and, I don't know, it was like I wanted to show Rojo I could handle the bad dogs." He closed his eyes. "He snarled, leaped, and took a chomp out of me that I'll never forget. I screamed like a lunatic, shaking the dog cage door in panic, and Zeus came at me again, but I got out. Half my family came running out, of course, and I...I...didn't tell them what I'd done."

"They thought he lost it?"

He closed his. "Yes. It was the worst bite any of us had ever had. I remember my mother bawling in the backseat, holding me on the way to the ER. The whole time my dad quietly telling her that Zeus had to go. He had to go."

She gasped softly. "They didn't—"

"My parents would sooner kill a kid than a dog," he assured her. "But my mom loved him and wanted to keep him, until then. I don't know where they sent him and, honestly, I don't like to think about it, Chloe. Not 'cause I think anything bad happened to him, but because of me, he left. And wherever he went, he had a cloud over his history because my parents, of course, had to let the new fosters know Zeus had attacked one of their kids. But he didn't *attack*. He *reacted*, as any dog would."

He sat up a little, taking her hand off the scar to hold it. "I drowned in guilt. And, God, I wanted to tell my mother. But I knew I would be a huge disappointment to her, and she was wrecked about the whole thing. Questioning if we should ever take a pit again, though, of course, we did. Zeus would have had the best life at our house. And I took that away from him and from her."

"I'm sure he had a good home," she said, knowing it sounded like a platitude but wanting to believe it as much as she imagined he wanted to.

"I don't know. I'll never know. But I know this: People are the monsters, not pit bulls. And so, I have my mission. To convert everyone who will listen to the truth about pitties." He managed a smile. "I do it all for Zeus."

"And your mom."

The smile grew. "Yeah."

"She'd have forgiven you, I bet."

"Oh yes. But not until she had a good long talk with me." He dropped back on the pillow with a sigh, looking up at the ceiling. "She was an expert talker."

"What was she like, Shane?"

He closed his eyes like the question hurt him, and Chloe put her hand on his chest, over his heart. "Tell me about her. Tell me everything you can remember."

"Now? In bed?" He turned, his eyebrows raised. "You want me to talk about my mother? I thought we were on Zeus."

"What upset you about losing Zeus was that you hurt your mother."

"You're right," he said on a sigh. "But why do you want to talk about her?"

"Because I want to know this amazing woman who raised you. I want to understand what made her tick. I want to..." Her voice cracked, but she didn't care. "I want to imagine what having a mother like that would have been like if she'd been mine."

"Oh, Chloe." He rolled over and wrapped his arms around her, pulling her into his chest with enough of a shudder that she knew he was fighting tears, too. "I wish she could be, sweetheart. I wish she could. I wish she were still here, damn it."

She bit her lip to keep from sobbing, pressing her face into his chest as she thought about his mother...and hers. "Tell me."

240

He didn't say anything for a long time, holding her head against him, stroking her hair with the same calming, comforting, loving touch she'd seen him use on Daisy. "I have a hard time talking about her, to be honest."

"Even to me?"

"Especially to you."

She lifted her head up. "Why?"

He looked hard at her, a few heartbeats passing. "It's like there's a hole in my heart that can never...I can never..." He sighed noisily. "I don't know why, but ever since I met you, I think more about her than ever. I was able to put it in a box, shove it away, not think about how much it hurt to lose her. I tried to make it not matter. Just, you know, part of life. My mom died. It happens to everyone. It happened to you, so shouldn't I be able to...deal?"

His voice shredded the words, and she rubbed his chest, making a small circle with her palm.

"Everyone deals in a different way," she said. "But you shouldn't put her memory away. You should share it. Help her memory to live. Please tell me about her."

It took him a while to talk again. When he did, his voice was low and calm. "She made friends with everyone. Everyone. Five minutes and she knew something about everyone, and then she'd remember it. I'd be in town with her, and we'd run into someone, and she'd know that their kid was sick last week or they got a new car. Not gossipy stuff, but personal. She always found something to compliment, but not to be fake, but because she only saw good."

Chloe closed her eyes and tucked closer to him,

listening to the tone and timbre of his voice as much as the words.

He told a story about her, then another. He laughed. He might have cried. He kept talking until Chloe was asleep, certain that that night, she'd dream of a woman with golden-green eyes.

And maybe the stories had been cathartic for Shane, but Chloe was the one who was soothed, warmed, and healed by the invisible presence of Annie Kilcannon.

Chapter Nineteen

For four, no, five, nights, Chloe had woken up with Shane next to her. And Daisy curled up at the bottom—yes, *on* the bed—waiting for them to wake up.

Nothing had ever felt quite so *normal*. Or good.

A training class was in full swing at Waterford, so Shane had to be at work almost all day, but Chloe had divided her time between polishing and practicing the presentation she'd give to the citizens of Bitter Bark in a few days and strolling through the town with Daisy. In the evening, they'd have dinner, share the highlights of their days, take Daisy out for "last pee," as Chloe had come to call it, and slip in between the covers together.

They stopped discussing how long Chloe would stay after the "popular vote" was taken. And she'd started checking her phone with one eye closed, dreading the call or text from her contact in Roatán, where they were currently deciding on a budget to bring in a tourism consultant for the rest of the summer to gear up for the fall and winter seasons.

Roatán, an island in the Caribbean, was so far from

the rolling foothills of the Blue Ridge Mountains that she actually couldn't think about it. But the thought planted itself that early morning, and Chloe pushed out of bed to shake it off. She slipped on sleep pants and a tank top, brushed her teeth, and headed for coffee. Daisy jumped off the bed with a soft thud and padded down the hall after her.

In the kitchen, she opened the back door to let Daisy into the yard, then peered out the window as she waited for the pot to brew. All the while, she was thinking about that call until her phone buzzed from the table where she'd left it charging the night before.

"Oh, not fair," she murmured, certain that merely thinking about her client had brought the call.

"What's not fair?" Shane asked, coming around the corner with sleepy eyes, no shirt, and boxers.

"That." She poked his bare chest on the way to get the phone, but he snagged her arm and pulled her closer for a kiss, long enough for the call to go to voice mail.

"You left me. Not fair."

She closed her eyes as the phone vibrated again, a text this time, no doubt with the news that she would eventually have to leave him for good.

He nuzzled her neck, not thinking that far in advance. "Come back to bed," he urged, the words and the promise they held melting her.

"I need…" Her words trailed off as she picked up the phone to realize that she wasn't getting a text from Roatán but Aunt Blanche, who'd texted and called three, four, oh, *many* times. The last message said WE HAVE A PROBLEM in screaming caps.

"What's wrong?" Shane asked.

"I don't know." She tapped the phone to start reading as someone pounded hard on the front door.

They looked at each other for a second, then both hustled to the living room, with Chloe still holding the phone she hadn't even read yet.

Blanche plowed in before the door was open. "Oh, someone's really done it now," she said.

Chloe's first thought was Daisy, who was safely in the backyard. Her second thought was Shane was darn near naked, but her aunt didn't even seem to notice, her eyes wild and locked on Chloe.

"Every single sign, Chloe. Every street sign, every business around Bushrod Square, the welcome sign, around the park and, of course, the tree. Every single one of them defaced during the night."

"Defaced?" Shane repeated in shock.

"With...what?" Oh God, Chloe couldn't even think about the possibilities of someone who hated her and dogs. That someone who left a calling card on her porch and broke the lock on the back gate. "What did they do?"

"Bitter Bark is now Better Bark, thanks to spray paint and markers."

Before she could answer, Shane sprinted back to the bedroom, presumably to dress.

"Oh, Aunt Blanche, I'm so sorry." Chloe reached for her, the woman's frayed nerves obvious. "I feel like I brought this on."

"You didn't change the signs, Chloe, but whoever did was vicious and sloppy and thorough."

"Jeannie," she muttered.

"She's out of town," Blanche said. "And so's

Mitch Easterbrook, which will come as no surprise to anyone."

Shane barreled back into the living room, wearing shorts and a T-shirt and sneakers with no socks, wordlessly passing the women to go outside.

"I have to see, too," Chloe said, glancing down at her bare feet.

Blanche kicked off her flip-flops. "Wear mine. I've seen enough."

"Go have coffee, Aunt Blanche. I'll be back." Without another word, she rushed to keep up with Shane, the two of them marching down the street toward town. At the first side street, they looked up at the sign where the round Bitter Bark logo was on the side of every sign within a mile of Bushrod Square.

Three lines with a thick black Sharpie next to the I in Bitter had turned it into an E.

She could still hear her voice in the presentation. *See how easy it will be? Just change one letter on every sign in town.* She hadn't meant *literally* and sure hadn't meant before the popular vote.

"Oh my God," she whispered.

They turned as they reached the square, and Chloe couldn't do anything but stop and stare.

Every single sign over every single store had been painted with three lines to turn the I to an E. Beautiful, expensive, wood-carved signs—all ruined. And windows. Someone had spray-painted right on the windows.

Better Bark Bakery.

Linda May came marching out. "Someone's going to pay for this!"

"I will," Chloe said softly, but Linda didn't hear her.

At Bitter Bark Buds 'n' Blooms, Max, the daisy-chain maker, stood in the doorway shaking his head, and Chloe stopped with her hand over her chest as if to say she was sorry.

Would they blame her? Probably. Would they forgive her? She had no idea, but she couldn't believe how much she dreaded the possibility that they wouldn't. Would they make Aunt Blanche resign?

She and Shane walked by to see the same damage on the bookstore, and Chloe imagined how sad Jackie would be when she arrived that morning.

Billy, the owner of Bitter Bark Bar, was just pulling up in his truck, his window going down as if he had to get a better look at the defaced sign. "What the ever-lovin'…" He threw his door open, his gaze moving from the sign to Shane and Chloe. "Really sucks, man. Someone really sucks."

Shane went to talk to him as Chloe turned to see the vandalized sign on the brick column that marked the northeast quadrant of Bushrod Square, and suddenly, her heart dropped. The tree!

"Not the tree!"

No one would paint a two-hundred-year-old tree, would they?

Without waiting for Shane finish talking to Billy, she darted across the street, flying into the square with her eyes on the tree. For some reason, she was flooded with relief to see it still standing. With no paint on the thick hickory bark.

Still she ran closer to where a bronze plaque had been erected, its raised letters telling the story of how Thaddeus Ambrose Bushrod founded the town after the Civil War and named it for the tree. Thaddeus had been no horticulturist, that was for sure.

But it was history and…

The plaque was wrecked, a marker having turned the I into an E.

Who would do this? Who? Why? If Jeannie and Mitch were out of town, could it have been Ned? An angry citizen? Kids?

"Chloe!" She looked up to see Shane coming toward her. "Billy said he has a security camera and might have gotten a shot of who did this, and if we get an ID, they will get the heat of my legal wrath, which isn't pretty." He stopped for a second, searching her face like he was trying to read her reaction. "Don't let vandalism make you stop, Chloe. Don't let this make you give up or leave."

She rubbed her bare arms, feeling a slight morning chill for the very first time. "I'm not going to give up. I'm going to do what I do best."

"Fight?"

"Clean."

By four o'clock in the afternoon, Chloe had finished three of the four main streets that ran the perimeter of Bushrod Square. Her arms ached from scrubbing and dragging around a step stool and a bag of cleaning supplies. Her whole body stank of vinegar, which she'd learned that, when mixed with water, could mostly erase Sharpie. But the worst discomfort was in her chest, where she carried a heavy heart as she confirmed her greatest fears.

An ugly seed had been planted and taken root, and any enthusiasm Chloe had drummed up for the idea of changing the town's name had been eradicated like the marker and paint she'd been wiping away.

And while some friends she'd made over the past ten days gave her sympathy, iced tea, and one more daisy chain for her four-legged partner, no one high-fived her or promised their vote at the town meeting the next day.

She huffed out a breath and looked down the length of the last street, which included the library, Jeannie's spa, Dave Ashland's real estate office, and a few other shops and town hall.

Oh yes, the meeting the next day would be right there in the general assembly room.

She should be working on her presentation and changing things to address what happened last night, but she was cleaning instead. As she reached the steps of the town hall, she stopped and looked up, longing for some air conditioning, water, and a conversation with someone who was on her side.

She texted Aunt Blanche and asked if she could come in with Daisy, and while she stood under a tree and waited for her answer, the heavy doors swung open and Blanche stepped out into the sunshine, looking for her.

"Can I come in?" Chloe asked, coming forward to greet her.

Blanche sighed. "I don't think that's a good idea."

"Because of Daisy?"

"Because of you."

Her heart sank as Blanche led her around the side of the building where a few tables with umbrellas were set up for people who worked at town hall to eat lunch. They were empty this late in the day, and private.

"I know people are pretty upset about this," Chloe said. "And they blame me."

"Not for the vandalism," Blanche said quickly. "But for...change. Honey, I underestimated how much a small town hates change." She folded her hands in a prayer position and rested her chin on her fingertips. "Frank had this uncanny ability to know how and when to push change and in what way. I..." She shook her head.

"You listened to me."

"Your idea is great."

"But too many people don't like it."

She frowned. "Most people did like it until last night. And now they associate all this mess with you. There's doubt and fear and uncertainty."

Chloe winced at the words, and Blanche instantly reached for her hand.

"But we can't sell this idea now. We can't vote for a name change or any new tourism program."

Chloe gasped softly. "So, no meeting?"

"We have the meeting scheduled and booked, and we have to have it, since James Fisker himself has decided to come in for it."

"The guy who owns a quarter of Bushrod Square?"

"The very one. And no one knows he's on his way, since he called me directly and told me to keep his arrival private, since he likes to pop in on his tenants and surprise them. While he's here, we need to have the meeting and make...other announcements. But no vote."

"And no chance to go in and change their minds? How about some new ideas? I can come up with something tonight, Aunt Blanche. I know the town so well now, I can come up with something wonderful. I know!" She snapped her fingers a few times, instantly getting Daisy's attention. "We'll petition the Arbor Society to have the bitter bark tree recognized as the newest species of..."

Blanche cast her eyes down.

"Okay. We'll make Thaddeus Bushrod a household name, somehow. Name a craft beer after him or...or have Thaddeus Thursdays when everyone dresses up..."

"No, Chloe."

"You're right, that's dumb. But he was a Civil War captain, so we'll arrange for one of those battle reenactments. We can have a..." Her voice trailed off.

"I'm going to resign as mayor tomorrow," Blanche said softly. "Dave Ashland's going to run unopposed."

Chloe stared at her. "Because of this?"

"Because I'm in over my head, Chloe. I'm no Frank Wilkins," she said on a soft laugh. "And everything here reminds me of him. I may be moving out and starting over somewhere else."

"Aunt Blanche!" Chloe put her hand over her mouth in shock. "No! This is your home."

"I don't know what I'm going to do yet," she said quickly. "And I don't want to upset you. You've done so much for me, dropping everything to move here, and..." Her gaze moved to Daisy. "Doing everything possible to implement your wonderful idea and sell this town. They all fell in love with you, you know."

Not deeply enough. "They fell in love with Daisy," she said. "Please don't do anything drastic like move or even step down."

"Oh, I've stepped down. I've been in transition meetings all day."

Chloe slumped in disappointment.

"Now, now," Aunt Blanche said, reaching for her. "Sometimes these things happen for the best. It's time to make a change, and this hasn't been a horrible few weeks for you, I imagine."

She gave a weak smile. "There were some highlights."

"Do you care very much about him?"

Oh so very much. "It was always temporary," she said, but even as the words came out of her mouth, they tasted bitter.

Blanche stroked Chloe's shoulders, holding her as if she could prop her up. "I had a little fantasy this morning when you and Shane went marching into town," she said. "I sat at your kitchen table and imagined that we won tomorrow. And that the town gave me the budget to offer you a job to stay here, and that you and Shane would get mar—"

She put her hand on Blanche's lips, not able to bear what was about to come out. "That isn't going to happen," she whispered, the truth of it hitting hard. "I've known Shane about two weeks, and I have a job and a life that aren't in Bitter Bark, North Carolina."

The other woman lifted a dubious brow. "Okay, now give me a *real* reason my fantasy can't happen."

Chloe swallowed and held her aunt's gaze. "I can't change who and what I am, Blanche," she whispered. "I need control, and if I don't have it, I panic, and I run. Shane's been very good at getting me to give up some control. The dog. The friendship. Yes, even intimacy, which obviously is happening."

Blanche smiled.

"But what you're talking about is…" A barrier too far. "Love. Life. Space. Sharing. I'm not sure I'm cut out for any of that. That's for people who are perfectly normal."

And she was Perfect Chloe, and there was nothing normal about that.

"How dare she do this to you?" Blanche's voice bubbled with an unexpected eruption of emotion. "It's child abuse, what my sister did. And I knew it all along but couldn't…wouldn't…" She fisted her hands in frustration. "I didn't *do* anything."

"No, no, Aunt Blanche. You did *so* much," Chloe replied. "You took me away when I needed it most."

"A dozen times? I should have taken you away for good, but no court would let me have you, and she *was* my sister." Her voice cracked as she fought a sob. "Don't let her shape who you are now, honey."

"I'm working on that every day," Chloe assured her. "And I've come a long way. But I don't know if I'm cut out for…that."

"That? You mean love and marriage? Everyone is cut out for it, especially with a fine man like Shane Kilcannon."

"He is fine," she agreed. "But what you're talking about are big, massive life changes that take time and compromise." They took normalcy, and Chloe would always live on the hairy edge of…not quite normal.

"You can compromise."

"I'd need time, Aunt Blanche. A reason to stay

here." She gave a smile that felt as broken as her heart.

"Then maybe you should find a reason to stay."

"I'll keep looking." Chloe sighed, picking up her cleaning supplies, tired of the conversation that hurt to have. "I still have to do one more street."

After a moment, Blanche stood, checking her watch. "I have a transition meeting with the finance department. I don't want to deal with any of it because I want..." She laughed softly. "To be planning a budget for Santa Paws next Christmas."

Chloe let out a sad grunt. "It was *such* a good idea. The right amount of corny and cute."

Aunt Blanche kissed her cheek. "I am so proud of you, Chloe. You came to Bitter Bark and gave it your all."

She sure did. All her ideas. All her heart. All her...love.

Aunt Blanche rose and blew another kiss, leaving Chloe to sit for a few more minutes to let the ache of this disappointment hit hard. When her cell phone rang with a call, she snagged it fast, eager to talk to Shane.

But the phone number was as unknown as the man's accented voice on the other end of the call.

"Is this Chloe Somerset?" he asked.

"Yes, it is," she said, putting on her professional voice. "Can I help you?"

"I'm calling on behalf of the Roatán Tourism Council with the wonderful news that we've accepted your proposal."

She closed her eyes.

"We have a beachfront condominium for you to

live in and an office where you will work. Your fee has been approved, and our only question is how soon can you start?"

The longer she stayed here, the harder it would be to leave.

"Very soon," she answered, absently reaching down to scratch Daisy's curious face. "I have to...finish up a few things."

Like the closest thing to love she'd ever known.

Chapter Twenty

S hane finished a long-ass day of training, his mood sour almost from the moment the day had started with an idiot trashing his hometown. He'd exchanged a few texts with Chloe, but hadn't heard from her since around four and hoped that meant she was done with her one-woman cleaning operation—well, one woman and a dog—and was home relaxing now.

He needed to give Dad a finalized contract for the DOD deal he'd finished and get out of here, but the hoopla out in the training pen told him that Garrett must have called the staff and family together before he'd leave to deliver an adopted dog, because that came with some ritual that couldn't be stopped.

As soon as Shane stepped outside, his mood lifted at the sight of people gathered around the lucky rescue who was being taken to its forever home. Of course, Garrett wore his "doggone hat," reserved exclusively for the delivery of an adopted dog. But, God help them, Jessie had one to match now, although hers looked fresh and new.

And damned cute, Shane had to admit.

Today, the happy farewell was for Louie, a two-toned Staffy who looked an awful lot like Daisy. This one was just as sweet and hadn't lasted long at Waterford when a warm, spirited woman named Mona started coming regularly to visit him and easily passed the home review and background check. She also passed Shane's pit bull test, showing a natural love for the breed that he required before he agreed to let one be adopted.

Gramma Finnie came out from the house, making her way toward the pen with a beaming smile, adjusting her signature colorful cardigan, red today, despite the midsummer heat.

"It's a happy day when a dog goes to a new home," she said, joining Shane and slipping one of her tiny arms around his waist. "It was always your mother's favorite day on the farm."

"Unless she was losing one she wanted to keep," he said, memories of Zeus still fresh after his recent confession to Chloe.

"That was Annie's goal, you know. To keep all the people and dogs happy," Gramma mused. "She used to say, 'You're only as happy as your least-happy kid.' Remember?"

"Sure do." He closed his eyes for a second, the move matching the mental sound of an emotional door shutting, as it always did when the subject of Mom came up.

"You happy, Shane?"

"I'm fine," he said. "Long day is all."

With her free hand, Gramma placed a crepe-papery palm on his cheek. "I heard about the vandalism in town."

"Good news travels fast."

"It's a darn shame she's done all that work and they've gone and canceled the vote."

"What?" He looked down at her. "They did?"

"There's still a meeting, but the subject of tourism is off the agenda. Seems Blanche is stepping down, and Dave Ashford is taking her place."

"Oh man. Chloe must be devastated." He gave a quick glance to the circle around Garrett, looking for his father to give him the contract. He had to get out of here and back to Chloe. "Where's Dad?"

"He's been behind closed doors all day."

That was weird. "Okay, I'm going to see him and leave. Bye, Gramma." He stepped away from her, but she held tight to the fabric of his T-shirt.

"One more thing, lad."

He stifled a sigh of frustration, waiting for some more bad news from town.

"You know what the Irish say about love?"

"Six hundred things that you have committed to memory or stitched on a pillow on your bed?"

"Cross-stitch? For this Internet sensation?" She gave a scoffing laugh. "Hashtag old school." She yanked him a little closer. "The only thing perfect about love is how imperfect it is."

He frowned. "I never heard that."

"Oh, I just made it up for my blog today. I wanted to test it out on you. Do you like it?"

"Kind of, yeah. Keep working on it, though." He reached down to give her a kiss, and she patted his cheek again.

"You keep working on it, too."

He wanted to, but if there was no vote and no

tourism push in Bitter Bark…why would Chloe stay?

An unfamiliar weight in his chest slowed him a little, but he hustled into the house, looking for Dad, surprised to find his office empty since Gramma had said he'd been behind closed doors. Didn't that mean working? Where would he be?

Checking out the downstairs, he took the steps two at a time to round the large center hallway to make his way back to his parents' room. Well, his dad's room now.

Sure enough, the door was closed. Shane tapped. "You in there, Dad?"

He heard some movement, a throat clear, some papers shuffle. "Something wrong, Shane?"

Yeah, Dad's voice sounded…weird. "I want to give you this DOD contract."

"Under the door."

What? He put his hand on the doorknob and turned it slowly, inching it open. "You okay?" he asked.

He heard his dad sigh. And sniff. Good God, was he crying?

He pushed the door all the way and got his answer, and the jolt of it nearly knocked him backward. Dad hadn't cried since the funeral, not since the day he'd come down from this very room and planted the idea that all the Kilcannon siblings leave their current jobs and move back to Bitter Bark to start a world-class canine facility.

All but Aidan, who was in the military, jumped at the opportunity. Building this business had been the thing that saved them all from grief, transferring their pain into creating something that Mom had always dreamed of.

"Dad." He took a few steps into the room. "Hey, man, are you all right?"

He was seated at the little blue settee that Shane always thought was more for form than function, placed in front of a fireplace about six or eight feet from the bed. On a coffee table, he spied a slew of pictures.

Oh boy. Someone was stumbling down memory lane.

"Fine, fine, Son." He wiped his reddened face. "Just got a little lost today."

Shane closed the door behind him, feeling that familiar kick of fury, but now wasn't the time to close off and walk out and be pissed off that life screwed him. 'Cause life screwed Daniel Kilcannon even more.

"What brought this on?" he asked, propping himself on a low wooden chest at the foot of the bed. There was another chair in that little sitting area, but he wasn't sure he wanted to get that close to what looked like about a hundred pictures that covered about thirty-six spectacular years.

"Stupid little anniversary."

Today? It wasn't their wedding anniversary, or the anniversary of the day she died. But Shane knew his parents well, and one of their "things" had been remembering dates. The first time they took a vacation together, the day they got engaged, the day they bought their first car.

"You two and your anniversaries," Shane said, memories drifting through his head. "Half the time nobody in the family knew what you were celebrating."

"That's why it was fun," he said, picking up a picture and putting it down. "Your mom and I had inside jokes. Not easy with six rug rats, but important. Kept us..." He swiped his eye again. "You know. Together."

"So what was today's anniversary, if you don't mind me asking?"

Dad looked up, his eyes the same blue as Gramma's, but much sharper, despite the fact they'd obviously been well-watered today. "I do mind you asking, and I don't think you want to know. It's, you know, private."

Private? Like...oh. He knew his parents met when they were both freshmen at Vestal Valley College and, yes, they got married young. But Liam's birthday was six months after their anniversary, so everyone knew why they'd gotten married at twenty and how it happened. But some things a son didn't want to think too hard about.

"But this anniversary took you to a dark place."

"Dark?" Dad laughed softly. "Nothing dark about reliving the best three and a half decades a man ever had. I've spent the day in the bedroom with her." His lips curled in a wry smile. "Just like we did thirty-eight years ago today."

Yeah. TMI. But something wended around his heart and squeezed so hard, Shane couldn't breathe for a moment.

Dad toyed with another picture, studying it for a long time. "She was pregnant with you here." He held it out to Shane, who stayed paralyzed like he had lead in his belly. "We still didn't have a real home, since we were here and Gramma and Grandpa hadn't yet handed over the Waterford reins. I'd opened my practice in town when we found out you were on the way. Take a look."

Shane relented and stood to reach for the picture, barely glancing at the image of a dazzling young twentysomething with a toddler holding one of her hands and the other resting on a sizable baby bump. He dropped it back on the table and returned to his seat.

"We were so happy," Dad said, picking up another photo. "It's the only thing that really matters, you know."

"To be happy?"

Dad snorted. "No, to be loved. To love. It's the only thing that lasts."

Lasts? Was he out of his mind? Shane knocked his knuckles together. "Except, you know, when it doesn't."

He didn't get an answer to that, but Dad cast his eyes down at the sea of photos. "You're so angry, Shane."

"Angry? Yeah, I guess I'm still mad about it. I want to punch walls if I think too hard about never seeing her again. Don't you?"

Dad shook his head. "If being mad at her or at what happened is some stage of grief, then I got through it quickly. God took her, Son, on the day and time He wanted her."

"A mother of six? Happily married? Fifty-five years old and healthy as an ox? What kind of God does that?"

"The one I'm going to face one day and account for how I handled it."

Shane fought the urge to flick that off, knowing better than to mock God in front of his Irish Catholic Dad. Hell, his parents had frowned at him when he'd even considered practicing family law, like it was his fault those crappy marriages ended up in divorce court.

"You'll never be able to find love of your own until you let go of that anger, Shane."

This time he did choke at the comment. "Not like you and Mom had, since that's pretty much the stuff of fairy tales. And didn't end that well after all."

Dad gave him a fiery, furious look, harsh enough to make Shane inch back.

"Don't you dare say that!" he exclaimed. "It ended, yes, but it lasted and will last forever."

Shane swallowed, a little damn sick of the platitudes and proverbs being strewn around this family. "Dad, come on. Love can't be reduced to a quote hanging on Gramma Finnie's wall. Nothing lasts forever. Even a relationship as nice and steady as you had with Mom, because look at you. Crying in your room all day. What the hell?"

His father stood, suddenly looming over him and throwing Shane back a few decades to childhood when he'd crossed a line in Dad's invisible sand. Criticizing the family in any way? A big, red line.

"I'll tell you what the hell, young man. I didn't have a 'relationship' with Annie. I had a *life* with her. And all the crap that entailed, from sick kids to low bank accounts to arguments that lasted deep into the night and the next morning."

"You never argued," Shane said quietly.

"Like hell we didn't. And I'll tell you something

else. There was nothing nice and steady about it. It was work. It took compromise. It got messy. It didn't always feel good and certainly wasn't always happy."

Shane blinked. "Sure looked that way to us kids."

"Because it was *real*, Shane Kilcannon. Our love for each other was real, down to the molecular level. Your mother and I loved each other the way we breathed, without thinking about whether or not there would be another breath. We just knew there would be."

Until there wasn't. Didn't he see that? "But then she died," he said softly, reaching out to calm his dad.

"Not here." Dad slapped his chest. "She's as alive in here as she was when she was in that bed behind you. I still hear her laugh. I still feel her touch." His voice cracked. "I still love her and always will."

Oh God. Poor, broken, delusional widowed Dad.

Shane nodded, standing slowly. He had far too much respect for his father to try to make him see the error of his thinking. "I got it, Dad." He put his hand on the older man's shoulder. "I'm glad you've found a way to come to terms with losing her."

"I wish you would—"

"I have," he assured him, cutting off the lecture before it started. "I'm never going to be happy about it, but I'm a big boy, and I get that this is the card life dealt our family."

"I wish you would listen to your mother," he finished.

Oh man. "She's *dead*. And I can barely hear the sound of her voice in my head."

Dad closed his eyes as if that comment had gone too far. But Shane didn't apologize for it, because he loved and respected his father, but he wasn't going to lie to him.

"If you *could* hear that voice," he finally said, "you'd know what she'd say about your situation."

"What situation?" As if he didn't know.

"This thing with Chloe."

"Oh, man, give it a break. There's no thing or, yeah, there's a thing. Just a thing. Just a meaningless, temporary, physical thing. Not everyone can take that and turn it into…" He gestured toward the table full of memories. "That."

"Not with that attitude."

Shane rolled his eyes. "Okay, Dad. It's my attitude. It's always my attitude, not, you know, life. Death. God. Fate. Bad luck. Whatever."

"Yes, Shane, it is your attitude. You're cocky because you're uncertain. You're angry because you're in mourning. And you're lonely because you don't want to lose, so you won't take a chance."

Really? He blew out a noisy breath. "Okay, then. There's the contract and…don't stay up here too long. Garrett's taking Louie for adoption, and they're probably still down there."

"I'm not going anywhere," Dad said, turning back to the pictures. "I'm staying with Annie today."

That. That was exactly what Shane didn't want to be, exactly the ultimate loss a man who loved to win could not endure. How could you win at this love thing? If you have a great marriage—no matter how tough Dad said it was, theirs was great—it can end in a bad heartbeat. And the majority of people never even had anything that good, since Mom and Dad had beaten ridiculous odds and *still* lost.

Shane gave him one more pat on the shoulder and headed out, already prepared to say his goodbyes to Chloe now…not later, when it would hurt even more.

As he trotted down the stairs, his phone buzzed with a text, no doubt from her. He pulled it out and glanced at the screen, then read the message, which wasn't from her at all.

Oh, poor Chloe. She was about to learn the same lesson Dad had just had driven home to him.

Love didn't last.

Test that on your pithy blog posts, Gramma.

Love didn't last.

Carve that in your memory box, Dad.

Love didn't last.

Sorry you weren't around for whatever anniversary this was, Mom.

Chapter Twenty-One

C hloe had no idea what to do when she got home, other than stop calling this little house "home" and start packing. A flight to Miami could be booked in minutes, and her two suitcases' worth of clothes packed in under an hour, so leaving Bitter Bark was way too easy.

But she moved like she was walking in quicksand.

She hadn't been there three weeks yet, an incredibly short assignment for her. There was no real reason to feel quite this attached, other than the fact that she'd picked up a lover and a temporary dog.

Feeling out of sorts, Chloe walked from the living room into the kitchen, down the hall to the bedroom, back to the other guest room, and then did the whole loop over again. Daisy stayed on her heels, loyal to the end, and probably confused as hell.

"I'm confused, too," she admitted to Daisy, ending up in the kitchen. "I guess I have two options."

Daisy barked twice, then flattened herself on the floor, as if dying to hear what they are.

"No, not 'stay' or 'go,'" Chloe said. "Chocolate or

wine, those are my options. Let's go with wine. You'll have no interest in it."

She pulled out an open bottle of white she and Shane had shared for dinner last night and grabbed a wineglass from the drainboard.

And suddenly she froze.

She'd done that. She'd put that glass there. She'd washed it by hand because it was too delicate for the dishwasher and…*put it on the drainboard.*

She hadn't thought about it. Hadn't debated or struggled or tried to do something so normal. But she *hadn't put it in the cupboard.*

A sense of victory washed over her, as potent and dizzying as if she'd slugged the rest of the wine directly from the bottle.

And, hell, another few weeks and she might.

Maybe you should find a reason to stay.

Aunt Blanche's words came back to her.

"Maybe I just did."

Suddenly, Daisy jumped up and barked, trotting to the living room door, announcing Shane's arrival. Should she tell him? Should she share this? Would that be normal or a little weird? Would he understand the magnitude of a glass on the drainboard?

Gingerly putting both glass and bottle on the counter, she went to the door to let him in.

Daisy leaped on him first, of course, licking his cheeks with abandon because she knew Shane loved that greeting. Chloe? Not so much. But the way things were going, Daisy might be licking her face soon, too. Change was in the air. *Normal* was in the air.

"Hi." He looked up from the tongue bath, something in his eyes she'd never seen before and couldn't begin to interpret. "I heard about the vote."

Oh, it was sympathy. "Yeah, I lost before I even got a chance to try."

"You okay?" He straightened and looked at her, absently touching his face. "Let me wash that off."

"No." She grabbed his shoulders. "No, you don't have to."

"But I want to—"

"Kiss me." She yanked him closer and lifted up to get her mouth on his, but he jerked back.

"You don't like to kiss me after Daisy did."

"But that's not...normal." She gripped him. "I want to kiss you. Right on the mouth for about an hour and a half."

That very mouth kicked up in a half smile. "Okay. Losing is the new muddin'? Turns you on?"

No, *he* turned her on. Being normal turned her on. Life with him turned her on.

"Or you need consolation?"

"I need...you." She pulled him closer, finally getting that kiss, which was sweet and tender, but maybe a little more tentative than she'd expected. No, definitely more tentative.

She broke the contact, easing back to search his face for clues. Something was definitely wrong. "What's the matter, Shane?"

"Marie wants Daisy back," he said softly. "Tomorrow morning, if possible."

She let that settle over her, the second blow to her happiness in a few hours. "That's sooner than you expected, right?"

"She got upgraded to a lighter boot, and she's more mobile. Misses Daisy like crazy."

Daisy came closer and panted, as if she instinctively knew she was the subject of the conversation.

"Who wouldn't? I sure will." Chloe reached down and gave Daisy's head a rub, getting her hand licked in gratitude.

"Hey." He took her chin and brought her face back up to his. "Where were we?"

No, the question was...where *are* we? But she didn't have the nerve to ask. Maybe...later. "We were here." She rose up to kiss him again.

No longer tentative, he angled his head and deepened the kiss, wrapping her tighter against him. "I'm covered with dirt, Chloe," he murmured, kissing her neck and already coasting his magical hands over her breasts and waist and hips.

"Just the way I like you." She doubled down on that statement by pulling at his T-shirt, tugging it up to get her hands on slightly sweaty, incredibly sexy skin. "Dirty Shame, take me to bed."

"Perfect Chloe, you've lost your mind."

She drew back, grabbing a handful of his muscles. "Don't you see? That's just it. I *haven't* lost my mind. That's my deepest fear, my greatest stumbling block, the reason I...I...put everything in the cupboard and not on the drainboard."

He laughed, shaking his head. "You're losing me, baby."

She pulled him in. "But I don't want to." Pressing her face against his solid shoulder, she bit back the sting of tears, a well of emotions so rich and complicated making her cling for dear life. "I don't want to lose you, Shane."

Very slowly, he tangled his fingers in her hair, cupping her head possessively and lifting her face to his. "I'm yours for the night."

For the night. *For the night.*

Didn't that tell her everything she needed to know?

She didn't have time to wrestle with that reality, because he kissed her so thoroughly and so deeply that the world spun out for a moment. Closing her arms around him, she let him guide her to the bedroom, barely feeling the floor beneath her feet on the way.

By the time they got there, half her clothes were in the hall. He kicked the door closed to keep Daisy out and guided Chloe to the bed, yanking his shirt off, stripping off his shorts, and helping her pull her cutoffs all the way off.

She wanted to slow down, to savor and taste, but this was different than any other time. This was a little desperate, a little frantic, a little…like the end.

She swallowed that thought and arched her back, concentrating on the delicious roughness of his palms over her breasts, shooting sparks and pleasure down her whole body. They rocked against each other, touching and kissing and not saying a word, not even a whisper of *please* or *yes* or *more.*

But she wanted to. Words bubbled up and echoed in her head. Every time she opened her mouth, he suckled her or caressed her or nibbled on a bit of her that melted in his mouth. The words lodged and seemed…daunting.

So while he laid her back and sheathed himself, she let the words sing in her head.

I want more than tonight.

He stroked her breasts and kissed the words silent.

I want it all.

He entered her with a fierce, furious thrust.

I love you. I love you. I love you.

Not trusting herself to not cry that out, lost in the glorious sensations that electrified her, Chloe bit her lip and choked back the confession. She rocked against him with a timeless, natural, perfect rhythm that rose and built and quaked them both.

Shane lost it first, bringing her with him, both of them shuddering with an exquisite release that lasted so long it almost hurt.

But she hadn't said a word. Not those words. Now, there was nothing but long, ragged, exhausted breaths and silence.

Absolute silence.

It sounded an awful lot like…the end.

Shane stared at the grass where Daisy was digging and sniffing and felt the familiar weight of a sadness he'd known since childhood. It came with the territory, and now Chloe would feel it.

Saying goodbye to a dog who'd stolen your heart was one of the hardest things he'd ever learned as a kid. Never really learned how to do it right, but knew that it was a helluva lot better to say so long to one that was going to a happy home than one that was dying.

And saying goodbye to a person?

Well, guess he would find out soon enough. He half expected to wake up to find her packing this morning, ready to run off to some Caribbean island

and help those people do what Bitter Bark wouldn't let her do. Maybe she'd meet a guy there and—

"I decided to go."

He whipped around and took in the sight of Chloe in work clothes, which was almost, but not quite, as good as Chloe in no clothes. She wore a crisp red and white dress as narrow as a pencil with a tiny, shiny red belt around the middle.

So she didn't mean *go* with him to take Daisy home to Marie.

"I feel like I should be at the town meeting even if there isn't a vote. If nothing else, I need to support my aunt Blanche when she makes her resignation speech."

"I get that. I know my whole family is going."

She blinked at that. "Are you?"

He threw a look at Daisy. "I promised Marie I'd bring Daisy back this morning."

"Um...what is she doing?" Chloe asked, her gaze following his. "Why is she rolling?"

"Dead snake? Maybe that mouse carcass? Something she wants to smell like."

She snorted softly. "Is that why she stinks after she's been out here?"

"Wow, have you changed when it comes to dogs. And...everything."

"I guess Marie won't mind if she shows up stinking like Eau de Snake. I usually use the hose, shampoo, and a big bucket."

Kind of like the shower they'd taken last night after sex, only nothing could have been as wet and intimate and cleansing as that. They'd skipped dinner and fallen asleep in each other's arms, both of them struggling with the inevitable goodbye.

Well, better start with this one. "I need to get on the road," he said, his voice a little hoarse. "So, this is your, uh, goodbye."

The slightest bit of color faded from Chloe's cheeks, leaving behind the soft powder blush she'd added when she put on makeup this morning. "With Daisy."

"I'm not going to live with Miz Marie."

She gave a soft laugh. "I could conceivably take a flight out this afternoon, following the meeting."

It hit like a sucker punch. "Would you do that?"

Swallowing hard, she looked at him. "What's the point of staying?"

"Well, when you put it like that…"

"What other way is there to put it, Shane? This has been…" She shrugged and let out a sigh that came from somewhere deep and bittersweet. "Fun seems like an understatement."

"Ya think?" He knew he sounded hurt, but he was the one who'd said *for the night* when she told him she didn't want to lose him. He was the one who'd held back every tender endearment and wretched confession while they made love. He was the one who was flat-out terrified of losing.

Of losing *her*.

Which was why he would.

As if sensing the tension, Daisy came bounding over, dirt on her paws and around her mouth, her gaze pinned on Chloe. These two had both fallen for each other. Chloe brushed some hair off her face, hooking the strands over her ears as she looked down at the dog.

"You…" she whispered. "You really shouldn't

have done that, you know?" There was no condemnation in her voice, nothing but love. Still, Daisy looked uncertain, knowing she shouldn't have rolled in dead things. "You shouldn't have stolen my heart."

Somehow, Shane managed to smile.

But Chloe hitched up her skirt, high on her thighs, so she could crouch down in front of the dog. Reaching both hands to Daisy's face, she stroked behind her ears.

"But you did," she said softly, holding Daisy's head with the skill and comfort of someone who had no fear of dogs or dirt. "You sneaked into my life when I wasn't looking and changed everything. You kissed me when it was the last thing I thought I wanted. You gave me ideas and took me on walks and taught me to conquer my biggest hang-ups. You got on my bed and made me want to spend every single day and night with you." Her voice cracked with a sob as she collapsed onto the ground and pulled Daisy right into her chest, snuggling her with two arms wrapped around the dog's neck.

Shane tried to breathe, but her words stole any chance of getting air.

Finally, she looked up at Shane, a mascara-stained tear running down a face of pure misery as she whispered into Daisy's floppy ear. "I love you."

I love you, too.

The words lodged in his throat like a dry bone, choking him.

Was it even possible? Could she ever say those things to him and not Daisy? Maybe she had, and he was simply…paralyzed with fear.

She kissed Daisy's head and then bent her own, no doubt the way she'd seen Shane do a hundred times, in complete submission, offering her hair and neck and cheeks for a tongue bath.

And got one.

"Now you be good," she said again.

Daisy answered by lifting both paws to Chloe's shoulders and dragging them down, leaving paths of filth on her white dress. Chloe didn't even flinch. "I'll never forget you," she murmured into fur that had to smell rank. "Goodbye, sweetheart."

She kissed Daisy again, then pushed herself up, looking down at the dirt marks on her chest. "I have to change," she said, wiping at the tears streaking her cheek.

"I'm pretty sure I just witnessed the most a person could ever change."

She smiled and reached up, touching his cheek. "Thank you for giving me Daisy. Even if it was for a short time, I'll never forget her." She stroked her thumb under his lips. "Or you."

Turning, she headed back into the house, leaving him to stand in the sun with Daisy, his heart shifting as some old pain melted away and made room for a whole different kind of loss.

Unless he changed, too.

Chapter Twenty-Two

Bushrod Square was almost empty. On a summer weekday morning, there were no Vestal Valley College students milling about, and most of the residents or owners of shops had poured into the assembly room in the Bitter Bark Town Hall.

Chloe took the longest way possible around the square to soak up the midsummer morning in one of her favorite places, her heels clicking with satisfaction on the brick pavement. She waved to Betsy, the lady who walked Jackson, that friendly golden she'd met while having lunch with Shane, and stopped to take one more picture of the *not* bitter bark tree because it looked majestic in the morning sun. Even the distant sound of the trash truck coming into town filled her with a sense of home and normalcy.

Goodbye, sweet town. There's nothing bitter about you. Well, most of you.

As she reached Ashland Real Estate Company, she curled her lip at the idea of Dave Ashland taking over Aunt Blanche's job as mayor. Would he sit on his phone for the entire town council meeting? Would he have any better ideas to help Bitter Bark?

As she reached a tiny side street that ran perpendicular to Bushrod Avenue, she heard a loud clang that startled her out of her thoughts, making her turn to look down what was really a small alley. It served as a passway between this street and the next behind the buildings, but Chloe had never ventured down because there was a dumpster in there, and she avoided them at all costs.

But it was the dumpster that had made that clang—or rather something that had been tossed into the dumpster. She couldn't make out a person, but someone was on the other side heaving black Hefty bags into the trash, and they must have contained metal.

Something else went over the side. A small can?

Just as she was about to look away, she saw a large figure step out from behind the dumpster. A man who had to have been crouching behind it to throw things away.

Was that Dave Ashland? What was he doing? She squinted into the shadows formed by the buildings on either side, catching a glimpse of him heaving an arm full of papers, flipping them over the top of the dumpster so that a few fluttered like white rain. One floated into the alley, and he ran after it, seemingly frantic, grabbed it, and wadded it up, shooting it in with the rest of the trash.

He stepped back and brushed off, then checked his watch.

The rumble of the trash truck, still a few blocks away, seemed to make his shoulders drop in relief as he turned toward her and started hustling out, as fast as a man that size could hustle.

Something made Chloe inch back, letting the brick

wall of his office building shield her, bracing herself for the inevitable encounter. He'd supported her efforts, with much to gain as a real estate broker if property values rose. But the fact that he was running unopposed to take Aunt Blanche's place really irked her. Should she confront him about it? Or maybe take the high road and suggest one of her alternative ideas so Bitter Bark wouldn't fail?

He stepped out of the alleyway into the bright light, a sheen of sweat on his broad forehead.

"Hi, Dave."

He nearly jumped out of his skin. "Oh! Oh. Oh, Chloe. Hello." He drew back, clearly stunned to see her. "What are you doing here?"

"I'm going to the same meeting you are, I suppose."

He nodded a few times, his gaze darting past her. "Oh yes. Big meeting. Big."

For a guy about to announce he was essentially a shoo-in for the mayoral position, he seemed pretty agitated.

"I'm sorry my ideas didn't work out," she said, trying to find a way to broach the subject of new ideas.

"Yeah, yeah." He nodded again, his attention pulled to the backup beeps from the trash truck that was now across the square.

"That'll be here soon," he said. "So..." He gestured for her to move. "They'll have to make that tight turn to get to my dumpster." He swiped his hand over thin hair, squinting at the truck.

"Are you worried about that?" she asked, trying to figure out why he seemed so uptight.

"Well, yes, of course. I want them to hurry because…" He glanced over his shoulder at the dumpster. "Because as the next mayor, I'm very concerned that we share trash collection with another town, and I want them to be speedy. And thorough."

He dabbed his sweaty forehead again, and as he did, Chloe caught sight of a black slash on the mound of his thumb. And another on the knuckle.

Was that…Sharpie? The impossible-to-wash-off marker, unless you had the vinegar and water mix she'd nearly drowned in yesterday?

Her heart skipped as he wiped his hands on his trousers, and she followed, her gaze on that mark. Okay, he might be sloppy with a marker or…he might be a *vandal*.

Is that what he'd tossed into the trash along with his papers? Evidence? Paint cans? Markers?

She had to know.

Beaming at him, she held out her hand. "Well, let me be the first to congratulate you on becoming the next mayor."

Hesitating, he shook her hand, and she peered down at his chunky knuckles. Oh yes, that was the marker she'd spent hours cleaning yesterday. And some paint embedded in his fingernails.

"Yes, yes, thanks." He shot another look at the trash truck, as if he could will it to move a little faster…so it would remove the evidence that the man who would be mayor was responsible for defacing every business in Bushrod Square.

Not on her watch.

"Well, you better go to the meeting," she said, pulling away. "I'm going to, uh…" She looked at the square and caught sight of the golden retriever on his second pass around. "Say goodbye to Jackson, one of my favorite dogs. And you better go. That meeting is starting, and your big client is there."

His ruddy complexion paled. "Not that he bothered to mention that to me," he grumbled. "Had to find out from a tenant ten minutes ago."

"Then go," she urged him. "You don't want to be late for your own party, Mr. Mayor."

She gave him a nudge in the direction of town hall, and he looked a little perturbed, but then nodded, taking off in that direction. She made a show of crossing the street toward the square in case he turned to look back at her, but his attention was riveted on that trash truck. Which had just moved to the next corner.

Chloe would have to go fast if she wanted to prove his guilt and save Aunt Blanche's job.

She took no time to think about it, though, running into the alley and thanking Daisy for ruining her first outfit and forcing her to change into white linen slacks. So perfect for…dumpster diving.

"You can do this, Chloe. You can do this," she told herself as she reached the rusty six-foot-high vat full of trash. "That dumpster is not going to hurt you."

But if that son of a bitch had vandalized this town, she'd take him down. She'd strut right into that meeting holding the evidence she got from his trash bin and show them what a mistake it would be to make him mayor.

It would be her parting gift to Bitter Bark. Maybe Aunt Blanche would reconsider stepping down. It would be a small victory, but she'd take it.

Holding that thought and her nose, she stood on

her tiptoes to peer inside the dumpster. There it was. Ashland's trash bag, partially covered in a sea of papers, and two small cans of paint and some brushes.

There was her proof.

Along with some soda cans, empty water bottles, a grease-stained paper bag, and plastic bags. Oh, not just any bags, but bags she recognized all too well. Bags and bags of dog poop from the cleaning stations around the park, with the expected number of flies feasting on the stench.

Oh God. She swayed and almost lost her balance.

Would she let a little disgusting trash stop her from taking down the man responsible for her loss? No way. No freaking way.

She gripped the side of the dumpster, lifted her leg to place her high-heeled sandal on a metal bar sticking out, and hoisted herself up, pressing her stomach against the edge to reach all the way in. Her fingers grazed the yellow ties of Dave's bag, but she couldn't quite get it.

The smell made her stomach roil, but she forced her arm to stretch more, focusing on one spot to concentrate, staring at the handwritten words she could read on Dave's discarded paperwork, reading them in her head as she challenged her body to reach that tie.

James Fisker. James Fisker. James Fisker.

Finally, she looped the tie and yanked the bag out, swinging it to the ground.

"Yes!" She ripped open the top and peered inside to see spray-paint cans, thick markers, and a few brushes caked in paint. And clothes. A pair of paint-splattered sneakers, jeans, and a once-white T-shirt that bore the words *Ashland Realty* with so much incriminating paint on it that she almost cried.

But her head was still echoing the words she'd read. James Fisker. James Fisker. James Fisker.

Why would someone have signed one piece of paper with the same name what had to be...fifty times?

She blinked. To practice it. To *forge* it. What the—

She spun around and hoisted herself up again, not even noticing the foul smell now, because her laser focus was pinned on that paper. And the ones next to it. Deed of Warranty. Land Sale. Mortgage.

Why was he throwing away important papers and forging the signature of a man who was his client— and on his way into town this very morning? The trash truck backup beeps screeched through the morning air.

And why was he so anxious that the garbage collectors take it all away?

She suddenly spied the balled-up paper she'd seen him throw in, resting precariously on a piece of metal jutting inside the dumpster. With a modest stretch, she snagged it and dropped to the ground again, spreading it open, smoothing her hand over the fancy letterhead.

National Security Lenders & Mortgage Company.

She scanned the words.

Dear Mr. Ashland...pleasure to secure your mortgage in the amount of $5 million...for the property parcel located along Bushrod Avenue...Bitter Bark, North Carolina...

This wasn't Dave Ashland's land! It belonged to James Fisker. How did he get a mortgage on it?

By forging the real owner's signature.

"Oh my God." This was damning, criminal evidence.

But why wouldn't he shred it? Because he just found out from a tenant ten minutes ago that James Fisker was in town, leaving Dave no time to destroy evidence. Oh, yeah. Desperate men did dumb things.

But her thoughts were drowned out by the sound of the trash truck, backing up to get into position to come down the alleyway.

Evidence that he was clearly anxious to have the trash truck remove.

Oh, no. They were not taking one single thing out of this dumpster, unless it was Chloe herself, because she was getting that evidence to take the son of a bitch down.

Two minutes later, she was standing in the dumpster, plucking through a mountain of what looked like damning evidence, each one clicking the story into place. But she couldn't be sure. There were so many contracts, so much fine print, so much...*legalese*.

She pulled out her phone and tapped one button and waited for Shane to answer.

"Chloe," he said, his voice low. "I'm so glad you called. I can't stop thinking about you. I can't let you—"

"No time for that! Where are you?"

"Just leaving town with Daisy. What's wrong?"

"I need a good lawyer. Right now. Right this minute, Shane."

"Where are you?"

She glanced to the side and then down at the bags of poop near her feet. "If I told you, you wouldn't believe me. Meet me in my aunt's office as soon as you possibly can."

"Okay, I'm on my way. But, Chloe, listen to me. I have to tell you something. You can't leave. You can't let us end. I can't. I love—"

A deafening bang cut him off, followed by the warning beeps and the rumble of a trash truck engine as it closed in on her dumpster.

"What the hell is that, Chloe?"

"Garbage truck."

"Where are you?"

"Dumpster diving."

After a second of stunned silence, he whispered, "I'm on my way."

She stuffed the phone in her pocket, gathered her precious papers, and managed to climb out, seconds before a shocked garbage collector reached her. But none of that racket drowned out the sound of what Shane had been about to say.

Clinging to the sound of his unfinished declaration, she ran to the town hall.

Chapter Twenty-Three

Chloe reeked.

And Shane couldn't remember anything ever smelling better. She smelled like hope and promise and a woman who was willing to do anything to get what she wanted.

With each passing moment, he was more certain that was him.

Daisy was pretty fond of Stinky Chloe, too. She'd had her snout all over Chloe from the minute the two of them had arrived at the mayor's office and, after Chloe washed her hands, had gone straight to work on the fastest legal argument he'd ever created in his life.

"Now I know why he was setting up Jeannie and Mitch when I saw him in the park that day," Shane mused as the evidence mounted. "From day one, he's been opposed to this idea, sabotaging you so it would fail, but trying to look like he supported it."

Chloe nodded, her attention on the papers she'd found while Shane called up the program to run a title search using her aunt's PC. He handed that over to Chloe when he finally reached the chief legal counsel of National Security Lenders. The other lawyer gave

Shane an earful of good information, and Shane repaid it by giving him the exact address the man needed.

The whole thing had taken less than an hour, but left them scant seconds to crash the meeting before her aunt took the podium to officially resign.

"Come on, come on," Chloe urged as Shane put the finishing touches on his notes and took one more look at the key documents he'd use. Dave Ashland was going down so hard, and not just off the mayor's podium. Someone was headed to prison. "It's almost ten o'clock."

"Okay, I'm ready." Out of the corner of his eye, he saw her leashing Daisy. "Don't you want to leave her here?"

She shot him a look like he'd suggested tossing the dog out the window, making him laugh and fall a little *more* in love with her.

A minute later, the elevator door whooshed closed and trapped them alone together, traveling from the fourth-floor mayor's office to the assembly room on the first floor.

He sniffed and leaned closer. "Eau de Trash is my new favorite fragrance."

She smiled. "You should have seen the look on the garbage collector's face when I climbed out of that thing."

"Would have paid huge money for that."

"I just hope it was worth it," she said. "I hope Dave doesn't have some excuse or rationalization. Fisker is there, you know. What if he's in on it?"

Shane snorted. "He's not in on this or Ashland wouldn't have been tossing state's evidence like yesterday's newspaper," he assured her. "When Fisker finds out what Ashland did, he's going to thank us."

"You're absolutely one hundred percent sure?" she asked, squeezing her hands together as if she couldn't contain the mix of anxiety and hope.

He leaned closer. "Absolutely one hundred percent sure." He lowered his head for a kiss, but she inched back.

"About this case."

"Oh, I'm only about eighty percent sure of the case." He winked. "About you? I'm one hundred percent." A thousand percent. A million.

The elevator clunked to a stop, and the doors opened in front of the closed assembly room on the ground floor of Bitter Bark Town Hall.

"Only eighty?" she asked.

"That wasn't the important number."

She gave a shaky smile and pointed to their destination. "It is now."

"Chloe." He reached for her hand before they walked out. "I've won cases with way less evidence and a real judge and jury. But I need to know one thing before I go in there. I need to know. Am I going to win or lose you? That's all that matters to me."

She searched his face for a long moment, her eyes as dark as he'd ever seen them, like bottomless pools that he wanted to climb into. "Shane Kilcannon doesn't lose."

"I will if I don't have you."

"Then win."

But he didn't know if she was telling him he'd win her...or ordering him to win the case.

So he had to do both.

With an easy nudge, holding all the papers from

the dumpster, printouts of the title searches he'd run, and the case law he'd had a friend in real estate law email to him, he ushered her toward the door.

"My family will be up front," he whispered as he reached to open it. "Sit with them."

"Really?"

"That's where you belong."

The smile that lit up her face was the last thing he saw before they walked into the large meeting room with at least three hundred familiar faces filling rows and rows of metal chairs. A few faces turned to see who'd come in late, but most were riveted on the woman at the podium.

Blanche stuttered a little at the sight of the new arrivals in the back, her gaze split between Chloe, who headed up the left-side aisle, causing a bit of a stir as she held on to Daisy's leash, and Shane, who went up the aisle on the opposite side.

In the middle of the front row, he spotted Dave Ashland, who glanced at him, did a double take, then returned his attention to the stage. Next to Dave was a very old man with white hair and suspenders whom Shane immediately recognized as James Fisker, a wealthy developer who'd lived in Bitter Bark until he retired to Florida about fifteen years ago.

Did old Mr. Fisker know he was sitting next to a man who'd essentially stolen five million dollars from him? Well, he was about to.

"And so, friends and citizens of Bitter Bark, it is with a heavy heart that I officially resign as—"

"I object." Shane walked right to the front of the room, not caring that his terminology and technique were all wrong. He had to stop her and get on that stage.

A rumble ran through the crowd and, although he was tempted, he refused to look directly at Ashland. Any clue could give the man a chance to find a way to escape.

"Uh, Shane, there's no objection here. I'm resigning."

"Not so fast." The stage was low, and he was up in one easy step.

Behind Blanche, the members of the town council sat at a long wrap table, looking at each other and him, confusion on their faces.

"I'm making a motion to stop you from saying another word until I speak."

The crowd noise rose, along with some specific complaints.

"Your girlfriend lost, Shane, give it a break."

"This isn't how we run these meetings."

"You don't own this town, Kilcannon."

"No, I don't," he said, choosing to answer that question as he calmly moved Blanche from the podium and set his papers down. "But that man, right there in the front row, James Fisker? He does own quite a bit of it. Is that not true, Mr. Fisker?"

The man sat up straight, stunned to be called on in the middle of the melee. "I suppose that is, yes."

"In fact, is it not true that you are the rightful owner of the parcel of land that runs from along Bushrod Avenue from Mountainview Street on the south to Vestal Road on the north, currently known as the western perimeter of Bushrod Square?"

Ashland visibly paled, giving Shane a boost. Shane stole a look to his right, catching a glimpse of Chloe, seated next to his sister Molly, then Gramma, Dad,

Darcy, and Liam in the second row. She gave him a secret thumbs-up, which shot even more adrenaline and confidence into his veins.

"I do own that land," Fisker said, leaning forward.

"Then may I present this exhibit as evidence that someone else has taken a five-million-dollar mortgage out on the property?"

"What?" Fisker stood now, gray brows furrowing. "That's preposterous. I've owned that land since the 1970s. I collect rent from every business on that property. You are sadly mistaken, young man."

But he wasn't mistaken about the look of horror on the face of Ashland, who went wide-eyed with disbelief and fear.

"What do you have there?" Fisker insisted, coming closer.

"The Warranty Deed, signed by you, selling that parcel outright."

"I did not sell it!" If he'd had a cane, which he almost needed, he'd have hammered the floor.

Behind Fisker, the audience went from momentarily rapt to grumbling questions and comments.

"But this deed says you have actually sold it to the Ashland Real Estate Company."

"I let him handle the leases," he said.

"That's right, Shane." Dave Ashland hoisted himself up, finally gathering his wits. "I don't know what it is you're up to, but this kind of shenanigan is exactly why we're running your girlfriend and her ridiculous dog ideas out of town."

That got another reaction from the crowd. But Shane took over with a booming voice in the microphone.

"Then can you explain this, Mr. Ashland?" He held

up the wrinkled letter that Chloe had rescued from the dumpster. "This is a note, supported with complete contractual documentation, confirming that you, as sole owner of this parcel, took out a five-million-dollar mortgage using this bill of sale transferring the property from Mr. Fisker to you."

"Impossible!" Fisker marched toward the stairs to join Shane. "I never sold anyone my land."

"Well, he didn't sell it…" Dave said, his voice less powerful now. "I handle the leases, and I think you got your paperwork mixed up, Shane. You're a dog trainer, not a real lawyer."

"Then you might have wished one of my dogs had eaten this." He lifted the page of practice signatures. "Your extensive attempts to duplicate Mr. James Fisker's signature, which you then, using your own real estate contractual creation skills, were able to forge on sale papers."

"I…I…this is crazy." He looked to the crowd for support, but about three hundred people were either slack-jawed or furious.

"And for that reason, is it not true that you have done everything in your ability to stop this town from increasing the flow of tourism?" Shane demanded.

"Why would I do that?"

"That you, in fact, used marker and paint to vandalize and deface personal and public property?"

He snorted. "That's patently ridiculous."

"Then will you explain the marker on your hand, in your trash, and on this Ashland Realty T-shirt?" He held up the shirt to a loud gasp from the audience.

"Why would I do that?" Ashland demanded.

"To keep the property value low!" Fisker

screamed, joining Shane at the podium. "So I wouldn't sell it, since I've asked you every year for a decade to tell me when the value would be right for me to sell. Several of the tenants have asked me about buying part of the land, and I'd like to sell, but you told me I'd lose too much money."

That got the crowd going.

Billy was first, shooting to his feet. "I've wanted to buy that bar for five years, but Fisker wouldn't sell!"

"We've made multiple offers to buy our piece of land." That was Jane Gruen, owner of the B&B.

"I'd love to own my spa." The bright red hair of Jeannie Slattery popped up from the back. "And if this is true, it's a travesty."

"It's not, it's not," Dave said, turning from one side to the other like there had to be someone to support him. His gaze landed on Chloe, and his eyes narrowed. "It's all her fault! She went through my trash and forged all this to make me look bad."

Chloe stood. "I went through your trash to find the markers and paint you used to vandalize every business in Bushrod Square."

By then, all three hundred people were up, and the place turned into a noisy free-for-all of insults and fury. Ashland stumbled backward, and Daisy started barking like gunshots through the assembly hall.

"Quiet!" Blanche smashed her gavel from the center seat on the dais behind Shane. "Return to order! Quiet!"

After a minute and a few more gavel drops, some semblance of order returned. Chloe quieted Daisy, and Dave Ashland started backing up toward the side door, holding out his hands.

"I can explain everything. I can show that I've been set up. I can—"

The side doors popped open, and two deputy sheriffs walked in. "Mr. Ashland, you are under arrest—"

The room exploded again, calling out their opinions as the officer finished his speech, handcuffing Dave. The other deputy came up to the stage to relieve Shane of the reams of evidence he had, and a low level of chaos ensued for another few minutes.

When it died down and Dave had been escorted out, Shane started to walk off the stage to get to Chloe, since she was all that mattered now that the work was done. He had to convince her to stay. But how?

"Just one minute, young man," Fisker choked into the microphone.

Shane froze, not liking the sound of his voice. He turned and eyed the other man.

"I owe you a debt of gratitude," he finally said.

Exhaling, Shane held up his hand. "It's fine. And it wasn't me, it was Chloe Somerset who realized what was going on. That's Blanche Wilkins's niece, right there. The tourism expert. The..." *Woman I love.* "The one who has a vision for this town."

"Then I owe her, too," Fisker said. "And I pay my debts. Just tell me how."

"Seriously, you don't have..." He let the words fade as an idea formed, and he took a step closer. "Mr. Fisker, you are the largest land owner in Bitter Bark, right?"

"I am."

"So you would have some say about what goes on in this town."

"I imagine."

Shane returned to the podium, taking the man's arm and inching him away from the mic, whispering in his ear. Fisker nodded, listening, and Shane continued.

Fisker drew back, blinking at him. "Stay right here next to me in case I forget something."

Shane nodded, inching to the side and locking his hands in front of him while Fisker pulled the microphone closer to his mouth.

"Ladies and gentlemen." Fisker's reed-thin voice in the mic managed to silence the room. "I make a motion that we vote our esteemed Mayor Blanche Wilkins to continue her term for the next four years."

After a second of stunned silence, the room burst into applause, making Blanche stand up and put her hand on her chest as if she couldn't contain her heart. Shane looked at Chloe, who covered her mouth with two hands and locked on his gaze with gratitude.

"Thank you," she said, blowing him a kiss.

He angled his head as if to say, *There's more.*

"And," Fisker continued, "I make a motion that we launch the Better Bark program to change the name of this town for the span of one year, during which time, under the direction of our mayor, we will undertake a massive promotional program to be known as the most-dog-friendly town in America."

Another roar rose with applause, with several people standing in support of the idea.

Residents hooted and hollered. Someone— someone who wasn't Daisy—did a loud dog bark.

Chloe leaned forward, her eyes glistening.

When it quieted, Fisker turned to Shane. "What was that last thing?"

Shane pointed to Chloe.

"Oh, oh, yes," Fisker recalled. "And I make a motion to offer a job as director of tourism to...what was her name again?"

"Chloe Somerset."

"Chloe Somerset," Fisker repeated.

She stood slowly as the old man said her name, and one more round of resounding approval rolled through the assembly hall.

Fisker, as if he'd had enough, stepped away from the podium, and one of the town council people helped him off the dais. Mayor Wilkins took his place, and pretty much all hell broke loose, but Shane didn't take in any of it.

All he could do was walk toward that beautiful woman in white as she walked to him. They met at the foot of the stage, and he folded her in his arms, the sound of the gavel falling over and over again.

Or maybe that was his heart slamming into his chest as Chloe reached for him, and he kissed her with all the love and certainty he felt.

Maybe it was one in a zillion. But he had a feeling his chance of winning this was in the bag.

A hand landed on his back and Chloe's, breaking their kiss. It was Gramma, beaming from one to the other.

"Welcome to Better Bark!" his grandmother exclaimed.

"We did it, Gramma!" Chloe said on a laugh. "We got the name change."

"One of them. We still have one more to get changed, Miss *Somerset*."

Epilogue

Chloe Somerset needed a dog. A precious, loving, needy, adorable, snoring, slobberfest of a dog.

But there were so many to choose from, she was a little overwhelmed.

So for her first month and a half of living and working in Better Bark, when she walked through the Waterford Farm kennels to accompany Shane for morning training sessions, she'd spend some time with the rescues that came and, she was happy to note, went with frequency.

She'd start to connect with one, but something was missing. Shane told her it would happen organically, but the rescues didn't stay long at Waterford. Garrett would announce he'd found a home, don his sorry-looking canvas fedora, and scoop up the pup to whisk it to happiness.

Today, Shane had awakened early with even more of a gleam in his green-gold gaze and a promise in his kiss. He held Chloe's hand extra tight as they drove to Waterford just after dawn, quietly watching the sunrise create prisms in the morning mist.

And now, at the kennels, he seemed distracted, checking his phone frequently while she spent some time with the dogs.

At the puppy pen, which was usually empty, they stopped at the sight of a golden ball of fluff bouncing around like a lunatic baby bear. "Oh my word! What kind of dog is that?"

"That's Cranberry, she's a Pomeranian who was found in a bog up in Maine, and Garrett got hold of her. And she recently passed an exhaustive battery of behavior tests with flying colors. Didn't you, Cranberry?" He scooped her up into his arms, her little bubblegum tongue out for a lick in no time.

"Why did she have those tests?"

"Because she's being adopted to work as a therapy dog at an assisted-living facility in Raleigh."

"Awww."

"Yep, she's going to make the old folks smile."

Chloe reached over to scratch Cranberry's head. "You lucky dog. And those lucky folks." She felt Shane's gaze on her, somehow more intense. "You okay?" she asked.

"I am now." Lowering Cranberry back into the pen, he pulled out his phone again. "Yes, very okay. I have a surprise for you."

"You do?"

"Yep. She's pulling in the driveway right now. You ready to see an old friend? Brace for some face licking."

She sucked in a breath, her jaw dropping. "Daisy?"

"Marie is bringing her for a visit. I thought you'd like that."

She slid her arms around him and squeezed. "I'd

love that. I think my problem is that I'm comparing every dog to Daisy, and no one measures up."

"You'll find your dog," he said, returning the embrace with a kiss on the top of her head. "Or your dog will find you. Now let's go see your girl."

"I can't wait." She tugged him toward the door, her heart actually kicking up a little at the thought of a reunion with Daisy. They stepped into the sunshine just as Marie, Daisy's real mom and a wonderful woman with spiky gray hair and camo pants, climbed out of a truck, her left foot no longer in the orthopedic boot she'd worn when they'd taken Daisy home to her the day after the town meeting.

But Chloe's eyes weren't on Marie Boswell. She waited for the next occupant of that truck, a familiar brown and white barrel-chested dog who came to the door and waited for permission to get out.

"Daisy!" Chloe stretched her arms out, ready to run.

Marie gave a command, and Daisy took off, and they sprinted toward each other, meeting in the middle, where Daisy jumped and Chloe dropped to the ground for a barky, licky, happy reunion.

Chloe laughed, maybe teared up a little, and finally settled cross-legged on the grass with Daisy in her lap. She looked up as Marie came closer, with another dog on a leash. This one was about the same size as Daisy, maybe a little smaller, a dark, dark chocolate color with a snow-white chest and a single white stripe down its nose.

"Hello," Chloe said, both to the woman and the dog. "I'd get up, but I'm too happy."

The woman laughed. "And so's my Daisy. She's

happy and healthy, but I think she needs to come and visit you more often."

"Anytime," Chloe said, nuzzling Daisy. "And who's this?"

"This is Ruby."

Shane got on his knees in front of the new arrival, greeting Ruby the way he always approached a new dog. Head down, offering his neck for inspection, giving her a chance to know him.

"Hello, Ruby," he said.

"Ruby?" Chloe studied the dog, knowing immediately she was a Staffordshire terrier like Daisy. "She's pretty."

"Gorgeous," Shane agreed, loving the dog with his two strong hands now, moving them over and around her head with skill and affection.

"Ruby came into the North Ames shelter yesterday afternoon, and I texted Shane," Marie said, dropping the dog's leash. "She's about three, I think. Has been bounced around a bit. But she's got a good heart."

"Hey, Ruby." Chloe held her gaze, mesmerized by her slightly tilted eyes that held a little fear and a lot of hope.

The dog angled her head, as if she wanted to ask a question or beg for consideration. And Chloe's heart slid all over her chest with a burst of love.

"Shane mentioned that you might be looking for a sweet Staffy when you had to say goodbye to Daisy," Marie said. "I really wanted to find you one so I could say thank you for loving my girl so much when I was laid up."

Chloe looked up at Marie, putting an affectionate hand on Daisy's head. Which, of course, got a juicy lick. "I should thank you, Marie. Daisy made a dog lover out of me, and I honestly never dreamed that would happen."

"She's a dear girl," Marie agreed. "And so is Ruby."

Chloe leaned toward the dog, and Daisy climbed off her lap, going to sniff Shane. "C'mere, Ruby. Come."

She didn't move except for her tail, which ticktocked hopefully.

"She's not trained as well as Daisy," Marie said. "She's gentle as a mouse but doesn't know commands."

"Good thing I know a decent trainer," Chloe teased, getting on her knees to crawl a little closer. "Hey, Ruby," she whispered. "Come and see me."

Ruby took a few steps. Chloe lowered her head to let her sniff, then lifted her face for a sweet, quick lick on the cheek. Except, Ruby picked her mouth, making Chloe laugh a little as she wiped her mouth with the back of her hand.

"Looks like you know a little about training yourself," Marie mused.

"I know how to get myself kissed." She put both hands on Ruby's head like Shane had taught her, and instantly, the dog sat down. Chloe got down with her, eye to eye. After a moment of staring at each other, Chloe sat up and crossed her legs again, and this time, Ruby climbed right into the nest of her jeans and curled into...her spot.

"Oh," Chloe sighed, stroking her smooth, brown back slowly. "I think we're bonding."

She looked up to catch Marie and Shane sharing a look that told her this little love affair had been planned.

"I'm going to leave her here for a few minutes." Marie reached over and unhooked Ruby's leash. "I'll take Daisy for a little stroll while y'all get acquainted. I don't want Miss Daisy to get jealous."

"Thanks, Marie," Shane said, ruffling Daisy's coat before guiding her to Marie. "I think you nailed it."

As Marie and Daisy walked away, Shane scooted closer to Chloe. "You like her."

"She's special." Chloe stroked her some more. "I love her," she admitted and then looked at him, her eyes misting over. "I want to keep her."

"Well, now you know exactly how I feel about you."

She laughed. "Then all you need is a collar and a leash, and I'm yours."

"Let me go get one." He pushed up. "I'll be right back."

"Okay." She barely noticed he was gone, leaning over to rub her head against Ruby's. She smelled like the shampoo Chloe had used on Daisy, and the scent of oatmeal gave her the first pang of true love. The way she'd felt when she'd cleaned Daisy after a roll in something disgusting and they'd sit on the sofa together and she'd tell Daisy how much she was falling for Shane.

"We're going to be good friends," she promised the dog.

Ruby whimpered and let out a soft, shuddering sigh that somehow expressed exactly how Chloe felt at that moment. Content. Home. *Normal*. Well, as normal as being this in love could possibly feel.

Across the grass, she spotted Shane in the training area, talking to some of his family. She hadn't noticed them all out there before, but Liam and his shepherd, Jag, were intently listening to Shane, and Molly came over with their father. Garrett was there, too, with Jessie, and a minute later, Darcy came bounding out from the grooming building, darting to join them all. Marie was right there in the middle, with Daisy watching.

Daniel put a hand on Shane's shoulder, guiding his son away from the others to talk to him. Chloe watched as the man they called the Dogfather spoke to his son, too far away to know what the subject was, but close enough to see Shane looking into his father's eyes, and nodding.

After a moment, the two men embraced and Daniel patted Shane's shoulder, then whispered something in his ear that made them both laugh. Shane turned toward Chloe, grinning, then pointed behind her to the house.

There, she saw Gramma Finnie standing on the back patio, gazing out at the big yard.

They must have all come out to see if she'd fall in love with the new dog, she thought with another jolt of love and joy. No family had ever cared about her happiness like that, and she was suddenly a little overwhelmed by it, folding over again to transfer that happiness to Ruby.

"We're kind of both being adopted," she whispered into a silky ear.

Shane left his family, carrying a long red leash, and Chloe finally stood. She curled her hand around Ruby's collar, not certain how she'd act if another dog came bounding out.

"Here you go." He handed her the leash, and when

she took it, he snagged her hand. "Are you sure?" he asked.

"Oh, completely. I am one hundred percent positive this is love."

"So am I." He pulled her closer. "This is definitely a forever, once-in-a-lifetime, lightning in a bottle love."

She kissed him, used to the exchange now, but not completely used to the thrill of the feelings they shared. "Yes, it is."

"Leash her up," he said.

She bent over to flick the clasp of the leash on to the collar...and her whole body stilled. There was something hanging on that leash. Something small and silver...no, that was platinum. And sparkling in the sun.

"Shane." She simply breathed his name, slowly standing up, holding the clasp in her hand.

"Oh, look at that. Ruby comes with a diamond." He took the leash from her shaking hands. "What do you think of that?"

"I think..." She pressed her hand to her chest, unable to speak. It was so unexpected, but not. It was so Shane. It was so perfect.

Behind her, someone hooted, and Molly hollered, "Do it right, Shane."

"On one knee, laddie!" Gramma called from the patio.

"Just like I told you, Son."

He laughed. "It's kind of a package deal with Kilcannons."

"I love that package," she whispered.

"Good, because they love you. And so do I."

Chloe's next breath caught as Shane followed Gramma's order and got down on one knee.

"Chloe Somerset," Shane said softly. "You really are perfect. I knew it the first time I saw you, and I know it today, and I'll know it when I breathe my last breath. I love you with my whole heart and soul. Will you marry me and raise a family of many two- and four-legged babies we can love forever?"

"Oh, Shane." Tears welled up and fell as she blinked. "I love you, too."

He took the ring off the clasp of the leash and held it up like an offering. "Please say yes."

"Yes," she breathed the word. "Yes, I will marry you. Yes, yes, *yes*."

He slid the ring on her finger and stood, not taking his eyes from hers as he kissed her. She heard the dogs barking and the family clapping and the beautiful, glorious sound of her heart beating with joy.

"Shane, how many times do I have to tell you I'm not perfect?"

He laughed and kissed her again. "But you are perfect for me."

The Dogfather

Don't miss the next book in The Dogfather series:

Leader of the Pack

Very few things ruffle law enforcement dog training specialist Liam Kilcannon. Stoic and steady, he has the patience and skill to transform a harmless puppy into a protective K-9, and the quiet strength to lead his five younger siblings through the storms of life. He's a former Marine who doesn't waste words or squander emotions, and he's also a man who very much wanted to spend his life with one special woman by his side. He found her...and lost her. And won't ever let himself be hurt by her again.

Architect and single mom Andi Rivers knows she made a big mistake when she let Liam slip through her fingers two years ago. Like every decision she's made for the past six years, Andi chose what she thought was best for her young son, and has vowed to stay single and unattached no matter how long and lonely her nights might be. But when Liam's father learns Andi's house has been broken into, he suggests she take Jag, a German shepherd watchdog Liam has been training. Andi sees the sense of getting a protection dog, especially when Jag seems to bring her son out of his shell.

But having Liam's specially trained dog puts her in close and constant contact with a man who is a sexy reminder that she's been sleeping by herself for far too long. Jag might be able to protect her home and family, but what will protect their hearts when Andi and Liam risk falling in love one more time?

If you want to know the day LEADER OF THE PACK or any of The Dogfather books are available for purchase, sign up for Roxanne St. Claire's newsletter!

Watch for the whole Dogfather series coming in 2017 and 2018! Sign up for the newsletter for the next release date!

www.roxannestclaire.com/newsletter/

SIT...STAY...BEG (Book 1)

NEW LEASH ON LIFE (Book 2)

LEADER OF THE PACK (Book 3)

BAD TO THE BONE (Book 4)

RUFF AROUND THE EDGES (Book 5)

DOUBLE DOG DARE (Book 6)

OLD DOG NEW TRICKS (Book 7)

Books Set in Barefoot Bay

Roxanne St. Claire writes the popular Barefoot Bay series, which is really several connected mini-series all set on one gorgeous island off the Gulf coast of Florida. Every book stands alone, but why stop at one trip to paradise?

THE BAREFOOT BAY BILLIONAIRES
(Fantasy men who fall for unlikely women)
Secrets on the Sand
Scandal on the Sand
Seduction on the Sand

THE BAREFOOT BAY BRIDES
(Destination wedding planners who find love)
Barefoot in White
Barefoot in Lace
Barefoot in Pearls

BAREFOOT BAY UNDERCOVER
(Sizzling romantic suspense)
Barefoot Bound (prequel)
Barefoot With a Bodyguard
Barefoot With a Stranger
Barefoot With a Bad Boy
Barefoot Dreams

BAREFOOT BAY TIMELESS
(Second chance romance with silver fox heroes)
Barefoot at Sunset
Barefoot at Moonrise
Barefoot at Midnight

About The Author

Published since 2003, Roxanne St. Claire is a *New York Times* and *USA Today* bestselling author of more than forty romance and suspense novels. She has written several popular series, including Barefoot Bay, the Guardian Angelinos, and the Bullet Catchers.

In addition to being a nine-time nominee and one-time winner of the prestigious RITA™ Award for the best in romance writing, Roxanne's novels have won the National Reader's Choice Award for best romantic suspense three times, as well as the Maggie, the Daphne du Maurier Award, the HOLT Medallion, Booksellers Best, Book Buyers Best, the Award of Excellence, and many others.

She lives in Florida with her husband, and still attempts to run the lives of her teenage daughter and 20-something son. She loves dogs, books, chocolate, and wine, but not always in that order.

www.roxannestclaire.com
www.twitter.com/roxannestclaire
www.facebook.com/roxannestclaire
www.roxannestclaire.com/newsletter/